Praise for the Vinyl Detective

"One of the most innovative concepts in crime fiction for many years. Once you are hooked into the world of the Vinyl Detective it is very difficult to leave." Nev Fountain, author of *Geek Tragedy*

"The Vinyl Detective is one of the sharpest and most original characters I've seen for a long time." David Quantick, Emmy Award-winning producer of *VEEP*

"Hilarious and thrilling." Ben Aaronovitch, author of the Rivers of London series.

"Cartmel has a gift for bringing you into his characters' world and making you want to stay there which simply makes this a joy to read." Blue Book Balloon Review

"Cartmel is getting a great tune out of the characters… Will have you chuckling out loud." SFBook Review

"Character is what Cartmel does well… An entertaining detective story with a slightly different vibe." The Dreamcage Review

"Crime fiction as it should be, played loud through a valve amp and Quad speakers. No digital writing here, it's warm and rich. Every delicate pop and crackle adding character and flavour. Witty, charming and filled with exciting solos. Quite simply: groovy." Guy Adams, critically acclaimed author of *The Clown Service*

Also by Andrew Cartmel and available from Titan Books

The Vinyl Detective series

Written in Dead Wax
The Run-Out Groove
Victory Disc
Flip Back
Low Action
Attack and Decay

The Paperback Sleuth series

Death in Fine Condition
Ashram Assassin

THE VINYL DETECTIVE

NOISE FLOOR

ANDREW CARTMEL

TITAN BOOKS

The Vinyl Detective: Noise Floor
Print edition ISBN: 9781803367965
E-book edition ISBN: 9781803367972

Published by Titan Books
A division of Titan Publishing Group Ltd.
144 Southwark Street, London SE1 0UP

First Titan edition: March 2024
10 9 8 7 6 5 4 3 2 1

Printed and bound by CPI Group (UK) Ltd, Croydon, CR0 4YY.

For Sarah Jane Docker, brilliant artist
and revered collaborator.

PROLOGUE

Body Found in Woods

Kent Chronicle's crime reporter Jasper McClew reports on a grisly discovery.

It's a little-known fact that Kent is home to a fragment of Britain's precious last surviving rainforest. This dense, ancient patch of stunning woodland, located adjacent to the beautiful tiny village of Nutalich, is home to many unique forms of life. But recently it was dramatically discovered to also contain a unique form of death.

Three young lads, brothers, were doing their regular workout, which involved a run through the wild, unspoiled woods, when they saw something that didn't look right. "It was Dermot who first spotted it," said Darra Bolsin (21). "That's right," confirmed Dermot Bolsin (21). "We saw it over between the trees and went to have a look." It didn't take long for the three young men to confirm the sinister nature of their discovery. It was Declan Bolsin (21) who used his phone to notify the police of their grisly find: the body of a middle-aged man, yet to be identified.

The three young men, non-identical triplets who are well known in the local area, were badly shaken by their gruesome discovery. Their manager, Julian Herald, hopes the experience won't blight the lads' chances of becoming a world-renowned boy band. "The Trippy-Lits are headed for the stratosphere," said Julian. "But they can't help but be upset by this terrible experience. We'll get through it. But I hope whoever callously dumped that body there in the woods burns in hell," he opined.

Music runs in Julian's family. His father is electronic dance legend Imperium Dart.

1: THE SUMMER I LEARNED TO DRIVE

"You know what I always say?" said Tinkler. "I always say that a luxury car delivery isn't a luxury car delivery until you've smoked a bong full of *really smelly weed* in the luxury car you're delivering."

He took out and brandished what was apparently a miniature bong—a squat cylinder possibly fashioned from Perspex, in an unearthly shade of neon blue.

"Wait, don't you fucking *dare*," said Agatha.

Because she was driving, Agatha's attention was unflaggingly on the road ahead, despite Tinkler's patently distracting presence beside her. But she did find time during her ironclad appraisal of the traffic situation to glance over at him with a look compounded of genuine outrage and just plain rage.

Delivering expensive cars was a good gig and, for a professional driver of Agatha's calibre, a laughably easy one. And, for a car nut of her calibre, a fun one. But it did involve getting the car back to its owner without the costly leather upholstery reeking of illicit cannabis use.

But then she saw, as we did, that what Tinkler was holding wasn't a bong at all, but rather a transparent and very trendy cylindrical bottle that contained a pretentiously packaged but otherwise blameless soft drink in an eerie shade of blue on which he was now feeding like a contented baby.

Tinkler lowered the bottle from his lips, gave Agatha a droll look and said, simply, "Got you."

"Very funny, Tinkler." Agatha fell silent as the light changed to green and she pulled away and slotted us into the traffic flow. Then she granted us her attention once more. "Look, I'm sorry to be dictatorial."

"You're not dictatorial," said Tinkler, instantly at his most emollient.

Nevada and I also quickly concurred that Agatha wasn't dictatorial.

"Well, good," said Agatha.

"Maybe a little *bossy*…" said Tinkler.

"You want to know about bossy? I asked Nevada not to wear any smelly perfume."

Nevada nodded. "She really did."

"I really did," said Agatha. "So the smell wouldn't linger in the car."

"Did this injunction on smelly perfumes dramatically narrow your choice of signature scent?" said Tinkler, swivelling around to look at Nevada with his big, and misleadingly innocent, puppy eyes. As usual when Agatha was driving anywhere, Tinkler was riding shotgun, and Nevada and I were in the back.

"It cramped my style," said Nevada, "let's put it like that. Most of my perfumes being smelly to one degree or another."

"Sorry to be bossy," said Agatha. "Or dictatorial, take your pick. But a lucrative gig delivering luxury vehicles is not to be sniffed at."

"Literally," said Tinkler.

"Also," said Agatha. "No eating food in the car. And, come to think of it, no drinking either. Stop it immediately, Tinkler."

"Too late. I've already consumed my beverage. But I can retrieve it if you like. Try and get it back in the container, out of my bladder and back into the container…"

"No, I think it's fine where it is for the time being, thank you," said Agatha. And then, as was customary when a complex driving situation loomed—in this case a junction that would have baffled most mortals—she fell completely and very reassuringly silent, all her concentration on the task at hand.

This task consisted of moving with consummate skill at an impressive rate of progress, ever forward through the most grisly traffic London could throw at her.

It was remarkable how Agatha spotted opportunities, changing lanes and darting in among the stream of vehicles. I commented on this as we settled into a new slot. "The trick is not to look at the cars," she said. "You look at the gaps between them."

"Very Zen," said Nevada.

"It's Agatha's School of Zen Driving," said Tinkler.

"The Clean Head School of Zen Driving," Agatha corrected him.

Indeed, her shaved-head look did go well with any Zen side of this proposed project.

"Great distinctive offer," said Tinkler. "And in a very crowded field."

"Are you stoned again, Tinkler?" asked Nevada.

Tinkler turned in his seat to peer at us. "Explain once more that subtle distinction between 'again' and 'still'?" he said.

"You're depraved."

Tinkler tutted. "I'll give you debauched. Depraved seems at little harsh."

"Actually, you know what, Tinkler?" Agatha smiled. "That concept of looking at the gaps instead of the cars…?"

"Yes," said Tinkler eagerly, swiftly swivelling to look at her. "Please tell me more about your philosophy of driving."

"It's not *my* philosophy of driving," said Agatha. "It was propounded to me one summer…" Suddenly her voice softened. "The summer I learned to drive. I was staying with friends of my parents in this little English village. It was a beautiful summer and a beautiful part of the world. My driving instructor and I drove down every winding country road, exploring, discovering all these little hidden places…"

"Your driving instructor?" said Nevada. Like me, she'd picked up on the change in the timbre of Agatha's voice at the mention of this person and was keen to know more.

Tinkler seemed equally aware of this but, it has to be said, rather less keen to know more.

"Right," said Agatha. "My driving instructor. He was the one who said to look at the gaps, not at the cars. It's something Horatio always used to say."

"Wait, your driving instructor was called Horatio?" Tinkler chortled. "He was called Horatio, and he was really Zen."

"Did I mention how good-looking he was?" said Agatha.

Nevada leaned forward, grinning slyly as she leaned on the back of Agatha's seat. "Did you have a thing for him?"

"A thing for Horatio?" said Tinkler, as though picking through ordure.

Nevada nodded. "It would not be unknown for a young lady to have a thing about her driving instructor."

"Well, let's just say that, *had* I had a thing for Horatio, it would have been entirely understandable," said Agatha. "As I say, he was a handsome devil and staggeringly skilled behind the wheel."

"Behind the wheel," said Tinkler.

"Yes, he was dynamite behind the wheel. He supported himself through uni by doing summer jobs as a stunt driver in the movies."

"Have I mentioned how much I hate this guy?" said Tinkler, and we all laughed.

"Anyway, it was beautiful that summer, the summer I learned to drive. I'll always be grateful to Horatio for that summer."

"I don't suppose old Horatio has tragically passed from this life?" said Tinkler hopefully.

"Nope, still very much with us," said Agatha. "In fact, I must look him up." She looked over at Tinkler, then smiled and winked. "Thank you for bringing his name up."

"I didn't bring his name up! And it's a fucking silly name."

Soon, thanks to Agatha's skill and daring behind the wheel, we were out of London and heading into deep countryside. "We're in Kent," said Agatha. "We've just officially driven into Kent."

"I know," said Tinkler. "I felt my IQ drop."

"Now," said Nevada, "while some might consider that a questionable or perhaps even offensive remark, Tinkler, I happen to know that you yourself grew up in Kent."

"I suppose there's no point denying it," sighed Tinkler.

"No, there isn't," said Agatha. "Anyway, as I was about to say, it's interesting that we happen to be talking about Horatio, because this is exactly the part of the world where he taught me to drive."

"Horatio," murmured Tinkler, followed by some sub-audible obscenities.

"Very near the place we're delivering the car," said Agatha. "Which, by the way, is a really beautiful house."

"You've been there before?" said Nevada.

"A number of times, on jobs like this. Collecting their cars from the airport and bringing them down to the house, things like that. And where they live is virtually next door to this lovely little village called Nutalich."

"Nutalich?" said Tinkler. "That's a fucked-up name for a village, even in Kent."

Nevada sighed. "Tinkler, you come from this region. You're a home boy."

"Well, Nutalich has the most amazing church," said Agatha. "The architecture is incredible."

"Okay," said Tinkler, "if she talks any more about church architecture, please could someone have a defibrillator at the ready?"

"I'm just saying it's worth a look," said Agatha. "Since we happen to be out in this neck of the woods."

"In this neck of the woods?" said Tinkler, adding a twang of yokel insanity to his voice. "Out in the dangerous backwoods of Kent, the four of us, thrown together by a quirk of fate."

"If by a quirk of fate you mean delivering a car, while at the same time giving my friends a lift to the address *they're* visiting," said Agatha, "then yes."

"Yes," said Nevada. "It's really useful that we all happened to have business in the same part of Kent."

Tinkler turned back in his seat to look at me and Nevada. "So do you guys have Vinyl Detective business out here?"

"Yes," I said.

"In the wilds of Kent?"

"Yes."

"What's the job?"

"That's what we're going to find out," I said.

"Oh, so it's like a job interview?" said Tinkler, dismissively.

"A very mysterious job interview," said Nevada. She didn't like our errand being so swiftly consigned to the mundane.

"Yeah, whatever," said Tinkler. "How close together are these two addresses? The car-delivery one and the job-interview one? And which one will be the most fun to hang out at?"

"The one with me, obviously," said Agatha.

"Yes," said Tinkler. "But, my hopeless amorous obsession notwithstanding, we must also give due consideration to the possibility that maybe the other place— the place where the cat slaves are going…"

"We prefer the designation Team Vinyl Detective, if you don't mind," said Nevada. "It's a little more dignified than 'the cat slaves'."

"Ha! More dignified…" said Tinkler.

"Only a little more," said Agatha.

"And you did get that I meant *you* were the slaves of your cats, right? I was never suggesting the cats themselves were slaves, when obviously they rule the roost. You two are the slaves of the cats."

"Yes, that did come across," I said.

"Just checking," said Tinkler. "Sometimes I'm too hip for the room."

"Sometimes you're too stoned for the room," said Agatha.

"Most of the time," said Tinkler. "Anyway, back to the crucial question. Where will I hang out? Which of our destinations will prove more entertaining? And, crucially, which one is the most likely to provide refreshments?"

"And how far apart are they?" said Agatha. "I'll check." She glanced back at us in the mirror. Or rather at Nevada, who'd made the arrangements. "What's the postcode at your destination?"

Nevada told her.

"It's the same postcode," said Agatha, "so they'll be close together. What's the full street address?"

Nevada told her.

After a pause, Agatha said, "It's the same street address. The same house where I'm taking the car."

"We're both going to the same house," said Nevada.

"Yes."

"We're both going to the same place."

"Yes."

We were all silent for a moment.

"Is it just me," said Tinkler, "or is that weird and just a little bit scary?"

2: WANDERING LAMB

"So we're all going to the same address," said Tinkler. "That's definitely creepy."

"It's not creepy," said Agatha. "We just didn't realise it was the same place. And here it is." Tall gates loomed in the headlights and she touched something on the dashboard, then the gates opened to reveal a big white house on a hill partially screened by lush greenery. The greenery and the house were on several levels, climbing a winding path up the black hillside.

The gates which had obediently opened in front of us consisted of tall vertical black struts topped with horizontal bars on which rested two words formed of elaborate wrought iron. On one gate it said: *Noise*. On the other: *Floor*.

As we drove in, the gates closed behind us. Agatha parked the car on a blue tarmac circle with a white circle inside it and a red dot at the centre—yes, a Mod roundel—in front of a white stucco garage. It was a big garage with two broad doors, one of which was open to reveal a gleaming new Mini parked inside. Agatha paused to examine this as we got out of our own vehicle, which was a Mercedes-Benz S-Class. I only knew this because she'd told us.

There were white stencilled letters on the blue circle at about two o'clock, which read *Noise Floor*, with a stencilled white arrow that pointed towards a gravel footpath that skirted around the side of the big hill on which, and into which, the house was built.

Stone steps led up from the garage, dug into the hillside, and cut through patches of flourishing greenery onto the next level.

And there stood a woman, awaiting our arrival. She waved to us. Night had fallen now and the many lights that shone around this big house were devoted exclusively to illuminating beguiling patches of shrubbery in the lovingly planned garden, turning them an intense luminous green.

But if you weren't a particularly interesting plant, you were consigned to shadow. All we could make out of the woman herself was that she was waving.

We waved back. "That's the lady who does the gardening here," said Agatha. "She's very nice."

"Is it her house or does she just do the gardening?" said Nevada.

"Sometimes I think one thing, sometimes the other," said Agatha.

We started up the steps. As we got closer and the woman emerged from the darkness, we saw she was middle-aged, stocky, with a halo of curly grey hair around her benign, smiling face.

She wore a black-and-blue check work shirt and faded ankle-grazer jeans, which had been patched at the knees with bright red material. Over her shirt she wore a sleeveless padded vest in khaki with a military look that was ameliorated by the gardening gloves and chrome secateurs stuffed into its pockets. Her sockless feet were shod in tennis shoes. Not great for gardening, I thought. Though maybe they helped her move spryly up the steep hillside.

"Hello," she said. "Hello, Agatha."

"Hi, Poppy," said Agatha. She performed the introductions, ending with Tinkler. "He's just along for the ride," she said.

"But I provide valuable entertainment value," said Tinkler.

"You can't have valuable value," said Nevada.

"I can," said Tinkler.

"Well, let's all go up to the house," said Poppy, whose cheerfulness seemed admirably undented by the arrival of these bickering strangers.

As we started up the steps, we saw a tall young man, very blond and very thin, walking down towards us. Poppy paused, so we paused too and waited for the young man to descend to our level. He gave us a dismissive glance and then, without preamble, addressed Poppy. "I thought that crap was going to be cleared out of the studio. I need to use the studio and it's full of crap. It's *still* full of crap."

"In fairness, Julian," said the woman, "it's mostly your crap."

"I need to use the studio," repeated Julian. "And you said it would be cleared out in two or three days."

"What I actually said, Julian, is that, if you were to put your mind to it, you could get it cleared out in two or three days."

"Ah, Christ," said Julian and kissed his teeth as he shoved past us and headed down to the driveway.

"Rude boy," murmured Tinkler, loud enough for us to hear but too low for Poppy. Not that it would have mattered, judging by the way she sighed.

We resumed our walk up to the house.

The house was dazzling in the glare of the spotlights that shone on it from the garden. It rose against the night sky in an imposing white rectangle with dark windows dotted across its face. The front door was at ground level instead of having steps leading up to it, which gave a cosy feeling quite at odds with the otherwise austere splendour of the façade. We went into an alcove which did feature steps, going up a metre or two.

Facing us at the top was a narrow band of wall with the framed front page of a newspaper hung in a position of prominence. To the left of this was an open door that led into the house.

But of more immediate interest was that framed front page. It was from one of England's more reprehensible tabloids, and featured a headline that blared *Rave Star Orgy Cult*. Further perusal of this fascinating piece of journalism was cut short as we followed Poppy through the open door, though Tinkler did pause to take a picture of it with his phone.

We walked into a high-ceilinged room that was so huge I thought at first it occupied the entire ground floor, in an open-plan design with a staircase on the far side. Then I saw there were doors in the wall at the back and realised that more rooms lay beyond it. This really was a big house.

The floor in here was tiled with terracotta squares, but these were mostly concealed by vast oriental rugs, evidently antiques. Or maybe they'd just seen plenty of hard use. Dispersed over the carpets was a lot of furniture, all matching, fashioned from dark wood and pale cream fabric. But the room was so large that it could accommodate all this stuff and still feel sparsely furnished, open and airy.

I liked the place immediately.

"Oh dear," said Poppy, patting anxiously at the pockets of her vest. "I don't have my glasses. Just let me get them. Back in a moment." She went out through one of the doors in the back of the room, leaving us alone.

"Are they trying to sell us this house?" said Tinkler.

"What are you raving about?" said Agatha.

"The smell of fresh baked bread."

It was true. I hadn't consciously realised it until now, but the place smelled wonderfully of baking. And it was also true that this was a recommended stratagem if you were trying to sell your home to someone. Full marks to Tinkler. For once.

We all took a deep breath. "I only wish we could afford to make them an offer," said Nevada. "The cats would love this place."

Somewhere deep in the house, music started to play. Pounding electronica. "Aphex Twin," said Tinkler knowledgably.

Agatha evidently liked it. She started swaying to the beat.

"Would you care to dance, mademoiselle?" said Tinkler.

"Not with you, thank you," said Agatha. "Now, if Horatio was here…"

Breath moved through Tinkler's mouth in the faintest of whispers. Nevertheless, the words "Fuck Horatio" were faintly audible under the thumping techno.

Poppy came back in. She was, as promised, now wearing spectacles. She had also removed her vest and exchanged her tennis shoes for canvas slippers with rope soles that scuffed across the tiles and fell silent as she reached the carpet. Under one arm she carried a folded pale pink shape. "Oh," she said, "please do sit down." She herded us over to a low rectangular table. I'd thought it was some kind of serving area, perhaps for drinks, but now I realised it was a desk.

She took the pink object from under her arm and unfolded it, revealing it to be a copy of the *Financial Times*, Britain's only pink newspaper. Carefully spreading it over the cream fabric of the chair's cushion, presumably to protect it from her dirty jeans, she sat down on it, positioning herself behind the desk. Nevada and I took chairs in front while Agatha and Tinkler settled close together on a small sofa nearby. For all their squabbling, they were very comfortable in each other's company.

Poppy opened a drawer on her side of the desk and took out a pen, a large diary and what I realised with a happy little pang of recognition was a chequebook. Nevada saw this too and she gave me a quick smile. Money. Or at least the prospect of it.

It was increasingly clear that Poppy wasn't just the gardener around here.

"Now…" she said. "Agatha, we already have your bank account info, don't we?"

"Yes, Poppy," said Agatha from the sofa.

"Yes, Poppy," piped up Tinkler in an identical chirpy voice.

Agatha punched him on the knee, but he appeared unrepentant.

Poppy smiled indulgently as she made a note in the diary. It seemed Tinkler had charmed her. He did occasionally have that gift. "Just send us your updated invoice," she said, "and we'll make a transfer to you, as usual. And thank you for delivering the car."

"My pleasure," said Agatha.

Poppy was now looking at me, holding the chequebook in one hand and tapping it on the desk. "But, if you don't mind," she said, "we'll make *your* first payment by cheque. A bit old-fashioned I know, but—"

"Nothing wrong with a cheque," said Nevada promptly. "And they're very secure. Totally unhackable."

"Well, that's what I think," said Poppy, smiling at her. Tinkler wasn't the only one with a gift for charm. "Right, so it's agreed," she said, looking at me. "We'll give you an initial down payment on your eventual fee in the form of a cheque."

"Eventual fee for doing what?" I said.

This seemed to give Poppy pause, as if she hadn't been prepared for the question. She stared down at the desk as though the answer might be there, perhaps written on a Post-it note for her. Then she looked at us again, pensively. First at me, then Nevada.

"You see," said Poppy, "my husband, and I'm using that term loosely, has a tendency to wander off." She paused for another moment as if expecting us to pour scorn and opprobrium on her. When we didn't, she tentatively continued. "And he's wandered off once more."

"Is he...?" said Nevada. And, remarkably, all of us instantly understood what she was getting at.

"Oh no, not at all," said Poppy. "Quite the contrary. He has full command of all his faculties, despite having poured drugs into his brain in preposterous quantities over many years."

At the mention of drugs, and in preposterous quantities, I sensed Tinkler suddenly taking an interest.

Nevada leaned forward in her chair. "When you say he wanders off..."

Poppy placed both hands palms-down on the desk and pressed on them as though bracing herself for impact. "He becomes... bored with his domestic situation."

"Ah," said Nevada.

"And looks for consolation—and stimulation—elsewhere."

"I'm sorry," said Nevada.

"Oh, we're quite used to it. And normally I wouldn't even be talking to you, it's such a commonplace occurrence.

But, this time, he's been gone rather a long while, and we have begun to worry about him."

"Okay," I said. "But…" I could see Nevada out of the corner of my eye, looking at me and willing me to keep my mouth shut. As she had done on other occasions in the past. And, also as on those occasions, I went on to say what I felt compelled to say. "The thing is, Poppy, while I am in business as the Vinyl Detective, I am not a real detective. I don't find people—"

"He has before," said Nevada. "He has found people before."

This was true enough.

"Nevertheless," I said, "what I really do is find records. If you have a missing-persons issue, and that's apparently the case here, then you should really go to the police."

"You do find records, though?" said Poppy.

"Yes."

"So you're a record hunter?"

"Yes."

"So you go to those things, don't you?"

"What things?" I said.

Poppy shrugged. "Record fairs, boot fairs, jumble sales. Second-hand shops. Places where they sell old records."

Perhaps Nevada was a step ahead of me, because she had started to grin. "Yes, he does," she said. "He certainly does."

Poppy nodded. "Then you're ideally situated to look for Lambert, and to find him. Because those are the places he is likely to be found." She looked at me. "You are the ideal man for the job."

"He certainly is," said Nevada.

"Is… Lambert… a record collector, then?" I said.

"Yes."

"What sort of stuff does he collect?"

"Tedious electronic dance music of the era." Poppy nodded, her eyes tilted upwards, to indicate that an example could still be heard playing in the background, an insistent, distant pounding. "Music of his era. Which is to say the 1990s. The more tedious the better. And esoteric and highly collectable. Including his own stuff."

"His own stuff?" I said.

"His own records."

"He was a musician?"

"He still is," said Poppy. "Theoretically. Though god knows it's been long enough since he went into the studio."

"What's his name?" I said.

"Well, his name is Lambert Ramkin, but the name he records under is Imperium Dart."

"Oh my god," said Tinkler suddenly. "Imperium Dart, of course. I thought it was Aphex Twin." He made a vague gesture as if trying to point at the invisible music in the air.

Poppy smiled a thin smile. "Yes, it appears that someone, either Jacquetta or Selena, thought it was a good idea to greet your arrival by playing you a selection of his greatest hits."

We all fell silent for a moment and listened to the music, its insinuating beat hammering away in some other room, deep in the house. "By the way, for god's sake don't tell him that. If you find him. *When* you find him. Don't tell him he sounds like Aphex Twin. Unless you want to get him angry. Very angry. Because there's no quicker or surer way of getting him very angry than telling him that."

"Okay," I said.

"They used to play Laser Quest together. They were quite chummy. But very competitive. And Lambert always resented the fact that Aphex has been more successful. Or at least that he perceives him as being more successful."

"What's Laser Quest?" said Agatha.

Poppy looked at her. "Do you know what paintballing is?"

"Sure."

"It's like that, except with lots of sci-fi trappings. 'Laser' guns instead of paintball guns, that kind of thing."

"Ah."

"Very popular back in the day. Very much a boy's thing." Poppy looked at me. "In fact, that might be one more place for you to look for him. If you can bring yourself to attend such a thing."

"Do they still do it?" said Agatha. "Laser Questing?"

"Oh yes."

"Okay…" I said.

"Okay we're taking the job?" said Nevada, turning to look at me. "Or okay, you're about to offer some further infuriating prevarication?"

"Only if asking where he was last seen counts as an infuriating prevarication."

"We're taking the job!" said Nevada joyfully.

"Well, he was last *seen* here, at home," said Poppy. "But his last known location was actually Heathrow Airport." She glanced at Agatha. "Where you picked up the car."

"He left the car at the airport?" I said.

"Yes. He drove it there, parked it in the long-stay car park and then effectively vanished."

"But if he's left the car at the airport he could have flown anywhere," I said. I could see Nevada was torn between disappointment at the potential terminal nature of this complication, and the possibilities it might offer for overseas travel on an expense account.

"I don't think so," said Poppy.

"Why don't you think so?"

"Because that's not why he drove to the airport. He went there because he was attending a record fair in one of the adjoining hotels."

That made sense. I actually remembered that record fair out at Heathrow. It was one of the big ones.

"Now, about your fee—" said Poppy.

"This is where my manager needs to step in," I said.

Poppy looked taken aback. "Oh. Who is your manager?"

"I am," said Nevada happily, hitching her chair closer to the desk.

I left the two women to haggle, and went over to the sofa to join Tinkler and Agatha. They rose up as I approached and we all wandered around the room together, putting a tasteful distance between ourselves and the sordid financial negotiations unfolding at the desk.

"Imperium Dart, eh?" said Tinkler.

"I've never heard of him," said Agatha.

"Well don't tell him that, for god's sake," said Tinkler. "When you meet him. Or that he sounds like Aphex Twin, apparently."

"Okay," said Agatha. "So you think I'm likely to meet him?" She addressed this question to Tinkler, but was looking at me.

I was thinking about the job. A missing-person situation. What was I getting myself into? What was I getting all of us into?

"Well, I'm sure he'd want to meet you," said Tinkler. "Who wouldn't?"

"There is that," said Agatha. "Isn't this a fantastic house?"

"Isn't it just," I said, dismissing my worries for the time being.

"And a very cool flying saucer," said Tinkler.

"Are you tripping?" said Agatha.

"Not just at the moment." Tinkler pointed to the window at the back of the room. We approached it and looked out and down at the very large back garden that spread below us. It consisted of a neatly mown and well-maintained lawn, a big and rather poorly maintained swimming pool with a lot of leaves and twigs and other debris floating in it, a low, white concrete bunker of a building with *Noise Floor Studios* painted above its doors in black art deco lettering…

And, yes, a flying saucer.

The flying saucer was located between the pool and the tennis court. It was about the size of a large car and stood above the ground on spindly but apparently sturdy legs, with a ladder running up to it. Illuminated by four lights spaced around its perimeter, it had a brilliant gleaming silver fuselage with bright red highlights, and its shape was that of a classic UFO from a 1950s science fiction movie. The fact it was just some kind of extraordinary garden decoration, or rich person's toy, rather than a real extra-terrestrial craft was confirmed or at least suggested by the large Day-Glo yellow smiley face painted on it.

"I want one," said Tinkler.

"So do I," said Agatha.

"You'd never fit it in your flat," said Tinkler.

"Or your house," said Agatha.

They both turned and looked at me. "Why are you looking at me?" I said.

"Because you're the only one in this assemblage of wastrels with a garden big enough to accommodate a flying saucer," said Tinkler.

"Only just," I said. "And I don't think my other half would countenance it."

We turned and looked back at the haggling duo at the desk. The fact that Poppy had now opened her chequebook and Nevada was sitting back and smiling seemed to indicate the bartering was reaching its conclusion, and a satisfactory conclusion at that. So Agatha and Tinkler and I went back to the sofa. It was a small sofa, so I perched on the arm and let the lovebirds sit on it.

Poppy signed the cheque with a flourish, set her pen aside, ripped the cheque out of the book with a particularly satisfying sound of perforated paper popping, and handed it to Nevada.

Just then, as if summoned by this action, a woman came down the stairs.

Blonde, with a long, rich spill of straight hair that fell to her elbows, she was tall and would have been dangerously skinny if not for her full breasts and hips. Very tight lavender jeans clung to her long, slender legs and contrasted strikingly with her baggy black sweater, which hung down low on one side to expose a pale bare shoulder and a black tank top.

They contrasted even more strikingly with the green rubber wellington boots she was wearing.

At first sight she appeared to be in her twenties but, as she drew closer, I revised this estimate upwards by a decade or two. Her face was smooth and unlined, but it was the sort of smoothness and lack of lines that seemed to have been achieved through considerable artifice. Her mouth was wide, her lips a vivid red, contrasting with her pale blue eyes.

She came into the room, gave us a dismissive glance that was oddly familiar, then turned to Poppy and said, "Is the Mercedes back?"

"Parked outside."

"About time," she said, and headed for the door.

"Are those my wellies you're wearing?" said Poppy.

The blonde answered this question with another question. "How petty can you get?"

Then she disappeared out the front door, leaving it wide open.

"Rude bitch," murmured Agatha to me.

Poppy sighed and got up from her desk, clearly heading for the door to close it. "Let me," said Nevada. She went and shut the door on the sound of tyres suddenly shrieking on tarmac down below. We all winced. The poor Mercedes.

"I hope she's not driving in those boots," said Agatha.

"Don't worry," said Poppy. "She'll have taken them off and she'll be driving barefoot."

"Barefoot's not a bad idea," allowed Agatha.

"Selena always says she'd go driving naked if she could."

"Really?" said Tinkler, his eyes big as saucers.

"Yes. Because she says it would make her feel 'free'."

"Has she ever done it?" said Tinkler. "Gone driving like that, I mean? Naked, I mean?"

To change the subject, though not entirely, I said, "Is Selena by any chance related to Julian?"

"Mother and son." Poppy delivered this clipped utterance as if it was a withering indictment. Perhaps it was. She added, "I was wondering where my wellies had got to."

Then, apparently hearing a sound that none of the rest of us had detected, she turned around and stared at the back of the room.

Sure enough, a door opened in the rear wall and another woman came in.

It would have been difficult for this person to present more of a contrast with Selena. A lack of green wellies was just the start of it. The newcomer wore yellow clogs, loose golden harem trousers and a baggy sweater striped liked Neapolitan ice cream, under an apron which bore the slogan, *Men Throw Punches—Women Throw Pies*.

Her inky black hair was cut short in a pageboy style. She appeared to be in her forties, but it was hard to say. Her skin was smooth and unlined—not, in this case, because of any artificial intervention but because she had cherubic, Rubenesque features with plump pink cheeks that were now gleaming with moisture.

The reason for that glow was obvious, since a flood of very warm air flowed through the door with her, carrying on it that wonderful scent of baking. The same smell was coming from the large blue platter she held, heaped with golden rolls dusted with flour, clearly fresh from the oven as they were literally steaming.

"Holy Christ," murmured Tinkler, a man driven by his stomach as much as by parts further south.

"This is Jacquetta," said Poppy.

"Hello, everyone," said Jacquetta, striding into the room and bringing her fragrant baked goods with her. "Do you mind if I pop these down here?" Without waiting for a reply, she set the platter on the desk, as Poppy hastily moved her chequebook, diary and pen out of harm's way.

"Would anyone like some home-baked ciabatta rolls?" said Jacquetta.

The disingenuous nature of her question was demonstrated by the fact that Tinkler had already sprung from the sofa and thrown himself towards the desk and the heap of steaming rolls. Managing to maintain some semblance of decency, just about, he refrained from snatching one up and said, "May I?" like a well-trained child, at the same time aiming his big puppy eyes at Jacquetta.

"*Wait*." This word was voiced with such sudden steeliness that it took a moment to realise that plump, inviting Jacquetta had uttered it. "I've forgotten something." She hurried back out the way we came.

We all stood there in silence, Agatha and I having abandoned the sofa and joined Tinkler, and Nevada and Poppy having risen from their chairs out of respect for the baked items. Our little group looked down at the pile of golden rolls and inhaled their scent and felt the warmth that emanated from them. It was almost a consecrated moment. Then Jacquetta came bustling back in. She was carrying another platter, this one smaller. On it were two glass bowls, one containing a golden-green liquid, the other dark brown.

"Sorry, I forgot these," said Jacquetta. "Olive oil and balsamic vinegar for dipping. And you'll need these." She took a stack of paper napkins from under the platter and set them on the desk beside it.

"Tinkler will need those," said Nevada, taking a roll and daintily tearing it open.

"Tinkler will probably need to be hosed down afterwards," said Agatha, selecting one for herself.

"Tinkler will respond to those insults after he's eaten," said Tinkler.

I took a roll myself, and Jacquetta watched us eat with an eager smile. At close range I could see she had a white smear of flour on her nose. It looked rather becoming. "Was that Selena I heard, roaring away?" she said.

Poppy nodded, licking balsamic vinegar off her fingers. "As soon we got the Merc back, she went haring off."

Jacquetta clucked her tongue. "What a pity. If I'd known, I would have served these sooner."

"Isn't she gluten-intolerant this month?" said Poppy.

Jacquetta shrugged. "It's impossible to keep track."

"Well," said Poppy, "I'd better get back to the gardening."

"In the dark?" said Nevada.

"Watering," explained Poppy. "I try and get it all done in the evening, but I started late today." She wiped her fingers on one of the paper napkins and then shook hands with us. "Lovely to meet you all."

"Especially me," said Tinkler.

Poppy winked at him. "If you're not careful I'll make you help with the watering."

"Oh, please don't do that," he said.

Poppy smiled and went out.

"Well, we'd better call for our ride," said Agatha.

"Wouldn't anyone like to see the kitchen?" said Jacquetta.

"My god, yes," said Tinkler, and she led him out.

Agatha busied herself on her phone. "Can we give you some money?" said Nevada.

Agatha glanced at her. "What for?"

"The ride back to London. It won't be cheap."

"It won't be cheap," agreed Agatha. "But it's paid for as part of my fee for bringing the Mercedes down here."

"In that case," said Nevada, "I withdraw my earlier offer."

The two women chuckled as Agatha put her phone away. "All done?" said Nevada.

"Yup. He should be here in a few minutes. Did you get a decent score for your fee?"

In reply, Nevada showed her the cheque and Agatha was making approving noises when Tinkler and Jacquetta came back.

"You should see the kitchen," said Tinkler.

"Maybe another time," I said. "Our ride will be here in a minute."

"I suppose it's someone local," said Jacquetta.

Agatha nodded.

"I hope it's not one of Julian's friends," said Jacquetta, her smooth brow wrinkling momentarily with concern. She looked at the platter, still heaped with food. "Aren't you going to have any more ciabatta rolls?"

"Can I have a bag to take home?"

"Tinkler!"

"I don't see why not." Jacquetta went out again, presumably to get Tinkler a bag for his rolls.

"*Tinkler*," hissed Nevada and Agatha in unison.

"If you don't ask, you don't get," said Tinkler complacently.

3: QUADROUPLE

When our ride arrived, Poppy came inside to announce it. We said our goodbyes to her and Jacquetta, and walked down the steps through the dark garden, Tinkler carrying his bag of swag. "Did you steal enough food?" said Agatha.

"It's not stealing if it's freely and willingly given," said Tinkler.

Long before we reached the bottom of the steps, we saw the vehicle waiting for us. It was a black London cab. Agatha stared at it. "One of your comrades?" said Nevada.

"Not really," said Agatha. "It looks like someone's bought an old London taxi, but that doesn't mean they're officially licensed." Agatha herself was officially licensed, although she drove a black cab only infrequently these days. "And heaven help them if they try and pretend they are."

It wasn't until we got to the bottom of the steps that we saw our driver, who had been leaning on the far side of the cab. He studied us with measured coolness and insolence as we approached. He was wearing a powder-blue Adidas tracksuit and had dark hair, cropped short on top and shaven at the sides, and a tiny and rather tentative moustache. All in all, he looked about fifteen years old. Agatha apparently thought so too because she insisted on seeing his licence.

Luckily for him, and I suppose for us, he had this with him and, after a pointedly prolonged inspection, Agatha handed it back to him. We got into the back of the cab while our driver surged into the front, slamming his door violently shut.

Agatha smiled. "Declan is annoyed at me."

Of course, having studied his licence she now knew his name. And Declan really was annoyed. He revved the engine and sent us charging forward with such abruptness and speed that the gates, which opened automatically at our approach, hardly cleared the sides of the cab as we shot through.

"That would certainly teach us a lesson," said Agatha dryly, "scraping the paint off the side of his own cab." Then she pressed the button that enabled communication with the driver. "Declan," she said sweetly.

"What?" replied Declan, considerably less sweetly.

"Could we please drive back by way of Nutalich?"

"We're going that way anyway." It sounded like Declan regretted this fact but that there was no way around it.

"Good. Thank you."

But Declan had already cut off communications with us. Agatha leaned back and stretched. "It's nice to be a passenger for a change."

"Even with Declan driving?" I said.

"Not so much with Declan driving, true. But at least you guys will be able to see Nutalich. I want you to see the church. It's fantastic. No remarks about defibrillators, Tinkler."

"Mouth-to-mouth resuscitation would be fine too," said Tinkler. "Providing it's you or Nevada." He looked at me. "Not you. No offence."

"None taken."

We all sat back and relaxed as the cab hurtled through the night. It was nice to sit here in the darkness, four old friends packed close together with the smell of Tinkler's pilfered rolls teasing our nostrils.

In this part of Kent, the roads were narrow and winding, and thickly forested on either side. But Declan was throwing us along them rather more quickly than I was comfortable with. Then a sign flashed up ahead of us, a streak of white against the greenery with heavy black letters, which read *Nutalich*. Agatha pressed the button to communicate with the driver. "Declan, could you slow down as we go through here so I can show my friends, please?"

Declan murmured something inaudible though no doubt uncomplimentary, but grudgingly slowed down.

The forest thinned out on either side of us and became meadowland, and then we were crossing a narrow brook on an old grey stone bridge. The dark, quiet water gleamed briefly on either side of us and then we were in the outskirts of Nutalich.

The lovely rural village seemed to rise from the land itself. What I thought was a hedge on one side of us was actually a thatched roof, sweeping up from the bridge and the brook to form a snug brown covering for the pale wooden front of a large wayside inn. There was a gravel parking area outside and it was full of cars, which rather spoiled the ancient sense of the place.

A sign that hung on a tall wooden scaffold beside the road read *Bird in Flight* and depicted an abstract modernist bird, yes, in flight, in the manner of Picasso or Miró. Clearly this wasn't your average pub and this wasn't your average village.

Across the road from the pub was a house with a thatched roof, which looked like a miniature replica of the pub itself. We passed more houses on both sides of the road, each one distinctive and different, all of them striking. Some appeared timelessly antique, others modern and even futuristic. None of them looked cheap.

Just when I thought the village consisted of nothing except a single road with homes on either side—plus that essential pub, of course—our headlights revealed that it split into two. Each section of road curved around to ultimately form a big circle. We were in the heart of the village now and in the circle at the centre of the roads was a village green with a duck pond and a large shed on it.

Lining the roads were shops of every variety— grocers, butchers, restaurants, fishmongers, bookshops, a comic shop, a shoe shop, a post office, antique shops and boutiques. Even a charity shop or two, which made my heart beat faster. There were also four more pubs. And every single one of these businesses was architecturally distinctive and appealing.

"This really is a lovely place," said Nevada.

"Didn't I tell you?" said Agatha.

Tinkler pretended to be snoring, but it was clear even he was impressed.

Once we were past the big circle, the two roads converged again into a single thoroughfare. We drove along this and saw more shops on either side, followed by more houses, and then clearly we were heading out of the village. Although I'd only spent a few seconds passing through the place, I felt a strange little pang of regret to be leaving it behind.

"The name Nutalich is from the Celtic for 'flying bird', *eun itealaich*," said Nevada.

"You speak Celtic?" said Tinkler.

"No, but I possess a small portable device called a smartphone. How was my Celtic pronunciation?"

"For all we know, spot on," said Agatha.

The shops were all gone now and it was just private houses on either side of us—and one last pub. That made at least six by my count. Not bad for such a tiny hamlet. The houses became increasingly large and grand. Then, to our left, there was a large stables with a high red-brick wall and a big wooden gate. And to our right was, at last, the church Agatha had been talking about.

Situated beyond a waist-high wall of natural stones and surrounded by graves and flower beds, it was a long, low, white-walled building of clean modernist design. But what was really striking about it was the roof. It didn't have a spire or tower, but was long and low and curved, echoing the lines of the building and sitting on it like a hat. A stretched, streamlined hat.

At the near end it narrowed to a point that curved earthwards. At the far end it narrowed again, but into an upraised curve almost like the prow of a ship. In between, it spread out broad and flat.

At first glance it appeared to be another thatched roof, but its thickness and smoothness revealed it to be concrete. Brown concrete, curved and contoured in the manner of a Henry Moore sculpture, which swept so low on either side in long wings that its eaves almost touched the ground. It was the word "wings" that triggered the realisation.

The roof of the church was like a bird taking flight.

Soaring heavenwards.

I'm not even a little religious, but the metaphor moved me in a way that no number of crosses or fish could. "Nice church," I said.

"As ecclesiastical architecture goes, it's not bad," said Agatha.

We passed the church and suddenly the village was behind us, confirmed by a sign that read *You Are Now Leaving Nutalich*. Declan took this as his signal to mash his foot on the accelerator and make up for lost time.

"So, no need for defibrillation after all, Tinkler," said Agatha. "Tinkler?"

But Tinkler was so deeply immersed in looking at his phone that he didn't hear her. And for Tinkler not to hear Agatha meant something very serious was afoot. "Tinkler, what is it?" said Nevada.

"He's engrossed in porn," said Agatha. "He's engrossed in gross porn."

"Tinkler," I said. And he finally looked up from his phone.

"How's the porn?" said Agatha.

"It's not porn," said Tinkler. "Or maybe, sort of, in a way…"

"What do you mean, 'maybe sort of in a way'?" said Agatha.

"Here, look," said Tinkler. He held up his phone.

"No thank you," said Agatha, turning her face emphatically away.

But I looked.

"What is it?" said Agatha.

Nevada was leaning forward, equally interested.

I said, "It's a photograph of that framed newspaper we saw when we went in the house."

"*Orgy Rave*?" said Nevada.

Tinkler corrected her. "*Rave Star Orgy Cult*, to be exact. When I saw it, I thought, what an outstanding headline. And that it would make a great T-shirt. So I took a picture…"

"And?" said Nevada.

"Well, first of all, do you recognise the photographs?" Tinkler enlarged the image on his phone. In the body of the newspaper story there were four black-and-white headshots. The first was of a man. "That's Imperium Dart at the top," said Tinkler.

"Lambert Ramkin," said Nevada.

"Right," said Tinkler. "A young Lambert Ramkin. But the others, the three women…"

"They can't be," said Agatha, leaning closer. Then, "Holy shit."

"Let me see," said Nevada.

I leaned in with her.

Tinkler held his phone out so we could all look at it. "Read the names," he said. "Poppy Claypool, Jacquetta Witton and Selena Herald."

"Poppy, Jacquetta and Selena," said Nevada.

"Holy shit," said Agatha again.

"Selena was the name of the green wellie nympho, right?" said Tinkler.

"Who says she's a nympho, Tinkler?" said Nevada.

"It's obvious. She likes to drive cars naked."

"That's merely an aspiration."

"Yes, Tinkler," I said. "Her name was Selena."

"Well, what does the story say about them?" said Agatha impatiently.

"Are they in a rave star's orgy cult?" said Nevada.

"Sort of," said Tinkler. "In a manner of speaking."

"In a tabloid manner of speaking?" I said.

"Right," said Tinkler. "Exactly."

"And, of course, the rave star is…"

"Lambert 'Imperium Dart' Ramkin. Yes."

"So the three women and him…" said Nevada. "I mean, and he…"

"They were an item?" said Agatha.

"A rather large item," said Nevada.

Silence descended on the back of the cab as the taxi hurtled through the night, moving at a reckless speed under

Declan's control—control being perhaps too generous a word for it—our headlights boring a bright green tunnel through the trees on either side of us.

"They were… a what?" said Nevada. "A throuple?"

"That's three people," said Agatha. "There's four of them."

"So, a quadrouple?"

"A quadrouple," said Tinkler. "Three women. He was living with three women. *Three*."

"Everyone keeps using the past tense," I said.

They all looked at me.

Nevada nodded, her eyes gleaming and serious in the dark back of the taxi. "You're right. They're all still living together."

"Although Lambert has pulled a disappearing act," I said.

"Nevertheless," said Agatha. "They're still living under the same roof. And they have been for—how long, Tinkler?"

Tinkler checked the date on the newspaper. "Around twenty-five years," he said. "Jesus. That's longer than a lot of marriages."

"Only they're not married," said Nevada.

"As far as we know," said Agatha.

"Well, there's a maximum of one he can be married to," said Nevada. "Maybe it's Selena. She's the only one he's had a kid with."

"As far as we know," I said.

"Jesus," said Nevada. "But wait—Poppy said he was her husband."

"Yes," I said. "But she also said she used the term loosely."

"Wow, that's pretty loose."

"Living together all those years," said Tinkler, "in a threesome? I mean a *foursome*?"

"Tinkler's little brain is going to explode."

"And not just my brain."

"Let me see the story, please, Tinkler." I took the phone from him. Story was actually a glorified term for it. It essentially consisted of nothing more than a bald statement of Lambert's domestic arrangement with the three women. But the fact they were all living together was enough to detonate a torrent of salacious speculation and prurient innuendo, balanced of course by stern disapproval emanating from the high moral ground of the gutter press.

It's almost redundant to note that the sensational headline bore no relation to reality, or even to the text presented immediately below it. Nothing was offered to justify the use of the word "cult". This was merely an account of four people who'd set up house together. As for "orgy", that was lascivious guesswork and frankly nobody's business but theirs.

A great deal was made of the fact that Selena, the youngest of the three women, was then still a teenager. This was repeated about six times in the text for maximum scandal value. But she was clearly of a legal age to do whatever she wanted and indeed, since her exact age was never specified, she might have turned twenty a few seconds after the newspaper was printed.

The story was bylined Timothy Purshouse, "Showbiz Journalist of the Year".

I handed the phone back to Tinkler, feeling a little unclean at having allowed Mr Purshouse's prose into my brain. "Wow," said Tinkler. "Think of all the sex they must have been having."

"Which was the entire thrust of the article," said Nevada.

"Thrust," chortled Tinkler.

With a manner suggesting a firm change of subject, Agatha said, "It's really beautiful around here."

I looked out at the forest flashing past us, trees flickering like a strobe. The woods seemed dark, mysterious and endless.

What I didn't think at the time was that this was just the place to dispose of a body.

"This is some of the most ancient woodland in England," said Agatha. "And we might actually be able to see it if we weren't going at warp speed."

"Hey, a *Star Trek* joke," said Tinkler.

But Agatha wasn't joking when she pushed the button and asked Declan politely to slow down. Declan ignored her and speeded up. Agatha pushed the button again and asked him to slow down again. Less politely this time.

Declan ignored her and speeded up some more.

We were moving so quickly now that it was starting to get a little frightening. We were on a curving stretch of country road, those curves unwinding and coiling again with ferocious serpentine swiftness. There was no way you could see what was coming towards you from around the blind side of the curves.

And it was a narrow road, seldom providing adequate space for two vehicles to pass safely side by side.

The London cab we were in was very big and solidly built. But you couldn't help wondering what would happen if this big solid piece of metal hit something equally big and solid coming in the opposite direction.

Just then headlights flashed in front of us. There was a blast of horns, a squeal of tyres. We lurched and rocked to one side, and I looked out the window to see a man's face in a car, staring in horror like a reflection of my own horrified face as his wing mirror was smashed flat against his vehicle with a gunshot sound. Then he was past us and gone.

"Is everyone wearing their seat belts?" said Agatha. Her voice was dangerously calm. When we had all confirmed that of course we were wearing our seat belts, she pushed the button again and said, "Declan, pull over to the side of the road as soon as it's safe to do so, and stop." The way she said it didn't allow any room for argument or disagreement.

Declan apparently didn't see it that way, though.

"Fuck off," he said. And switched off the intercom.

Then, unbelievably, he *increased* his speed.

We were all now staring as if hypnotised, as the uncurling lash of the racing road was carved out of the darkness instant by instant in our headlights. As we hurtled around each blind bend, all we could do was pray we wouldn't find another vehicle coming towards us on the other side.

But finally we did.

It was at a point where the road funnelled through a dense cluster of trees and then opened out into a straight, narrow stretch. As soon as we rounded the curve, we saw the car. It was shooting towards us at a speed comparable to our own.

Even Declan realised we were in trouble now and he hit his horn—as if that would do any good.

And he hit the brakes.

As if that would do any good.

The car came straight at us, growing in a split second from toy-sized to full-sized.

Directly in our path.

I closed my eyes and tried to brace against the inevitable impact.

Tyres screamed on the road surface. Our taxi juddered and shook and jolted to a halt. I counted to three like a child saying a prayer, and then I heard seat belts clattering as they were unbuckled, and I opened my eyes. We were still alive and in one piece. The headlights of the taxi were shining point blank on some trees and we seemed to be at an odd angle to the road.

But we were still alive.

I managed to open my seat belt. My hand was steady and I felt tremendously calm. I looked at Nevada and our gazes meshed for a wordless instant, then we opened the doors and got out with the others. As the cold, fresh night air hit me, I began to feel a lot less steady and calm.

Declan had got out, too, and was inspecting the front of the taxi for damage. We ignored him and turned to the other vehicle, which was stopped at an angle on the verge on the other side of the road.

It was a very familiar car. A Mercedes S-Class.

I said, "Is that—"

"Yes," said Agatha. "It's the car we came down in. Selena may be a rude bitch, but my god she can drive. She just saved all our lives."

But as we started walking towards the Mercedes, we saw that Selena was in the passenger seat. The driver was a man. He was getting out of the car now. Perhaps not surprisingly, he looked furious.

He was a tall, muscular young guy with dark, curly, shoulder-length hair, a full beard and dark eyes that were blazing with rage.

But when he saw us that rage changed to bewilderment. And then delight.

"Agatha?" said the man.

"Horatio?" said Agatha.

"*Shit*," said Tinkler.

4: BACK HOME

Several days later, we were back home in London feeding our cats. Or at least trying to.

Nevada was currently chasing Turk around with a bowl of food.

Our other little darling, Fanny, had consumed her breakfast without hesitation or complaint, then gone outside to sun herself in the garden. But because breakfast today was the expensive, organic and environmentally sourced cat food, Turk regarded it with great suspicion, despite Nevada having helpfully mashed it up in her bowl with a large wooden spoon to make sure it more closely resembled the cheap feline junk-food mess Turk would have much preferred.

Now, holding the bowl in one hand and the big wooden spoon in the other, Nevada had Turk cornered in our living room. She smooshed the spoon into the bowl and then presented the food-coated spoon to Turk, who averted her head, grudgingly sniffed the spoon and then licked her lips.

"She licked her lips!" cried Nevada triumphantly, setting the bowl down on the floor in front of Turk. "We've got her now."

And indeed Turk, her previous reluctance quite forgotten, proceeded to set to with enthusiasm, devouring what until very recently had been reprehensible muck to be spurned.

All of which explains why, when our guest arrived, we looked like the sort of people who feed their cats in the middle of the living room.

Luckily for us, our guest was Tinkler.

"More cat nourishment hijinks?" he said, giving us a knowing look.

"It gets the cattle to Abilene," said Nevada cryptically.

"Glad to see you're keeping the slaves busy, Turk," said Tinkler. "Don't ever relent. They only respect a harsh master."

Turk treated this advice with the disdain it deserved and continued to eat her breakfast.

"You're just in time, Tinkler."

"Oh, indeed? For what, pray tell?"

"A bit of celebrating."

"Perfect. My sixth sense must have sensed that and prompted me to turn up here unannounced."

"You're always turning up here unannounced," said Nevada.

"Well, that's true. What are we celebrating?"

"The cheque from Poppy has cleared and the funds are in our bank account."

"Poppy," said Tinkler. "My goodness. I've been researching pictures of her when she was young…"

"'Researching'?" said Nevada, her upturned eyebrows providing the ironic quotation marks for the word.

"Poppy was so *hot* back in the day. So was what's her name, the cook…"

"Jacquetta," I said.

"She was scorching," said Tinkler. "I bet she had better things to do in those days than bake ciabatta rolls. They were both really good-looking. All three of them. The Green Wellie Nympho, too."

"Selena."

"Yes. Mind you, she's still pretty good-looking."

"Tinkler," said Nevada, "I think it's creepy you googling these women and checking them out."

"Checking out the way they *used* to look," Tinkler corrected her.

"That doesn't redeem anything. It's still creepy. It's *molto* creepy."

"Molto being…"

"Italian for 'very'," said Nevada.

Tinkler sighed. "Well, that's my language lesson for the day." He settled down on the sofa, carefully positioning himself right in the centre. Apparently he thought we were going to be listening to music and that this was the best place to be situated for that pastime. And he was right on both counts, since this was the sweet spot where the soundstage of the two Quad electrostatic speakers would intersect and be at its most transparent and three-dimensional. "Anyway," he said, "what were you saying about Poppy? Hot, hot Poppy of yesteryear, as was?"

"Her cheque has cleared."

"Was there any doubt it would clear?" said Tinkler, looking through the books and magazines on our coffee table.

"No, but we couldn't start celebrating until the money had actually landed in our bank account, could we?"

"Of course you could," said Tinkler. "Why should you be different from everyone else? Spend money you don't have like the rest of us, instead of thriftily waiting for it to arrive. Who do you think you are, the metropolitan elite or something?"

"Yes," said Nevada succinctly, and went into the kitchen—I strongly suspected to fetch some wine. I sat on the sofa beside Tinkler.

"Isn't celebrating a bit premature?" he said. "After all, you haven't done any work yet."

"Who says I haven't done any work?"

"I mean on the case. The new case. The case of the missing techno musician. Or 'Rave Star', as a certain tabloid might have it."

I said, "Who says I haven't done any work on that?"

Tinkler shifted around on the sofa to look at me. "You mean you're already on the case? Have you found him yet?"

"That really would be cause for celebration," I said. "Not yet."

"So what are you doing?"

At this point, Nevada came in from the kitchen and said, "Is he cadging food again?" She was carrying two bottles of white wine and half a dozen glasses. It was a lot for one young woman to carry, but she managed it easily; she'd had plenty of experience.

"No, as it happens," said Tinkler. "But now that you mention it…"

"I'm sure I can fix something," I said.

"If it should chance to be the one-pot macaroni and cheese, so much the better," said Tinkler. "The one that doesn't require making a white sauce."

"I know which one you mean, Tinkler."

"But first perhaps some wine?"

"Today we're on Marsanne," said Nevada, opening the two bottles. The corks had been pulled earlier today and then gently reinserted so the wine had had a chance to breathe and was ready to go when we wanted it. It was a similar principle to keeping the amps warmed up. "We were comparing one actually grown on the north banks of the Rhône with one from Australia."

"An A/B test?" Tinkler chortled with delight as Nevada poured the wine. "How perfectly marvellous."

Meanwhile I put Sonny Rollins on the turntable. *Way Out West* on an original US Contemporary green label with Roy DuNann engineering. We all squeezed onto the sofa together. Tinkler clinked glasses with Nevada. "Your beloved was just about to give me a progress report on the search for Imperium Dart, aka Lambert Ramkin. Or is it the other way around?"

"He's certainly been busy," said Nevada, looking at me as she sipped her Marsanne, dark blue eyes providing a charming contrast with the pale golden wine.

"Doing what exactly?" said Tinkler.

I said, "Visiting various record shops…"

"In other words," said Tinkler, "just doing what he does every day anyway."

"Isn't that sort of the point?" said Nevada. "Isn't that exactly why Poppy hired him?"

"And that's the masterplan, is it?" said Tinkler. "Just wander randomly into record shops and hope you bump into the man you're looking for."

"Not quite," I said. "Poppy has provided some recent photos of Lambert and I've been showing them to people who work in the shops."

"And asking if they've seen him?"

"And asking them to let me know if they *do* see him," I said.

"That all sounds pretty thin," said Tinkler. "And I can tell from the way your missus is grinning that there's more to it than that."

"There is," said Nevada.

"So has he cooked up some kind of cover story?" said Tinkler, leaning across me to better address Nevada.

"He certainly has," said Nevada.

I considered reminding them I was sitting right here, but they were both so happy that it seemed a shame. "I told everyone I was looking for him because I'd done a deal with him on a record," I said. "And I wanted to let him know I'd found it."

"But you'd lost his contact details or some such?" said Tinkler.

"Something like that."

"Plausible enough, I suppose, but still pretty weak."

"Which is why I added money to the equation," I said.

"Ah, money. How so?"

"Well, I said it was a very rare record that cost a lot of money."

"And he owes you for it?" said Tinkler.

"Well, I thought about that," I said. "And I decided people might be reluctant to rat someone out if they believed he owed me money."

Nevada was nodding with approval. Tinkler started nodding, too.

"Good point," he said.

"On the other hand," I said, "if I cooked up the opposite story, that *I* owed *him* money and was looking for him so I could pay it, then people would think that was too good to be true."

Again Nevada nodded, and again Tinkler joined in.

"Would they believe I was really going out of my way to find someone to pay him money I owed him? They might smell a rat."

At this point Turk suddenly came over and joined us, almost as if the conversation had roused her interest. After all, she had once killed a rat and left it under our bed for us to discover, one memorable morning.

"Again, a very good point," said Tinkler. "And what was the solution to your quandary?"

"To do *both*," I said. "I told them he'd paid me a substantial deposit to find this record for him and that I had found it and now I needed to get in touch with him—"

"So he can pay you the rest of your fee," said Tinkler.

"And so he can get his record," I said.

"Isn't it clever?" said Nevada, gazing at me proudly. And I liked to think it wasn't just the wine talking.

"It's okay," said Tinkler. "But there's one way it could be improved…"

"By offering a finder's fee to anyone who can help me find him," I said.

"Exactly. A bit tautologous, but exactly," said Tinkler. "So is that what you've done?"

"That's exactly what he's done," said Nevada, pouring more wine for all of us.

"So, now you sit back and wait for results?"

"No," I said. "Now I go on visiting every record fair, boot fair, jumble sale and second-hand shop where they sell old records. To quote our client."

"Well, I may be able to help you there," said Tinkler. "There's going to be a big record sale in Barnes."

This was just up the road from us. "I haven't heard anything about it," I said.

"They've done a very bad job of publicising it," said Tinkler, "which is all to our advantage."

"Because it reduces the competition," said Nevada.

"Exactly. If they don't know it's taking place, the other bastards can't beat us to the good vinyl."

"How do you happen to know about it?" I said.

"Inside information. From an old flame of mine."

"Would this happen to be Stinky Stanmer's sister?" said Nevada.

"It might be," said Tinkler guardedly.

"No need to be defensive," said Nevada sweetly, pouring us all some more wine. Turk jumped up onto the arm of the sofa and patrolled across the back of it so she could lie down behind us. "Stinky's sister isn't to blame for her family connections. We can't control who our siblings are. And she seems to be a perfectly nice girl."

"I wouldn't go that far," said Tinkler.

"She seemed quite sweet that time we met," said Nevada. "I saved her from drowning, you know."

Turk began to purr contentedly behind us, adding some low-level audio warmth and presence to the Sonny Rollins jazz, like a tiny subwoofer.

"I remember well," said Tinkler. "And you didn't save her from drowning. Agatha saved her from drowning. You just stood around and looked pretty."

"It's what I do best," said Nevada, contentedly sipping her wine.

"Okay," I said, doing my best to keep the conversation on track. "Where exactly is this big record sale taking place?"

"In a church called, I think I've got this right, St Drogo's. Can there be such a place?"

"There certainly can," said Nevada. "Agatha went to a massive paperback sale there."

"Right, exactly. That was such a success…"

"Not for Agatha. She was very disappointed with the selection of crime paperbacks."

"Well, it was a big success for the church, and they've decided to try a record sale next."

"Brilliant," said Nevada. "We'll all go together."

"Including Agatha?" said Tinkler casually.

"I'll see if she's free and if she fancies it," said Nevada equally casually. "I'll see if she's fancy free." Then she chuckled. The wine was beginning to work its magic. "Incidentally, Tinkler," she said, "you seem in surprisingly good spirits."

"I am. Why surprisingly? Why shouldn't I be in good spirits?"

"Because of Agatha bumping into the love of her life the other night."

"Are you referring to the whore ratio?" said Tinkler. "Get it? Like the ratio of a whore?"

"Oh very good," said Nevada. "How long did it take you to think of that one?"

"Not more than several endless days fuelled by constant bitter brooding. And he isn't the love of her life."

"They seemed pretty pleased to see each other," I said.

"They were just thrilled that Declan the boy taxi driver hadn't killed them both."

Well, there was that.

"They exchanged phone numbers," said Nevada. "Agatha and Horatio."

"So what? In this age of the internet and social media they could have got in touch any time they wanted.

Exchanged phone numbers—big deal. And besides, he's clearly fully occupied banging the Green Wellie Nympho."

This was all true enough. Yet I had the impression that Tinkler was a man who was whistling in the dark.

"The whore ratio," said Nevada, and chuckled.

"It is pretty good, isn't it?" said Tinkler. "Can I have some more wine? And where's that macaroni?"

5: EYES FOR YOU

The following morning an interesting and rather important-looking letter arrived in the post. Our address was handwritten on the envelope, which was made of some kind of classy heavyweight paper, and featured stickers and barcodes which indicated someone had paid a premium to post it for guaranteed next-day delivery.

Nevada watched with curiosity as I slit open the envelope, as did our two cats.

The first things that spilled out were two colourful concert tickets for a gig at the Fridge in Brixton. I thought this famed club had closed some years ago but, according to the tickets, this was their grand reopening, featuring Orbital as the headliners, supported by Dominic Glynn and a number of other acts of the same and similar genres of electronic music.

Not Imperium Dart though, I noticed. Oh well, that would have been too easy.

Next out of the envelope was some kind of voucher and, finally, a handwritten note from the same hand that had written our address. The bright red poppies printed on the margins of the notepaper meant we hardly needed to see the signature at the bottom of the note. Above that, it read:

Hello there!

We have a very strong reason to believe that Lambert will be attending this gig tonight. We don't want to attempt to intercept him ourselves because he is liable to see us coming from a mile off and make a run for it. But could you please, please go to the concert (two tickets attached) and try to make contact with him? I know this is terribly short notice and you probably already have other plans for tonight, but we'd be extremely grateful to you if you could see your way to doing this. And, by way of apology and compensation, we're also attaching a coupon we've purchased for you for two meals from this very trendy food van which will be in the vicinity. Their cuisine is said to be excellent!

Thanking you in advance and with very best wishes, Poppy.

"She's not kidding about the cuisine," said Nevada, looking at her phone, holding it in one hand and the voucher in the other. "The ratings for these people are through the roof. I'm almost willing to forgive them for their name, which is 'Food Wagon' but involves a U with an umlaut instead of two Os in 'food'. And no O at all in 'wagon'. Like this."

She showed me the Füd Wagn logo. "Maybe they have something against the letter O," she said.

"Does she really expect us to drop everything and go to this gig tonight?" I said, looking at the tickets.

"That wouldn't actually involve us dropping very much," said Nevada.

"More to the point," I said, "how are we supposed to find him there? Go around with his picture saying, 'Have you seen this man?' In a crowd of two thousand people?"

"No," said Nevada, slowly and judiciously. "But if you circulate you might spot him."

"Again, in a crowd of two thousand?" I was guessing about the capacity of the Fridge, but a later check online showed I wasn't far wrong. About eighteen hundred.

"You can keep your eyes open," said Nevada. "You might get lucky."

"Me?" I said. "Not we?"

Nevada smiled her sweetest smile. "You're right about it being a long shot spotting him. But I think we owe it to Poppy to at least give it a try. Considering she's paying us rather handsomely."

"When you say we owe it to her to give it a try, you mean we owe it to her, but it's me who is going to give it a try."

Nevada added her widest blue-eyed gaze to her sweetest smile. "The music really doesn't appeal to me much. And Agatha and I were going to have a girls' night."

"I thought we didn't have anything to drop tonight?"

"Not 'very much', I said," said Nevada. "And I will come along if you really want me to. But I know someone who'd actually be eager to use that ticket. And hear that music."

She wasn't wrong about that. When I got Tinkler on the phone he said two things. "Yes please." And, "Bring your earplugs."

One advantage to going to the gig with Tinkler was that he could drive us to Brixton in his little red Volvo DAF. We parked outside a friend's house in Dalberg Road then walked to Max Roach Park, partly to pay our respects to the great eponymous jazz musician but mostly because this was where the letter-O-free Füd Wagn was parked.

It was a bright orange vintage Citroën van with Mexican-style floral skulls and buxom bikini-clad girls in sombreros painted on it, and had been modified so that one side opened to reveal a brightly lit kitchen and serving area with a blackboard menu beside it.

They were doing booming business and we had plenty of time to scrutinise that menu while waiting in line.

"The Füd Wagn?" said Tinkler.

"Nevada thinks they don't like the letter O."

"Maybe they bought a font set missing that character," suggested Tinkler, ever the cyberneticist.

"Great theory."

"Thank you."

When we finally got to the front of the queue, I was so focused on placing our order that Tinkler had to remind me about the coupon. "Free food!" he said.

The guy who was serving us seemed puzzled by this document when I handed it over, but the woman working with him plucked it from his fingers and said, "I've got this."

She smiled at me. She had vivid green eyes. Her hair colour was a mystery because it was concealed inside a cylindrical white paper cap. "She's got eyes for you," Tinkler whispered in my ear as the woman turned away to get our food from the grill.

"Why does no one ever have eyes for me?" he lamented as we walked away with our meals, hot and fragrant in their eco-friendly disposable paper containers. "It's always the guy who already has the hot girlfriend that other girls hit on."

"No one hit on me, Tinkler."

"I get the picture. I won't tell Nevada."

"There's nothing to tell."

"Got it."

"There's nothing to get."

"My lips are sealed. Your secret's safe with me."

We ate in Max Roach Park. The food was superb. I'd chosen Asian chicken with shaved coconut and kimchi mayonnaise. It was the sort of elaborate meal I wouldn't have prepared for myself at home.

However, I had indeed prepared a meal for myself at home that evening and eaten it with Nevada before we'd come out. So I could only manage about half of the enormous portion I'd been served. When I set it aside, Tinkler said, "What's going on?"

"I'm full."

"For the love of heaven, don't let that stop you. I never do."

"You eat it then."

"Okay, I will," said Tinkler.

And he did.

Then we disposed of our food containers in a responsible fashion and made our way to the venue. Here, our attempts to spot Lambert Ramkin in the crowd, if indeed he was present, proved as futile as I'd expected. Tinkler didn't help matters by offering frequent random sightings.

"Is that him?"

"No, Tinkler. That's a woman."

"Is that him?"

"No, that's a rubbish bin."

"Behind it."

"That's a woman with a child."

"It could be him. Either of them could be him."

Finally, we were the last people left in an empty lobby. Well, empty except for venue staff, security people and merchandise sellers. We gave it a little longer in case Lambert Ramkin was the type to arrive fashionably late, which seemed plausible enough. So we stood there, getting some odd looks from the venue staff, security people and merchandise sellers while music pounded away inside.

There was indeed a steady trickle of stragglers and latecomers. But they were all so obviously not our man that not even Tinkler bothered suggesting them as possibilities. Finally, we gave up and went in for the gig, having missed some of the opening acts. "Maybe we'll spot him in here," said Tinkler.

"Because the conditions for spotting him will be so much better in the chaotic darkness and noise?"

"You're just a negative thinker."

The interior of the venue had been reconfigured for a standing-only performance. Instead of the seating being removed, an elevated platform had been installed above it, creating a kind of false floor a couple of metres above the actual floor level. This in turn had required the stage itself to be raised to prevent the acts being at the same level as the audience. After all that work it probably would have been easier for them to have taken out the seats.

We went up a temporary set of stairs onto the temporary floor and joined the throng just as Dominic Glynn began playing the *Doctor Who* theme, to a rapturous response from the audience. I wasn't an electronic dance music kind of guy but there was something about this communal experience, surrounded by an ardent, ecstatic crowd, all moving in time to the pounding music, that went into me at a primal level. I felt my heart hammer and sweat seemed to pour out of me.

Tinkler was unashamedly dancing, as were so many fellow ravers. I might even have done some dancing myself, to use the term loosely. I was surprised at how carried away I was by the music. It seemed to be entering into my body and making itself at home there, co-opting the pounding of my heart, the thudding of my pulse.

Then, after thunderous applause and a strange timeless interval, it was Orbital's turn to take to the stage.

"Did you know that they're named after the M25, London's orbital road?" said Tinkler. Or rather, shouted Tinkler, since there was considerable ambient noise and we were both wearing earplugs.

"I know that, Tinkler. Everyone knows that."

"Because that was the access route for rural raves in the 1990s," continued Tinkler.

"I *didn't* know that," I said.

Tinkler smiled with satisfaction. He looked very sweaty and very happy. I was glad we'd given him the ticket. He was having a splendid time.

I wished I was having a splendid time. But I was beginning to feel very strange indeed. This feeling of strangeness wasn't helped by the eerie sound loops playing to welcome the headliners onto the stage. Endlessly repeated and vaguely menacing dialogue from some science fiction movie I couldn't identify. Then Orbital came on, the Hartnoll brothers two dark figures taking their places amid shadowy heaps of technology. And the audience convulsed like a single organism as they began playing, smashing, echoing, metallic swells of sound.

Tinkler leaned close to me, grinning. "It's like being in an MRI scanner," he shouted. "But with a better light show."

Tinkler actually had once been in an MRI scanner, after sustaining a serious head injury, so he ought to know.

That was our last chance at communication because a moment later we were separated in the crush as the audience surged around us. It reminded me strangely and fearfully of a time when we had all been in the water together, swiftly rising tidal water, and had been swept apart. I felt the same helplessness now as I was carried along by a force that was beyond my control.

I looked everywhere for Tinkler, but he was gone. I felt simultaneously very alarmed and very relaxed, as if I was standing to one side of myself and regarding my anxious self with utter detachment.

The darkness was abruptly slashed with giant slices of shuddering blue light, fixing the dancers all around me in their abandoned poses in frozen subdivisions of time like still photographs, then accelerating with stroboscopic speed. The light turned white and I was in a black-and-white world, sliced into segments.

Convulsed in dance, the crowd rose and fell around me like ocean waves. The great mass of people moved with a single synchronous impulse and once more I was swept away from where I stood, carried along helplessly. I managed to keep my footing, but only just. I knew that if I went down the crowd would close over me. The waves would close over me.

Then suddenly the waves parted, and she was standing in front of me. Dressed all in black, abandoned in dance, her silver hair thrown around her head, seeming to drift in slow motion in the strobe light, like seaweed in the shifting tidal currents.

She was looking at me while she danced. White sheets of light blasted the blackness. Her face was white, her hair was white, but her eyes were the most intense green.

It was the girl from the food van.

At least I thought it was her.

"Eyes for you," Tinkler whispered in my ear. But Tinkler wasn't there.

She was staring at me and, as the white light washed her face, I could see those green, green eyes.

Her eyes opened like flowers, the emerald green of them opening like flower petals in response to the light, opening wide and the great black pupils at the centre of each eye growing like the mouths of a black abyss you could fall into.

I fell into them.

The waves closed around me, the crowd closed around me, and I felt myself going under.

She reached out and took my hand. I realised what she was now. She was a spirit of the sea, a mermaid, and I was the drowning man she'd come to rescue.

She pulled me from the waves and drew me through the crowd. The waves seemed to part, people seemed to part to make way for us. She led me out of the deep waters into the shallows, towards dry land…

Like a siren leading a shipwrecked mariner to safety.

But wait—didn't sirens lead mariners to their doom?

We emerged from the ocean onto the shore. We emerged from the crowd into the area at the back of the elevated floor, at the far end from the stage. Here the floor had diagonal black-and-yellow hazard stripes painted on it. Actually, the floor surface was already black, so they'd only had to paint the yellow stripes. This struck me at the time as a profound observation. The words *Keep Clear* were also painted on it. We went and stood on the words.

The woman leaned in close to me so I could hear her as lights and music exploded around us. "Stay here," she said.

Then the lights changed.

And then she was someone else. And then she was some*where* else.

She was gone.

I stood there on the words *Keep Clear*. They seemed to lift off the floor and float above it. So did the yellow stripes. I felt myself begin to float, too. In front of me was the great moving mass of the audience, beyond them the slow-motion firework display of the stage. Behind me was a small strip of the floor, then a drop, then the expanse of empty concrete floor below. Further back from that, there was a bar area with people standing by it.

Something happened on the stage. I couldn't see what it was, but it caused the audience to move back, like a giant organism flowing unstoppably towards me. The audience was expanding the way water expands in rippling circles when you drop a stone into it. The ripples reached me, the swell of the crowd, it forced me back. I backed away and the crowd kept coming.

I kept backing away.

The crowd kept coming.

I kept backing away.

And then suddenly there was nowhere left to back away to.

I'd reached the edge of the elevated floor. There was no guard rail. There was nothing to cling on to. In front of me there was just an expanding mass of humanity, their backs all turned to me, being forced back by the oceanic swell of the crowd.

And in turn forcing me back towards empty space and a drop to the concrete floor below.

I flailed helplessly.

I began to fall.

I fell.

I fell onto a hundred hands reaching up to catch me and hold me safely.

The hands pushed me gently, firmly, strongly back up onto the elevated floor. I found my feet again. I stood up. The crowd in front of me had moved forward, back towards the stage. There was plenty of room around me now. I was safe.

I looked back, over the edge of the raised floor, and saw that the crowd from the bar were standing below. A hundred strangers smiling up at me. They must have seen me start to fall and come to save me.

I felt tears sting in my eyes and then I couldn't see anything at all, just jagged fractured lights as my eyes filled and the music danced and lunged, and the crowd danced and lunged.

When my vision finally cleared, I saw the words *Keep Clear* on the floor below me and decided it was good advice.

I went to the edge of the floor and sat down, legs dangling. Then I placed my hands at either side of me, and carefully jumped down. For a moment after I landed it seemed like I couldn't move, as if I'd jumped into some kind of sticky quicksand, but then I found I could move again. I started to walk.

I looked at the people at the bar, the people who had saved me. None of them were looking at me. They'd forgotten me. I went out through a swinging door into the lobby. The door swung shut and instantly cut off the sound of the gig behind me. The lobby was dazzlingly, painfully bright. All white light and dirty black-and-white tiled floor. And standing in the middle of the floor was Tinkler.

He shook his head impatiently.

"Did it really take you this long to work out where to find me?"

"I'm so glad to see you," I said.

"Are you tripping?"

"Yes," I said.

"I thought so.

"Did you dose me?" I asked him.

"Not this time. Come on. Let's get you home."

We walked out of the venue, out into the night, along streets. The warm air smelled of food and traffic fumes. I heard cars. I heard music. I saw lights. I saw the sky, clouds as heavy and solid as a cement ceiling, hanging low, reflecting the lights of London. I was lost in the infinity of this city. It didn't matter. Tinkler was beside me. I was all right. We came to Dalberg Road. We got into his car. The familiar smell of it was infinitely moving. I felt the enormous emotional swell of homecoming, being back in this friendly, familiar space. There was a thunderous noise, strangely musical, repetitive and intricate, positively apocalyptic.

I realised Tinkler had started the engine.

We pulled away as if the car was being released from glue. I told Tinkler about almost falling off the elevated floor. "I probably would have been all right," I said. "It wasn't so far to fall."

"Don't kid yourself," said Tinkler. "That's about how far Zappa fell off the stage at the Rainbow and he was in hospital for months. One of his legs was permanently shorter than the other afterwards. And his voice dropped a couple of octaves. Neck injuries."

"Oh," I said. There was a silence that echoed down the ages and then I said, "It was the food from that van. Dosed with acid or something."

"Must have been," agreed Tinkler.

"Don't you feel anything?" I said.

"A bit. I feel a bit like when you're coming down with the flu," said Tinkler. "You know, a bit out of it and glassy. But that's it. That's all. But you know what I'm like. I'm a big disappointment to people who try to drug me. But it was enough, feeling like that. To tip me off. That's how I knew you must be really tripping. Are you really tripping?"

"Yes."

"Well, you might as well enjoy it," he said. "Look out the window and enjoy all of the pretty lights as we speed along."

At that point we stopped at a red light.

"Okay, so we'll speed along in a minute," said Tinkler. He took out his phone and made a call while we waited for the traffic signal to change. The red light was enormous, like the sun.

"Hi," said Tinkler into the phone. "Get prepared for psychedelic sex. Your boyfriend is tripping. No! Why does everybody always think it was me? It was the people at the food wagon. In fact, it was the girl at the food wagon. Sorry, the Füd Wagn. She was taking an unusual interest in your beau. It seemed a bit suspicious, even at the time. Oh, stop moaning. I ate half of it myself. No, I'm fine. You know me. Immune to psychedelic drugs. Of course I'm driving. Of course I'm all right to drive. I could drive and play chess and water-ski. Assuming I could water-ski. Or play chess. Right. See you soon."

He hung up, the light turned green.

Enormous, infinite green. As green as the girl's eyes.

As we pulled away, I said, "I think I saw the girl from the food wagon."

"You mean the Füd Wagn. What, she was at the gig?"

"Yes. She led me to the edge of the floor. I think she deliberately left me there."

"Are you sure it was her?" said Tinkler.

"No."

"Are you even sure there was anyone there?"

"No."

"Well, just sit back and enjoy your trip," said Tinkler. "You've got psychedelic sex waiting for you at home, after you receive a scolding for flirting with the girl in the Füd Wagn."

"I didn't flirt with her."

"And you might not want to mention hanging out with her at the gig. At least until after you've had your psychedelic sex."

"I didn't hang out with her."

"That's your story," said Tinkler. "Now just enjoy the pretty lights streaming past. Aren't they like little spaceships shooting at each other? 'Just like Beggar's Canyon back home.' Oh look, isn't that a black monolith, floating in space? Now it's opening and brilliant-coloured lights are beginning to stream out towards you…"

"If you're just going to make clumsy references to vintage science fiction films, I'm going to go to sleep," I said.

"No you're not. Look at those coloured lights streaking towards you. Get ready for some very baffling antique French furniture."

6: PRINCESS SATAN

Not surprisingly, I felt very peculiar the next day. I wandered like a stranger through our house which seemed much larger and emptier than ever before. There was something immensely odd and sad about the sunlight that poured through the windows. I felt bereft and lonely.

I thought the cats were avoiding me, but I couldn't tell if that was really the case or if I was imagining it. So I asked Nevada.

"I think they might be avoiding you because you smell funny. It's the drugs. They're coming out of your system. I can smell them myself."

"I'm sorry," I said.

"Don't worry," she said. She put her hand on my shoulder. It felt like a small animal tentatively perching there. The phone rang and she answered it. It was Tinkler, so she put him on speaker.

"How's the raver?" he said.

"In recovery," I croaked.

"Well, I'm feeling bright and chipper. Whoever dosed us didn't realise that I'm a freak of nature and immune to psychedelic drugs. They didn't know that was my superpower."

"They didn't even know you were going to the gig," said Nevada. "It was supposed to be me."

"Good point. So, what are you going to do now?"

"What we should have done in the first place," said Nevada. "Check whether it was actually Poppy who sent us the letter."

"Want to know what my bet is?" said Tinkler.

Tinkler would have won his bet. We arranged a video call with Poppy and emailed her a photograph of the note. When the appointed time arrived and we were all on the same screen together, her first words were, "I didn't send that letter."

"We guessed as much," said Nevada. "But is that your handwriting?"

"No, I just told you—"

"No," said Nevada, cutting in. "I didn't mean, did you write it? I meant, does it *look* like your handwriting? Is it a good imitation?"

"No, it's nothing like it," said Poppy. She sounded worried and exasperated. "Do you want a sample of my handwriting, for comparison?"

"No," said Nevada. "What I'm getting at is that, if it *had* been a good copy, that would have told us something."

"What?" said Poppy. "What would it have told us?"

"That whoever sent the letter knew you well," I said.

"I see," said Poppy. She didn't seem impressed. "But it might still be someone who knows me well; they just didn't want to bother imitating my handwriting. That certainly isn't my notepaper. They made no effort to get that right."

Since the paper in question featured poppies on it, I thought they actually had gone to some effort to get that right. I also thought that whoever had written the note might not have done a good job of imitating her handwriting, but they'd done an excellent job of imitating her syntax and speech patterns. I didn't mention any of this, though, because the eponymous Poppy seemed defensive enough already.

Not that she should be the one who was feeling defensive.

To make this point, I told her the story of our evening. With a heavy emphasis on being drugged against my will.

"My god," said Poppy, now sounding agreeably contrite. "That's why they sent you the food voucher."

"Right."

"Do you think they actually intended to hurt you by leaving you at the edge of the floor like that?"

In my account I had also emphasised my close call with a Zappa-like plunge.

"The jury's still out on that," I said.

"I think we have to assume that was the case," said Nevada. "For our own safety."

"I certainly hope it wasn't the case," said Poppy. "And I don't really believe that was the intention."

"Why?" said Nevada.

"Because it wouldn't be like Lambert," said Poppy.

"Lambert?" Nevada sounded as surprised as I was.

"Nevertheless, this is very good, positive news," said Poppy.

"In what way good and positive?"

"It means Lambert is alive and well. And feeling playful."

"Playful?" said Nevada. "Jesus."

Poppy quickly added, "Although, of course, it was enormously distressing for you. And naturally we'll have to significantly increase your fee to compensate for the unpleasantness involved."

The mention of a significant fee increase immediately mellowed Nevada. She didn't actually start purring, but you get the idea. I then tuned out and checked my emails as the two women proceeded to negotiate over money, and eventually tuned back in to hear Poppy saying, "Once again, let me say how terribly sorry I am that this should have happened to you."

"It's our own fault," said Nevada, happy to cop a mea culpa now that our salary had been beefed up. "We should have double-checked that it was you who actually sent us the tickets and food coupon. Rookie error."

"I'm afraid it wouldn't have done you any good," said Poppy.

"What do you mean?"

"Either by accident or by design, whoever sent you that letter timed it to arrive on a day when I wasn't at home. I was out visiting gardens at stately homes in the area. I do that from time to time to get tips for our own garden, and also because I just like doing it. I find gardens very calming. And when I'm out on a day like that, I have my phone turned off, for virtually the whole day. It's so peaceful. So, you see, you couldn't have reached me even if you had wanted to."

"All of which," I said, "argues strongly for it being someone who knows your routine."

"Well Lambert knows my routine. In broad outline, so to speak. But since it was more or less a spur-of-the-moment thing, I don't really see how he could have known I was going to go out on that particular day."

"Or how he could have known you'd hired us in the first place," I said.

"Good point," said Nevada.

"All of which argues," I said, "for someone in your household being in touch with Lambert and telling him what's going on."

"Selena or Jacquetta?" said Poppy.

"Or Julian," I said.

"Oh, highly unlikely."

"Why?"

"Because Julian has significant father issues and is seldom on speaking terms with Lambert, so they are hardly likely to be in clandestine contact. In fact, Julian is the one person who doesn't really want Lambert to be found. He'd be quite happy for him to stay away forever."

"But it could still be Selena or Jacquetta," I said.

"I don't see why they would do such a thing," said Poppy. "And you shouldn't jump to the conclusion that anyone at all is helping Lambert."

"Why not?"

"Because he's quite capable of finding out things on his own. He is very resourceful."

I wasn't particularly convinced by this, but I didn't argue the point.

"So, we're back to Lambert being behind everything?" said Nevada.

"Yes, apart from the possibility of harming you," said Poppy, looking at me, "which would be so utterly unlike him. Otherwise this whole situation is very much the kind of intricate intrigue that Lambert enjoys orchestrating."

"You mean he plays pranks on people?" said Nevada.

"I wouldn't use the word 'pranks'. They are considerably more elaborate than that."

"Well, if it was Lambert," I said, "that means he knows we're looking for him."

"I suppose it does," said Poppy. "Nevertheless, I hope that won't put you off. Finding him, I mean."

"Just knowing that he's all right isn't enough?" I said. "You still actually want us to find him?"

Nevada shot me a look that told me to button my lip and belay any line of chat that might lead to cutting short our employment.

"But we don't know that he's all right, do we?" said Poppy.

"Well, he's certainly alive and well enough to be arranging elaborate hoaxes on me," I said.

"But we can't be sure it was him who did that," said Poppy, neatly reversing her earlier position without so much as batting an eyelash. "By the way, have you thought of getting in touch with the people at the food van? Surely if this woman was responsible for drugging you, she must know something?"

"We're way ahead of you," said Nevada with justifiable pride. "I rang them this morning, posing as a potential customer, and asking to hire the same team who worked in Brixton last night."

"Because we were so impressed with them," I said. Actually, I *was* rather impressed. I still had treacherously pleasurable memories of how wonderful that Asian chicken had tasted. Not to mention the kimchi mayonnaise. Oddly enough, everything that had occurred subsequent to this had done nothing to alter the disloyal judgement of my tastebuds.

"That's right. Because we were so impressed with them," said Nevada. "And they told me that, unfortunately, we couldn't have exactly the same team because the woman has now left their employ."

Was there a note of venom in the way Nevada uttered the words "the woman"? It was always reassuring to know she had my back, although I pitied "the woman" if Nevada ever got her hands on her.

"But at least you have her name," said Poppy. "And that's a start."

"Oh, we got her name, all right," said Nevada.

"That doesn't sound very promising," said Poppy, who was anything but obtuse. "What's the problem?"

"The problem is that her name is Princess Seitan. Seitan spelled like the vegan foodstuff."

"Made from wheat protein. I know it well. Jacquetta is a dab hand with it and she's made some lovely dishes with it which we've all enjoyed, especially Selena when she's going through one of her vegan phases. Although her greedily tucking into it does tend to make a hilarious mockery of her gluten-intolerant phases... because it's almost pure gluten, you see, seitan." Poppy came to a halt at this point as if realising she'd gone off on a tangent, or perhaps was oversharing. "Anyway, are you saying that's the only name this woman is known by? Princess Seitan?"

"Yes," said Nevada.

"That must have made processing her national insurance and income tax a challenge for their payroll."

"I don't think they're very big on national insurance and income tax at the Füd Wagn," said Nevada. This name also got the venom treatment.

"And, seriously," said Poppy, "this is what everyone went around calling her all day? Princess Seitan?"

"No," said Nevada. "According to the bloke I spoke to, she was mostly just called Princess."

"Well, that's a little less bizarre, anyway," said Poppy.

"And it might even be her name," I said.

"True," said Nevada.

"I've heard odder Christian names," said Poppy. She paused briefly, apparently to mentally review the salient bullet points, then said, "So, the situation is that a person or persons unknown, pretending to be me, sent you off on a wild goose chase, in the course of which they did or did not deliberately intend to do you harm. And, either by accident or by design, chose a day when it would have been impossible for you to confirm whether or not it was actually me who had sent you that invitation. Is that a fair summary?"

"My money is on 'persons', 'did' and 'by design'," said Nevada.

"And while I believe, on the contrary, that no harm was intended and that it was Lambert who was responsible, we need to keep an open mind on both those scores." Poppy looked at me.

I actually thought this was a very fair summary and said so. Nevada grudgingly agreed.

"But the main thing is that you're going to keep looking and find Lambert?" said Poppy.

"We are going to do our best," I said.

"I truly hope you do find him." She sighed. "This incident has made me miss him all the more keenly. It was just like the good old days."

I dreaded to imagine what those good old days must have consisted of. It really didn't bear thinking about, at least by me in my current fragile condition.

"Can I see that letter again?" said Poppy.

We put it up on the screen for her.

Poppy looked thoughtful for a moment as she studied it. "The most distressing aspect to this whole situation is the suggestion that I would use that dreadful notepaper."

"We thought there was a more distressing aspect to the situation than that notepaper," said Nevada as she topped up our wine glasses.

"I should imagine so," said Agatha, looking at me with concern. "How are you feeling?"

"I've just about got it out of my system."

"He's *fine*," called Tinkler, opening the garden gate.

Nevada, Agatha and I were sitting in the garden, enjoying the evening sunlight and the intermittent company of our cats. Tinkler had just arrived. Before he could come in through the gate, Nevada stopped him with a sharp, imperative command.

"Don't move."

He froze obediently and said, "Okay, why not?"

"Don't break the spiderweb."

Tinkler paused and stared at the very large spider's web that extended down from one of the lower branches of the sycamore tree to our purple sage, planted in a position of honour in the centre of our garden. "Okay, why not?"

"Because that poor spider put so much work into making that web. And she might have children to feed."

"You're sure it's a lady spider?" said Tinkler, ducking carefully under the web.

"We're not taking any chances," said Nevada.

"Very wise."

Once safely past the web, Tinkler came over to join us. Nevada and I were in garden chairs and Agatha was on the garden sofa, so no prizes for guessing where Tinkler sat. "Now, what was I saying before I was so rudely interrupted by some disgustingly anthropomorphised arachnids?"

"Just one arachnid," said Agatha.

"Because she hasn't had her babies yet," said Nevada.

"But nevertheless, full marks for vocabulary," said Agatha.

"And alliteration," added Nevada.

"Thank you both," said Tinkler. "I remember now. I was talking about our friend here." He nodded at me. "I was saying he's fine."

"How do you know?" said Nevada.

"Because having your food spiked with vast quantities of unknown powerful psychedelic drugs has never done anyone any harm," said Tinkler. "Allow me to rephrase that. It has never done *me* any harm. Anyway, he looks all right, doesn't he?"

In fact, I was feeling considerably better than I had this morning. And the cats had started to let me get near them again, which was reassuring.

"He's just a sissy where drugs are concerned," continued Tinkler. "The poor fool doesn't like to challenge his brain with anything stronger than coffee."

"And wine," said Nevada, clinking glasses with me.

"And wine."

"You're so lucky you only ate half your portion of that food," said Agatha.

"I ate the other half for him," said Tinkler. "And I felt *great*. Have I mentioned my superpower?"

"Not in the last five minutes," said Agatha. "Now what's this about St Drogo's in Barnes?"

"They're having a record sale there tomorrow," said Tinkler casually. "If you fancy coming along?"

"Sure," said Agatha. She looked at us. "Will you be looking for your missing person there?"

"Yes," I said.

"Do you think you'll find him?"

"Who cares," said Tinkler. "Just as long as we find some records."

I woke up in the middle of the night—around three in the morning, to be more exact—with Nevada awake and tense beside me. "Did you hear that?" she said.

"It sounded like our garden gate," I said. Our front garden had a steel gate that made a distinctive screeching sound, especially if you'd neglected to oil the hinges, as I had lately. However, our neighbours had identical gates, which made virtually identical noises. And I pointed this out to Nevada.

"Fanny thinks it's our gate," she said.

It was true. Our cat, who had been sleeping contentedly between us, was now poised on the edge of the bed in a taut listening pose, her small head pointed in the direction of the front garden.

It was also true that the cats, with their more sensitive hearing, could easily distinguish the sound of our gate from those of our neighbours, and the way Fanny was behaving pretty much clinched the matter.

Nevada slipped out of bed and pulled on a T-shirt. I did the same while she rifled through the cupboard. "What are you looking for?" I said.

"A non-lethal weapon." She emerged with the Taser we'd bought some years ago but never, fortunately, had occasion to use.

Perhaps it made me a dull fellow that I was also hoping we wouldn't have to use it now.

I went through to the kitchen and looked out the window. "I can't see anyone there," I said.

"Let's find out," said Nevada. She slipped on her shoes, quietly unlocked the front door and then flung it open, the Taser ready in her right hand. Cool air and the honeysuckle and lavender smell of our plants flowed in past us. The front garden was very small and there was nowhere for anyone to hide. Nevertheless, Nevada stepped outside. Fanny appeared from the bedroom and called out after her.

"You stay indoors, little one," said Nevada.

Just then the cat flap rattled and Turk hurried in from the back garden to join the fun.

"You shut the door and wrangle the cats," said Nevada.

And that was what I did. I poured out some dry food for them, then pulled on a pair of jeans and some shoes, and went out to join Nevada.

I shut the door behind me, making sure I had a key in my pocket to prevent hilarious complications.

Nevada was sitting in one of the chairs we kept beside our planters. I sat in another one next to her. "Nothing?" I said.

She looked up from the Taser, which she'd been turning over in her hands. "The gate's open," she said.

I looked. She was right. It was slightly ajar.

"Could Tinkler and Agatha have left it like that?" said Nevada.

I wished I could say yes, but I shook my head. "They know better than that."

Our friends were aware we were rather particular about the gate being shut, and they scrupulously did so.

"So, someone's been here," said Nevada.

"It looks like it," I said.

We both got up and went out the gate, and stood there looking at our estate, silent and tranquil under the yellow security lights. It was deserted except for us. There was the occasional sound of traffic on the main road and somewhere a night bird called out.

"Maybe it was just some drunk," I said. "He realised he'd got the wrong house and went away and found the right one."

"Maybe," said Nevada.

We went back in, closing the gate behind us.

I slept badly. I'm not sure Nevada slept at all.

In my dreams, I was talking to the green-eyed woman from the Brixton gig. I asked her why they spelled the name of the Füd Wagn without the letter O.

"The question you should be asking," said Princess Seitan, "is why I'm not spelling my name with E I anymore, but with an A."

7: CHURCH SALE

St Drogo's was a church in Barnes, a village in suburban London, which was just a short walk from where we lived. Not quite as picturesque as Nutalich, although it did have a duck pond of its own, Barnes was a pretty little high-end hamlet inhabited by the rich, the very rich, and the very, very rich.

We came from the other side of the tracks in every sense. In fact, we walked over those tracks on our way there, waited patiently for a train to pass, and then carried on to rendezvous with Agatha and Tinkler at the arts centre café on the village green.

From here it was about a minute and a half to St Drogo's. The church was an elegant art deco confection of green and white with an impressive and rather austere modernist stained-glass window that could only be seen in its full glory from inside the big central hall of the church. The window was all the more impressive when Agatha told us it had recently been smashed by a tree branch in a storm and had to be painstakingly reconstructed.

The repairs certainly didn't show on the stained glass, which in a sombre palette of black, white, greys and greens depicted the saint the church was named after—a handsome fellow, surrounded by some remarkably ugly people. "St Drogo is the patron saint of the physically unattractive," explained Agatha.

"My tribe," said Tinkler.

Of even more interest than the stained glass, at least to me, were the rows of tables which currently filled the church's central hall, laden with crates of vinyl, and crowded with people buying and selling.

My tribe.

I was familiar with many of the dealers here, but there were a number I'd never seen before. So naturally I explored those first. As is traditional with people selling records in any situation, there were plenty of crates inconveniently situated at ground level, under the tables, so I was glad I'd worn my vinyl-hunting shoes, which are cut low at the sides and therefore allowed me to crouch comfortably, or at least not too uncomfortably, as I went through the crates.

I also, of course, went through the crates more accessibly situated on the tables themselves. No special footwear was required for examining these.

Nevada and Agatha had volunteered to take over Lambert Ramkin-spotting duties while the menfolk, such as we were, obsessively combed through the crates of vinyl. This was kind of them, and practical, since our attention would inevitably have been divided between our real job at hand and our ever-present obsession.

Occasionally, as I emerged from my plunges into the piles of vinyl, I checked, with a small but real feeling of guilt, on the women. The big room had become very crowded by now and they were both circulating in the throng, apparently looking casually at their phones, on which there were a selection of recent photographs of our quarry, and then equally casually scanning the people around them.

Overcoming my guilt, I returned to looking through the records, occasionally running into Tinkler as we randomly ended up at the same seller's table together. I noticed Tinkler had a bag under one arm, indicating he'd found something. Personally, I'd found nothing. And soon I'd have nowhere left to look.

Except one place.

This was at the biggest and, though the word stuck in my throat, grandest record stall present there today. They had taken possession of several tables, which ran the full length of one of the narrow sides of the big rectangular hall. A banner hung on the wall behind them said, *Mindy Indie Vinyl—Your Trustworthy Independent Record Seller. Rare Vinyl Bought and Sold. Best Prices Paid. Highest Quality Accurate Grading. No Quibble Refunds.*

"Mendacious Mindy," said Tinkler.

I turned to see he was standing beside me.

"Hard to count the number of lies on that thing," he said, indicating the banner. "But have you looked at all the other sellers' tables?"

"Yup," I said.

"And are you now wrestling with the temptation to look at *their* stuff?"

"I'm afraid so," I said.

Mindy's had a lot of stock and they were doing a thriving business. And no doubt there were some fine records lurking there, waiting for someone to come and rescue them. But I was still deeply reluctant to give these people my business.

"Aren't they the idiots who sold you that faulty British promo copy of the Art Pepper album?" said Tinkler.

"That's right," I said.

"And they refused to give you the guaranteed full refund they make such a big deal about promising."

"Don't you ever get tired of being right?" I said. "And that's not all. They then blacklisted me, because I complained."

"Really? Holy shit, I didn't know that part."

"If I ever want to order anything from their website, god forbid, I'll have to get you to do it for me."

"I'm your man," said Tinkler. "Wherever any duplicity is required."

"Thank you."

"Now," said Tinkler, "just so we're clear about this, these guys are despicable, dishonest, vindictive swindlers whom we should boycott and never shop with again."

"Absolutely correct," I said.

"So, shall I start with their crates on the left and you work from the right?"

"It sounds like a plan," I said.

The thing about Mindy's was that they thought they knew all about rare vinyl, while they simply didn't. They didn't have a clue. But this cluelessness cut both ways.

Their stock was often wildly overgraded or overpriced.

But sometimes it was wildly undergraded or underpriced.

This maxim was brought home to me dramatically when, after looking through all the genres of music I was personally interested in, I then, purely as a matter of business, checked the electronic dance section.

I didn't actually expect to run into Lambert Ramkin in person while I was flipping through the records here, but it wouldn't do any harm. And I was also beginning to acquire some expertise and knowledge about Ramkin's own records, recorded as Imperium Dart.

Know the music, know the man, was my thinking.

Plus, I was honestly interested.

That honest interest sharpened dramatically when I found a copy of his album *The Magus* on clear vinyl, released on his own ID record label. I pulled it out of the crate and examined it carefully. When something seems too good to be true, it generally is. On the other hand…

Over my years of record hunting I'd occasionally made staggering finds. And if you adopted a too-cynical attitude, you'd end up passing these by and missing out on treasures.

Now, *The Magus* wasn't exactly a rare album. Even its silly coloured-vinyl variations. There had been a mass market pressing of the clear vinyl edition, for example, and hundreds of thousands of copies were floating around. But there had also been a special very limited edition, which was rather rare and valuable.

Also on clear vinyl.

As I examined the record, I realised Nevada was standing beside me. "Have you found something?" she asked.

"Yes," I said, "How could you tell?"

"By the way you were standing. By the way you were holding that." She nodded at the record. "I immediately knew something was up. It was obvious."

"Well let's hope it's not obvious to those fuckers." I sneaked a glance at the Mindy's staff behind the table. At least one of the Mindy's crew was already giving me a suspicious look. It was the guy who was the father of one of the others, and he was the worst of them. He was quite capable of refusing to sell me this record at the sticker price if he thought—correctly, of course, in this case—that I was getting a huge bargain.

"Look," I said to Nevada. "Can you hold on to this record for me while I check it out on my phone without looking like I'm checking it out on my phone?"

"I can do better than that," said Nevada. And then she said in a loud shrill voice, "Haven't you booked a table at the restaurant yet? We'll *never* get in if you haven't booked a table at the restaurant."

She continued on this theme for a time and then bad-temperedly snatched the record from me as I took out my phone while looking sheepish, which wasn't difficult because everyone was staring at me. Some with amused contempt, some with male we're-all-in-this-together camaraderie. And

Agatha and Tinkler with impressed respect for Nevada's acting skills.

But, most importantly, the suspicious look from the Mindy's guy had ceased and he'd gone back to pricing— overpricing—records.

Nevada winked at me while I confirmed on my phone that this really was the rare, limited edition and was, as I now whispered to Nevada, worth many, many times what the clowns had priced it at.

I bought it, for cash to avoid any chance of blowback, and we turned away proudly with our little treasure.

"What did you find?" said Tinkler, closing in immediately.

"An Imperium Dart album," said Nevada.

"Is it a clue?" said Agatha.

"Better than that," said Nevada. "It's a bargain. It's worth many, many times what we paid for it."

"Suddenly you're an expert on Imperium Dart albums?" said Tinkler.

"I've learned from the master," said Nevada.

"By the way, has the master seen this?" said Agatha.

While Nevada and Tinkler wandered around the sale, she led me to a table I had visited briefly earlier and quickly dismissed. I had visited it briefly and dismissed it quickly because I had been able to see, even at a glance, that their vinyl stock consisted of nothing but recent reissues, all sealed and shiny and not great sonically, and of no interest to me whatsoever.

But what I hadn't seen and what Agatha had spotted was that they also had a stack of books, everything from amateurish self-published discographies to lavish coffee-table volumes of album cover art, and biographies of musicians and bands.

Among the latter was a glossy paperback volume entitled *Dart to the Heart*, which had a cover photo of a young Imperium Dart bent over his sound system, face looking like he was transported in ecstasy, and probably *on* ecstasy, head flung back in wild abandon.

I picked it up. It was a hefty volume, featuring a comprehensive index and discography, and an appendix section that contained several interviews with the man himself. I was going to have to have this. It might well prove very handy in our search for the elusive Mr Dart, aka Ramkin. At the very least, it would allow me to form a clearer picture of the person we were looking for.

"Thank you," I said to Agatha, reaching in my pocket for money. "Good find."

"Tell him what you told me," said Agatha, addressing the seller behind the table, a chunky, cheerful woman with many tattoos who was watching as if hypnotised as the money came out of my pocket.

"Oh," said the woman, her trance broken, "I was just saying to your friend here, if you want it signed, he's over there." She pointed to the crowd of punters behind us.

I turned to see a man standing in isolation under the stained-glass window, carefully positioned in the panel of light that fell through it as if he was trying to get a suntan. Which, admittedly, would have been a very odd thing for him to do.

He was a remarkably small man, not much taller than a child, wearing jeans and a leather jacket of the retro American Air Force variety with fake insignia on it. Both jacket and jeans appeared well-worn but in an artificial kind of way, expensively and synthetically distressed, and had probably looked that way when he'd bought them. Which might have been yesterday. His shoes were bright, white trainers of dazzling newness.

Emerging from the sheepskin collar of his leather jacket, his face was hairy and very pale, as though he'd never been exposed to the sun. Maybe because he always tried tanning through stained glass. His small, black beard was very unkempt and disorderly, and transitioned imperceptibly to the unkempt and disorderly black hair on his head. He wore circular wire-rimmed glasses with the lenses tinted lemon yellow.

Despite being small in stature, or perhaps because of that, he looked combative and cocksure. And his standing there in the light from the big church windows suddenly seemed no accident. It was as if he had chosen this spot all the better to show himself off. Not that anyone was paying attention to him.

Except for me, of course.

"He'll sign it if you like, all right," said the woman behind the record stall. "If you don't mind paying him thirty quid. Which is twice what the book itself costs."

I confirmed this by turning the book over and reading the price on the back. Also on the back was a photo of the author. It was unmistakably the man standing over there, though a few years younger and somewhat less hairy. And, for the first time, I registered his name.

Tim Purshouse.

I looked at Agatha. She was watching me with a sardonic expression, waiting for me to get up to speed, which I now was. This was the man who had written the tabloid story that hung in a position of honour at the house called Noise Floor.

I paid the helpful woman and we went over to join Tim Purshouse where he stood, in divine isolation and illumination.

He didn't bother looking at us as we came towards him. But I'd seen him quickly and surreptitiously glance our way and register us. Particularly Agatha. Now he seemed to be pretending to be absorbed in thought. Deeply absorbed in very important thought.

"Hi," I said.

He ignored this.

"I understand you'll sign this for us." I held up the book, just in case he hadn't seen me buy it. This was vanishingly unlikely, since he'd obviously chosen this vantage point specifically to keep an eye on his sales. But I was beginning to think he was going to ignore this comment of mine, too, when he suddenly reached out his hand to me, palm up and fingers spread.

I tried to put the book in it, and he hastily moved it away.

"Thirty quid," he said. He had a croaky, rasping smoker's voice, very deep and actually quite agreeable.

I got it. I put three ten-pound notes into his hand. He rolled them up into a careful cylinder as if planning to make a cigarette out of them. I hoped not because they were plastic bank notes. "Have you got a pen?" he said.

"Nope." I did, but I thought, for thirty pounds, the least he could do was provide his own writing implement. And he did. After making a sound that could have been either a sigh or a snarl, he delved into the inside pocket of his jacket and took out a black Sharpie.

"Here," he said, impatiently reaching for the book he'd been so reluctant to take a moment ago.

I gave it to him and he brutally folded the cover back, flagrantly and unnecessarily creasing it—I could see Agatha wince—and scribbled his name on the first page.

He handed it back to me and was about to turn away when I said, "Showbiz journalist of the year, eh?"

He turned back and looked at me properly for the first time. He also smiled for the first time. "Five years running, mate. Five years running." He held his hand out for the book and I gave it to him again, a little reluctantly because I was wondering what other damage he might inflict on it. But he seemed to be aware of this and even rubbed the crease he'd created on the cover, as if soothing a wounded animal. "It doesn't say that on this, does it?" He meant the "showbiz journalist of the year" bit.

"Not that I've noticed," I said.

"No," he said, inspecting the book. "We missed a trick there. Well, that's publishers for you." He looked at me shrewdly. "So you knew it already?"

"I didn't know about the five years running," I said. I saw that Nevada and Tinkler had come over and joined us, which, on the one hand, was good because I was about to do something that involved money, and I always liked my sweetie pie to be involved where financial matters were concerned.

On the other hand, it was annoying because it was so clearly gratifying for Tim to be the centre of attention. It was as if he'd been waiting for a crowd of people to form around him. Admittedly, this was a small crowd, but it was still more than he deserved.

"And how do you come to have heard of me?" he said. He was addressing me, but he wasn't looking at me. He was looking at Nevada—he'd instantly dismissed Tinkler as of no consequence. He looked at Nevada for a long moment and then at Agatha. He began looking back and forth between the two women. It was as if he was making a comparison and taking notes.

It was also, as my darling might have said, *molto* creepy.

"Rave Star Orgy Cult," I said.

Tim laughed delightedly and looked at me again, the erotic spell cast over him by our female companions apparently broken. "My best headline ever. I don't think it's in here…" He flipped through the pages of the book to the various photo sections but couldn't find it. "No. I was aiming for a somewhat more serious tone for this bio."

"Have you ever met him?" I said.

"Old Lambert?" Tim regarded me with disdain. "Of course I've met him. Innumerable times."

"Would you say you know him quite well?" I said. "And not just his music, I mean."

"Of course I know him quite well. I know him very well."

Nevada and I looked at each other. "I wonder if you might be able to put us in touch with him."

"I doubt it," he said dismissively.

"Actually," I said, "we don't so much want to be put in touch with him, as to find him."

"Good for you," said Tim.

"And we want you to help us find him," I said.

"Why should I do that?"

"Because we'll pay you."

The thirty pounds he'd demanded for his autograph had been cheap at the price, because I believed it had given me the key to the whole man. And it looked like I was right, because I now had his full attention.

"How much?" said Tim.

I looked at Nevada. "That would be up to my business manager."

Tim looked at Nevada. "You're his business manager?"

"And devoted lover," said Nevada. She hadn't been unaware of his creepy attention and clearly wanted no misunderstandings.

Tim, to his credit, took this in his stride. Perhaps because the talk of money overrode all other concerns. "And you want me to help you find Lambert Ramkin?" he said.

"We'll make it worth your while."

"You will, will you?"

"In purely monetary terms," said Nevada, again allowing for no misunderstandings.

Tim laughed. "He's gone walkabout again, has he?"

I didn't see any value in playing our cards too close to our chest, so I said, "Yes."

"Has a tendency to do that," said Tim. "The wandering Lamb as they call him."

"And do you think you can help us find him?" said Nevada.

"Oh, I wouldn't be at all surprised," he said. "Why don't you take my phone number and we can work something out."

He dug in his pocket and, somewhat surprisingly, took out an elegant little antique silver case that contained business cards and handed us one. I took it. For some reason, I didn't want Nevada to touch anything he'd touched. For that matter, it looked as if Nevada felt the same way. I pocketed the card.

"Well, I'll be seeing you," said Tim. He was smirking at us. And then he turned away. He literally turned his back. Apparently, we'd been dismissed. I stood there, furiously trying to think of a reason to stay here and continue looking through the records so it wouldn't look like we were leaving because he'd sent us packing.

But I couldn't think of a damned thing.

So we all started for the door. At least our visit to St Drogo's hadn't been a bust. Not only had we made the charming acquaintance of Mr Purshouse, but Tinkler and I had also scored some vinyl.

Evidently as keenly aware of this as I was, Nevada said to Agatha, "It looks like we had a better time here than you did last year."

"You mean at the paperback sale? I should say so. I had such high hopes for that and I didn't find a thing. In fact, it's been a long time since I've been to a really good book sale." Agatha sounded despondent. Then she rallied. "I'm thinking of going to Hay-on-Wye."

Hay-on-Wye was a town full of bookshops, famous for its festivals and events.

"Would you guys come, too?"

We all said we would and she smiled, her good mood restored.

As we walked through the hall, Agatha looked thoughtfully around us at all the keen little buyers and the somewhat less keen sellers of vinyl. And she said, "They should have a Hay- on-Wye for records."

She said it casually. And, for a moment, I didn't give it another thought.

Then I stopped walking. I must have stopped rather suddenly because Nevada stopped too and looked at me with concern. Then the concern vanished from her face and she smiled. I was smiling too. The others had also stopped and were looking at us.

"Hay-on-Wye for records," I said.

Nevada was nodding.

"If only we knew a lovely little village, not too far from London…" said Nevada.

"You're not serious," said Tinkler.

"Nutalich," said Agatha.

I nodded happily.

"Do you think you can pull it off?" said Tinkler.

"The Vinyl Detective presents a village full of records," said Nevada, improvising advertising copy on the spot. "For one weekend only. Come to the garden of England and buy rare and second-hand vinyl in one of Kent's most renowned beauty spots."

"Don't get too carried too away," said Tinkler. "On the other hand, count me in."

"I'll be there, too," said Agatha. "And I expect a kickback for introducing you to the place in the first place."

"If by a kickback you mean as much wine as you can drink and as much food as he can cook for you," said Nevada, her hand on my arm, "then it's a deal."

"It's a deal," said Agatha.

By the time we got home, the sun had disappeared, blotted out beyond grey, threatening clouds; our summer afternoon swallowed by imminent thunder. When we all trooped into the cool quiet of the sitting room it was so dark that I switched on the big floor-standing lamp. Or at least I tried to. The switch clicked but nothing happened.

"Dead bulb?" said Agatha.

"You know they have these new-fangled things called long-life light bulbs?" said Tinkler. "Widely available since the late twentieth century."

"It isn't dead," I said, reaching inside the lampshade and tightening the bulb, instantly being rewarded with warm ivory light that filled the room and cheered the place up. It was a stylish lamp with three long wooden legs. The problem was that the slightest jarring of one of those long wooden legs, say through the impact of a mischievous cat colliding with it, was enough to loosen the bulb in its fitting so that it wouldn't come on. It was easily remedied, though. "It just loses contact when a furry little comet bashes into it," I said.

Lying on her belly on the arm of the sofa, Fanny blinked in the sudden brightness as if acknowledging the justice of my statement.

"Entirely your fault for choosing mid-century style over practicality," said Tinkler, looking at the tall, elegant lamp. He had a point, actually.

Nevada went to fetch some wine and Agatha flipped through the Imperium Dart book while Tinkler and I examined—some might say gloated over—our purchases. Tinkler had found some classic British blues, including a nice copy of an early Fleetwood Mac album, *The Pious Bird of Good Omen*, on Blue Horizon.

And of course, I had my rare and valuable pressing of Imperium Dart's *The Magus*. "Not to be confused with the movie *The Magus*," said Nevada, handing out the wine. "Which is a mess."

"The movie may have been a mess," said Agatha. "But it was based on a great novel by John Fowles. Which has a fantastic cover, or covers, by Tom Adams. There are at least two different versions of his art for it."

She picked up the album, which had a very striking cover painting of a nude woman wearing an inscrutable mask. "And this is one of them. They've borrowed it from the book cover. Let's see if Tom Adams gets credit." She checked the back of the sleeve. "Yup. Full marks to Imperium Dart. I like to see an artist getting his due. Tom Adams also did all those fantastic cover paintings for the Fontana Agatha Christies in the 1960s. Am I giving too much information?"

"It's all right, we'll be drunk soon and it won't matter," said Tinkler, sipping his wine.

"The album is actually inspired by the John Fowles novel," I said.

"You're kidding," said Agatha.

"No, there's a quote from the book on the inner sleeve," I said, handing it to her.

While she inspected it and the others enjoyed their wine, I took out Tim Purshouse's business card. I began to speculate about what sort of odyssey of infuriating complications I was about to embark on in my attempts to "work something out" with Mr P.

But, in fact, two days later we were booked to see him at his home.

8: THE TWELFTH POSSIBILITY

Like Lambert Ramkin, Timothy Purshouse had a house on a hill. But in Tim's case it was a considerably smaller house on a considerably smaller hill, and located in Surrey rather than in Kent.

We went out there in two separate cars, Tinkler and Nevada and I in one and Agatha in the other. Agatha's presence had actually been a stipulation of Tim's. I'd thought he'd been suspiciously helpful and hospitable when I'd rung him up. True, he had insisted on a meeting in person, at his house, but that didn't seem particularly troublesome or strange. Until he'd added, "Make sure you bring your beautiful friend with you."

I had thought we'd made this clear at the record sale, or at least Nevada had. But apparently not. "Look," I told him, "Nevada and I are going out. In fact, we're living together. In fact, we've been living together for years."

Tim said, "No, not her, not the white girl. The other one. The one with the shaved head."

I told him I'd see what I could do, planning to completely ignore this creepy request in the way it deserved to be completely ignored, but he added, "If you can't bring her, I might just find that I won't be available."

On that not-so-veiled threat, we concluded our conversation. Nevada and I discussed the situation with Agatha and she agreed willingly enough to accompany us. On one condition of her own. Which we explained to Tinkler as we drove down to Surrey to meet with Tabloid Tim, as Tinkler had aptly dubbed him.

"Don't get too excited," Nevada said, "but you have to pretend to be Agatha's boyfriend."

"A role I was born to play," said Tinkler. "But why?"

We explained about Tim's demand that she had to accompany us. "And it seemed safest and easiest for her to have someone with her as a…"

"Cock block," said Tinkler.

"More or less," I said.

"Very poetically put," said Nevada.

"Thank you."

"And Tabloid Tim's already seen you with her at the record sale, so it will seem natural enough."

"Of course it will seem natural," said Tinkler. "Because I'm perfect for the role. But, pray tell, why didn't Agatha just get Albert to come along and play the part of her boyfriend since Albert actually is her boyfriend?"

"Because he isn't," said Nevada. "Not anymore."

"Oh, really?" said Tinkler, barely able to conceal his joy. Albert was the guy who ran our local gastropub and he and Agatha had been dating for some months now.

"I'm afraid so," said Nevada. "They've had a parting of the ways."

"What a shame," said Tinkler with magnificent insincerity.

"And Agatha has decided it's time for a more serious and lasting and deeper relationship," said Nevada. "With someone she has known for a long time."

"Really?" said Tinkler, suddenly on high alert.

"Someone she had not previously seen in that way. You know, attraction is a strange thing."

"Yes! Yes, it certainly is."

"Agatha's thoughts have turned to someone she had previously ruled out as too inappropriate."

"Turn! Let them turn! Let those thoughts turn. Yes, yes, I was sure of it, I never doubted it. Yes, yes, yes!"

"And so now, in consequence, Agatha has said farewell to Albert and is going on a date with her old driving instructor."

"What? *Horatio*?"

"Afraid so."

"That *motherfucker*."

As unpleasant as Tabloid Tim was, his house was a thing of some beauty. It consisted of two rectangular glass boxes that intersected at right angles with another smaller rectangular box, concrete this time, at one side, which was the garage. All of these boxes had grass planted on their roofs, which was odd because somehow Tim didn't seem the sort of person who cared about the environment or green issues. Maybe he just liked the energy efficiency and ensuing money saved.

This elegant house came into sight as we drove through an open gateway between low hedges and up a small hill to stop on a parking area that consisted of a rectangle of concrete. I sensed a rectangular theme here. Agatha was waiting for us, sitting in her car.

"Sorry we're late," said Nevada as we got out of our car. We weren't really late. But there was very little chance of getting anywhere before Agatha if she was on wheels. "Been here long?"

"Not long," said Agatha. "But I thought I'd better wait before I called on our host." She nodded towards the house which, thanks to its glass walls, was revealed to be apparently unoccupied. However, there was the faint sound of music playing, which was promising, if this word could be used in any connection with Tabloid Tim. "I thought I'd better wait for my escort."

"I'm an escort," said Tinkler contentedly, falling in beside Agatha as we walked towards the house. "Can we hold hands?"

"Only in the event of an emergency," said Agatha.

"Like if he takes his trousers off?"

"That would certainly count," said Agatha.

"Here's hoping, then," said Tinkler.

Tabloid Tim had apparently eschewed the presence of grass anywhere except on the roof of his home. As we left the concrete parking platform, we crossed an area that I suppose you'd call the garden, although it only consisted of reddish-brown gravel planted with some widely spaced beds containing large cactuses. The desert-style garden ended at another flat rectangle of concrete sited at the inside corner of the intersecting glass wings of the house.

This formed a patio, equipped with white metal all-weather furniture with plump cushions in shades of reddish brown, which matched the gravel, and dusty green, which matched the cactuses.

I wasn't willing to concede that Tim had good taste, but I was willing to concede he'd hired someone who had good taste.

The door of the house—which was simply a section of the glass wall that slid sideways—was wide open and the music was louder now. "What's that? Vivaldi?" said Agatha.

"Something from that era," said Nevada. "Baroque, anyway. We'd need Saxon Ghost to tell us exactly."

Saxon was our friend who knew about classical music.

We stood there for a moment, listening to the spare, elegant music and staring through the open door into the spare, elegant house. There was no doorbell or intercom I could see anywhere. Perhaps it would have spoiled the spare elegance. And knocking on the glass seemed like a waste of time.

So we stood on the threshold and I called out, "Hello?"

No reply.

Nevada tried calling and then Agatha and finally Tinkler. None of this elicited any kind of response. Music just kept playing somewhere inside the apparently empty house. "Maybe we should all try calling together," suggested Tinkler.

"Let's just go in," said Nevada, stepping over the threshold.

The interior of the house was cool and smelled faintly of patchouli. It had pale wood walls and dark wood flooring with thick shaggy white woollen rugs randomly spaced on it. The furniture was all made of chrome and cream-coloured leather. Above a fireplace with a chrome surround was a large, framed charcoal drawing of a nude. A woman, of course. We walked the length of this wing of the house until we came to the other wing, set at right angles to it. The music was coming from here.

As we turned the corner and entered the other wing, we immediately saw Tabloid Tim.

He was in what seemed to be a breakfast room. There was a doorway and serving hatch in the wall behind it, leading to a kitchen. Tim was seated alone at a table.

On this was a variety of tea accoutrements and two covered bowls, one large, one small. These were all in a blue-and-white Chinese pattern. As was the silk bathrobe our host was wearing.

He looked up at us through his yellow-lensed spectacles and gave us a polite smile of greeting. He lifted one hand, pointed a remote control at something in the wall and turned the music off. "You made it, then?" he said, standing up.

The creepiness of his greeting us in his bathrobe was ameliorated by two factors. First, the childlike size of the man made it hard for him to seem dangerous however he was dressed, or undressed. Second, he was not, thankfully, naked under the robe. Or at least he was wearing grey woollen leggings. Nevertheless, we weren't spared the sight of his bare chest, covered with wiry black hair, peeking through the robe's open neck.

"Come and have tea," he said.

It took us a moment to realise there were chairs like the one he was sitting on ranked against the wall. He watched us patiently while we each took one of these and brought it to the table and sat down. Apparently this was, like the open door, some kind of initiative test.

Once we were all seated at the table, he started to pour tea for us without being asked. I glumly considered and dismissed the idea of requesting a coffee instead. Nevada gave me a look that said she understood my sacrifice and appreciated it. When he'd finished pouring for all of us, he spread his hands out in a gesture of offering towards the other things on the tray.

"We have milk. We have lemon. And we have sugar." He lifted the lid off the smaller of the two covered bowls, revealing irregular little golden brown sugar cubes. "Brown sugar," he said. "Proper brown sugar. Not white sugar dyed brown like you normally get."

"Well, thank god for that," I said.

To my surprise he laughed, and then everyone else laughed, too. It would be too much to say this broke the ice, but we all relaxed a little.

"How did you manage to create such a beautiful house?" said Nevada, in full charm-offensive mode.

"Showbiz journalist of the year, five years running," I said, answering for our host.

He seemed to like this because he nodded vigorously and pointed at me with a teaspoon. "What he said. Exactly what he said." He waved the spoon in a more expansive motion, pointing all around at his glass domicile. "The house that journalism built."

"The tea's very nice," said Nevada.

For all I knew she might have been telling the truth. I'd tried mine and it was tea. That was about as much as I could tell you.

"When you're finished drinking it, we can start on these," said Tim. He lifted the lid off the larger of the two covered bowls, revealing a remarkable number of neatly rolled joints tucked tightly inside. The sweet, sticky smell of skunk filled the room.

"I'm driving, so I won't, thanks," said Agatha politely.

"The same with me," I said.

Tinkler shot me a grateful look. He'd driven us down here, but there was no reason I couldn't do the honours on the way back and let him have his fun.

"I'll refrain until we've finished talking business," said Nevada.

"Then let's start talking," said Tabloid Tim.

"We want you to help us find Lambert Ramkin."

"No," said Tim. "You want me to find him for you."

"All right," said Nevada, doing an admirable job of retaining her temper. "We want you to find him for us. Is that something you can do?"

"I said it was, didn't I?'

"I can't honestly recall."

"Well I can. Find him. What's it worth to you?" He grinned a salacious grin. "I'm talking about money, just for avoidance of doubt."

"Have you looked at your messages recently?" said Nevada.

"Not recently."

"Well you might like to take a look." She had texted Tim with an offer before we'd set off, after consulting with our employer and doing some esoteric calculations of her own.

Tim fished his phone out of the pocket of his robe, examined his texts for a long moment and then put the phone away again with a grunt which didn't tell us much.

"So?" I said, not wanting Nevada to be in the undignified position of having to press him for an answer.

"Yeah, that's all right," said Tabloid Tim, which was both a surprise and a relief.

Apparently this ended the discussion of business because he took joints out of the bowl for Tinkler and Nevada, and one for himself. As he was lighting them, Agatha and I excused ourselves and went out into the open air so as not to get stoned on ambient smoke. We chatted for a while, sitting on the outdoor furniture and admiring the cacti, until we calculated it was safe to go inside again.

The room stank of skunk, but everyone had finished smoking and they looked just like they had when we'd left them. Tim's eyes flicked up at Agatha as we came in. "So, this is your boyfriend?" he said, nodding at Tinkler.

"He's my man," said Agatha with such understated conviction that I almost believed her. She sat down beside him.

"She can't get enough of me," said Tinkler.

"Well, if you ever want to add another body in your bed…" said Tabloid Tim.

"What?" said Tinkler. "You mean…"

"Me. As well as you, of course, mate."

"No way, José. The devil's threesome? Absolutely not. Get thee behind me, Satan. No wait, when I say get *behind* me, I don't mean…"

"You shouldn't be so boringly conventional," said Tim. "The man you're looking for certainly isn't."

"Rave Star Orgy Cult," I said.

"That's right," said Tabloid Tim. I don't think he was aware of it, but he was actually licking his lips, which glistened an obscene red in the hairy nest of his beard. "You see, Lambert worked out that with him and three women there would be seven different sexual combinations."

"S-seven," stuttered Tinkler. He'd never manifested a stutter before but then he'd never encountered such a carnal cornucopia before.

"That's right," said Tim. "Like on Monday he has Selena, then on Tuesday he has Poppy, then on Wednesday he has Jacquetta." He was counting on his fingers and Tinkler began to do the same. "Then on Thursday he has a threesome with Selena and Poppy. On Friday it's him and Selena and Jacquetta. On Saturday him and Jacquetta and Poppy. And then on Sunday everybody has everybody."

"I thought Sunday was supposed to be a day of rest," said Nevada.

"I'm not saying he would abide by those actual days," said Tim, wiping his mouth with the back of his hand. "The point I'm making is that good old Lamb had created a Rubik's cube of erotic possibilities."

"The Rubik's cube has quintillions of combinations," said Agatha.

"That would probably be too many even for good old Lamb to cope with," said Nevada.

"At least without some really good Viagra," said Tinkler, who had regained some of his composure.

"The point I'm making," repeated Tabloid Tim, beginning to manifest some exasperation under the verbal fire of my dearest friends and companions, "is that he had an amazing setup. He still does, for that matter. It's a crying shame he's not taking advantage of it. If I was him, I'd just stay at home and reap the benefits instead of going out wandering. I'd still give any of them one, any day of the week. Especially Selena, but I'd still offer it to Poppy or Jacquetta, too. There's many a good tune played on an old fiddle."

This seemed like as suitable a time as any to say our farewells. We drove back to London in our separate cars and convened at our house for a debriefing. Plus feeding some hungry cats.

As we sat in the sitting room, drinking coffee, Tinkler wouldn't shut up about Lambert's erotic Rubik's cube, and I guess Agatha had decided to shut him up and done some thinking about the best way to achieve this.

"Actually, Tabloid Tim got it wrong," she said. "There are in fact *eleven* possible sexual combinations."

Tinkler was astonished and indeed overjoyed. "Really?"

"Yes," said Agatha, with the satisfaction of one who has carefully set a trap and watched an oaf blunder into it. "The four permutations of the three women, which don't involve Lambert at all."

"But he could still watch, right?" said Tinkler, clinging to the noble vision of this sexual utopia.

"And then there's the twelfth possibility," said Nevada. Everyone looked at her expectantly. "Which is to say, no one having sex with anyone," she said.

"Well, that's just plain perverted," said Tinkler. "Trust you to think of it."

Agatha smiled. "Now, how long before Tabloid Tim thinks he'll be able to come up with a lead on your missing person?"

"Oh, he already has," said Nevada. She showed Agatha a flier he'd given to her.

For a record fair in Wales.

9: RED SUNSET OVER SEA

Nevada and I discussed the Welsh record fair. It was a long way to go on the off-chance of finding our missing person. But Tabloid Tim had been absolutely adamant that Lambert would be there, and he stood to receive a hefty payment if he was right. And Tim was a man with a high regard for money.

So we decided we had to give it a try.

I attempted to talk Tinkler into coming with us. If Agatha had been part of the deal, there was no doubt he would have been up for it. In fact, there would have been no stopping him. But it so happened that she was busy that weekend and Tinkler's enthusiasm for accompanying us dwindled accordingly. Nevertheless, I got on the phone and attempted to cajole him. "Come on, Tinkler," I said. "It's a record fair."

"On the one hand it's a record fair. On the other hand, it's Wales."

"Don't be so negative," I said. "Aberystwyth is beautiful."

"I'll tell you what," he said. "If you can spell Aberystwyth, I'll come with you."

Unfortunately, he had me there. But although he didn't come with us, Tinkler did lend us his car.

Aberystwyth was on the far side of Wales, indeed on the far side of this fair island, in relation to our happy home in London. If we'd taken the motorway and driven hell for leather we probably could have done the journey in six hours, even in Tinkler's little car. But to avoid stress, and since we were on expenses, we decided to take the scenic route, break our journey in Bath and spend the night there before driving on.

Proceeding thus in a leisurely fashion, we arrived in Aberystwyth on Friday afternoon, with the record fair scheduled to start the following morning.

The first untruth about the Zobole Marine Hotel was the marine part. It turned out to be three streets away from the sea. The Zobole part transpired to be none too accurate, either.

Zobole was apparently a renowned modernist Welsh painter (1927—1999) and the intention seemed to have been to honour his aesthetic by creating the kind of arty boutique hotel you might find in Barcelona or New York.

But then they'd either run out of money or lost their nerve, and gone for the standard soulless corporate model instead. So essentially the building was an air-conditioned, carpeted concrete box full of rooms which were also air-conditioned, carpeted concrete boxes. The exterior concrete box was narrow but five storeys high, so virtually a skyscraper by Aberystwyth standards, with a grey stone and glass exterior relieved only by a sign—a thin, vertical rectangle of bright orange, pale green and blue, which turned out to be a slice, or "detail", of one of the great man's canvases—*Painting and Subject Matter No. 5*.

I couldn't help knowing this fact because it was repeated, along with the image, on just about every scrap of paper in the hotel, including the menus and placemats, and on every fixed surface, including the interior of the bathroom doors.

There was a large car park around three sides of the hotel, which was unsettlingly empty when we arrived. But then, we told ourselves, the record fair hadn't started yet.

We parked the car and went into the lobby. There were no posters or advertising of any kind to indicate that a record fair was, in fact, taking place here, so I was very relieved to see a number of overweight middle-aged men in jeans and T-shirts wrestling with luggage trolleys containing crates of LPs. There were even some familiar faces among them.

It seemed we were in the right place after all.

We checked in and were promptly ambushed by a young woman in a navy blue blazer and skirt, wearing a badge featuring that slice of *Painting and Subject Matter No. 5*. She had a chubby, cartoon-chipmunk cheerfulness and introduced herself as Bronwen, our concierge for the duration of our stay, and gamely set about trying to sell us assorted goods and services. While politely fending her off, Nevada happened to remark that the work of the great Zobole reminded her of Chagall.

At this point, something in Bronwen's eyes came to life and, although she persisted in her business spiel, you could see her heart wasn't in it. Or even less in it than before. Then Nevada said, "He also reminds me of Toba Possner. Her middle period."

"You've heard of Toba Possner?" said Bronwen, making no attempt to conceal how impressed she was, and definitely giving up on her concierge routine now.

Nevada had made another conquest. One that became overwhelming when she added, "We haven't just heard of Toba—we know her. In fact, she owes us a painting of our cats." This led to Nevada taking out her phone so she and Bronwen could make fond noises over photos of our little savages. Then we invited Bronwen to have a drink with us.

"I really shouldn't," she said, glancing over her shoulder. But she did. The hotel bar was empty except for ourselves and a bored-looking bartender. After a swift and ruthless inspection of the drinks list, Nevada ordered three large red wines. "Staff discount on these, Benny," said Bronwen, handing the bartender a swipe card with the inevitable slice of *Painting and Subject Matter No. 5* on it.

It turned out Bronwen was an art student, which accounted for her working here. "Poor Mr Zobole, having this terrible hotel named after him," she said. "I only applied for the job here because I thought there might be an artistic aspect to it, but no such luck. They wouldn't even let me choose the paintings for the rooms. And I know more about art than any of them. I wanted to have *People and Dogs, Ystrad*, for a room or maybe even up in here." She looked around the empty bar. "It's one of my favourite

Zoboles. But I was vetoed because one of the dogs depicted in it is doing a wee."

"That's just not right," said Nevada. "I mean rejecting it for such a petty reason."

"No, it isn't."

Just then another staff member, a young man in a business suit and a *Painting and Subject Matter No. 5* badge looked in and Bronwen instantly picked up a menu and showed it to us. "For your evening meal," she said in a loud voice, "we have artisanal, hotel-made sauerkraut and a garland of other locally sourced vegetables personally fermented by the chef."

"Do you recommend it?" I said.

Bronwen looked up to make sure the young man had withdrawn, which he had. "Not unless you want potential food poisoning," she said. "With a side order of ferocious flatulence."

"Thank you for your candour," said Nevada. "We shall give it a miss." She took out her phone again but, this time, instead of our cats, she showed Bronwen a photograph of Lambert Ramkin as he looked these days, a big, burly man with thinning grey hair and a neat grey beard, and asked if she recognised him.

Bronwen nodded. "One hundred per cent. And I expect I won't forget him in a hurry."

"Why not?"

"He's the first person I've ever seen who actually has an actual entourage with him. An entire entourage. They got here yesterday and they've been partying ever since."

"And they're in the hotel now?" said Nevada.

"Oh yes. Up on the top floor, in *Red Sunset Over Sea*, which is our biggest room and also our nicest."

"Are all the rooms named after paintings?" I asked.

"Yes. Let me see your room card."

I showed it to her.

"You're in *Rhondda Landscape*. It's a nice idea, I suppose, using the paintings instead of numbers. But it is a bit confusing for the guests. I think they'd prefer a simple 'third room on the second floor' sort of approach."

"Must be fun trying to find your way back when you're drunk," I said.

"Oh yes, as more than a few guests have discovered to their peril." She leaned towards us and lowered her voice, although the only other person in the room was Benny the bartender and he was down the far end of the bar, sorting out a stack of coasters with Zobole paintings on them as if he was dealing a deck of cards. "To tell the truth," said Bronwen, "the hotel isn't doing too well. Which is why they were so glad to get the record fair. To help them do a bit of business for a change."

This information didn't particularly surprise me, though I tried to look sympathetic, as did Nevada. "Well hopefully your job is secure," she said.

"Oh, I'm not bothered about that. It's only a stopgap to get me through college. And I only do the weekends, from Friday afternoon to Sunday evening. Which is nice, because it meant I got to meet you." She looked at her watch. "Oh well, back to the coalface. Did you know that Zobole's father actually worked down in the pits? When they first emigrated to Wales from Italy? I could bore you on the subject of Mr Zobole, but I shan't. I don't suppose you'll be wanting dinner in our restaurant?"

"We'll make other arrangements," said Nevada.

"If you want to bring in your own meal, I promise I shall turn a blind eye," said Bronwen. "Your friend in *Red Sunset Over Sea* has been bringing in his own food. And drink. Lots of drink. There have been complaints about the noise. Quite a few complaints."

We did indeed bring in our own dinner. Bread and cheese and wine, which we'd carried with us from London in our retro 1950s-style Polarbox cooler, the yellow-and-cyan model. It was a good job Bronwen had offered to turn a blind eye because it was difficult to miss this baby. We picnicked on the bed and strategised how best to approach Lambert Ramkin tomorrow, then turned in early.

After we showered and dressed the following morning, we went down to see if we could get something unfermented for breakfast, only to find that the place, instead of buzzing with activity, was strangely quiet. And still no posters or signs for the record fair. There were a few middle-aged men trundling trollies of record crates, all right, but they were all heading for the exit.

"This does not look good," said Nevada.

Then Bronwen came hurrying over to us. "I'm afraid your convention has been cancelled," she said. "The people organising it have gone bust."

I said, "Do you know if our noisy friend with the entourage is still here?"

"I'm sorry, I only just came on duty. What a shame about the record fair."

We took the lift up to the top floor and hurried along the carpeted corridor to *Red Sunset Over Sea*. The door of the room was open. As soon as we touched it, it drifted slightly inwards, silently and with a certain hint of sinister invitation.

We looked at each other.

Then we knocked and waited. No response. So we knocked again and waited again, and eventually, after what seemed like an acceptable interval, we pushed the door open and went inside.

"Hello," we called.

Once again, no response. The air conditioning hummed over silence.

It was big in here, a suite rather than merely a room, and this was the central lounge. It was a mess, with bottles and cans, both booze and soft drink, and fast-food cartons scattered everywhere.

"Looks like the party is over," said Nevada.

"And we missed it," I said.

"Nothing to indicate where Lambert might be headed next?"

"Doesn't look like it," I said.

There was movement behind us and we both whirled around, but it was just the door. It had drifted shut.

And it hadn't locked.

Indeed, we could see now it had been rendered unable to lock by the expedient of a strip of silver gaffer tape stuck down the edge of it, across the latch and wrapped around the inside of the door. It hadn't been visible from out in the hall, and clearly that was the intention.

Nevada and I looked at it and looked at each other. "Why the hell would anyone do that?" I said.

Nevada nodded thoughtfully. "Say you had a lot of people crashing in your suite, more than it could officially accommodate, and they were coming and going all the time and you didn't have enough key cards to go around and you didn't want the hassle of coming to the door all the time to answer it…"

"Makes sense," I said. "Providing security wasn't a big thing for you."

"No doubt there was always somebody in the room."

"Not anymore," I said.

While I stared at a large print of an abstract painting on the wall—*Red Sunset Over Sea*, of course—Nevada wandered idly around the periphery of the big lounge, pushing open doors at random. The first two were bathrooms but the others all led to bedrooms. Each one presented a similar picture of mess, replicating the disorder of the lounge on a smaller scale but with the addition of thrashed-up bedding.

Then Nevada pushed open the last door and we saw the girl.

"Shit," said Nevada. She moved quickly through the door and I followed her.

The girl was lying face down on a big double bed. She looked to be in her twenties. And she was naked except for a pair of panties, white with tiny pink hearts printed on them, and a matching bra that was unfastened at the back. She had carrot-coloured hair and pale, freckled skin.

The bed was less messed up than the others we'd seen. But, as if to compensate for this, there was the vomit, spattered in a large, irregular orange halo around the girl's head, which showed starkly on the white duvet. Nevada kneeled on the bed and gently lifted the girl's head and studied her carefully for a moment. "She's alive," she said and, as if to confirm this, the girl emitted a loud snore.

Nevada lifted the girl by her shoulders and began to manoeuvre her away from the patch of vomit and put her into the recovery position. As she did so, the bra slipped off, exposing the girl's small, pale vulnerable breasts. I looked at them and then realised I was looking at them, and looked at Nevada instead. She was gazing at me sardonically. "I didn't mean to look," I said.

"Forget it, you're only human. If you want to make yourself useful, see if you can put her bra back on."

I was more than a little alarmed at this suggestion. "Where are you going?"

"To the bathroom to get something to clean her up."

She gave me a casual look that could have meant anything and then went out. I kneeled gingerly on the bed and adjusted the girl's position so she was lying on the bra the way she had been before she slipped out of it. Then I fastened it at the back. Her skin was clammily damp but very warm, which was a relief because it suggested health in a way that cold, damp skin wouldn't have.

Any danger of this being an erotic experience was negated by the smell of the vomit and also of the girl herself. She stank strongly of beer. The yeasty reek of it seemed to be pouring out of every pore.

Nevada was gone such a long time that I began to get irritated. When she finally came back in, I said, "You didn't have to leave me here to test my virtue. I didn't grope her."

"I never imagined you would. I'm sorry I was gone so long but it took me forever to find a clean towel. Or something resembling one." She held up a damp white hand towel then came and went to work on the girl, cleaning the vomit out of her hair and wiping her face.

The girl murmured contentedly in her sleep as if she was enjoying the attention and my fears for her wellbeing diminished still further. "Do you reckon she's drugged or just pissed?" I said.

"Just pissed. She smells like a brewery."

"She certainly does."

As she worked, Nevada said, "What do you think happened to her?"

"Somebody brought her in here and tried to undress her."

Nevada nodded. "Someone who was undeterred by the state she was in."

"Or perhaps spurred on by the state she was in."

"Right," said Nevada. "She was in no condition to say no. Which they regarded as a plus. So they started to undress her…"

"And then she threw up. And that put them off."

"Poor rapist," said Nevada. "Such delicate sensibilities."

"And they just left her here."

"Chivalry really is dead," said Nevada.

I asked the inevitable question. "What do we do with her?"

Nevada looked at me.

"*We* can't just leave her here," I said.

She smiled at me with approval. "Maybe chivalry isn't dead after all."

"Should we notify Bronwen?"

Nevada shook her head. "It won't just be Bronwen we have to deal with. And it would tend to lead to embarrassing questions about what we were doing in someone else's suite. See if you can find her clothes."

This didn't take long. A quick search located them scattered on the floor around the bed and there wasn't a lot to find. Socks, jeans, a T-shirt and a pair of slip-on shoes.

"Let's see if we can get her dressed," said Nevada.

"And then what?"

"We'll see if we can find an address on her. If not, we'll take her to the local hospital and park her in the Accident and Emergency department. I'm sure it won't be the first time they've had a drunk sleeping one off in there. And, if anything goes wrong with her, she's in the best place to be taken care of."

"Sounds like a plan," I said. "Are you sure you don't want to wait until she sobers up and then ask her some questions?"

"I suspect it would be a very long wait for some very unsatisfactory answers."

"I agree," I said. There was no guarantee that the girl was anything more than some random stranger who had drifted into Lambert's circle.

"I'll go to reception and check out and settle up," said Nevada. "You bring the car around to a parking spot as near to the door as possible. We don't want to have to manhandle her too far."

"Okay."

"First let's try and get her dressed."

This wasn't easy but, with both of us working together, we managed it and left the girl, now fully clothed, snoring on the big double bed. While Nevada headed for reception, I went out to the car park, paid the parking charges and moved the car. I got lucky and found a space right next to a quiet side door of the hotel. I went in through it, memorising the layout in relation to the lifts for when we came back with our drunken burden.

I met Nevada in the lobby and we went up together.

We had just stepped out of the lift and turned the corner in the corridor when we saw the man. He was big and broad-shouldered, wore a black leather jacket and blue camouflage combat trousers and was moving slowly down the corridor away from the room where we were headed.

He was moving slowly because he was dragging the girl with him.

"Hey!" said Nevada.

The man turned and glanced at us, then turned away and began to move more quickly. Nevada and I broke into a run, our footsteps whispering on the hotel carpet, and, in a moment, we were beside him. The man had the girl's left arm flung over his shoulder and her lolling head beside his. When he turned to look at us, her head turned too. Her eyelids flickered open and then shut again.

The man snarled at us, "This is none of your—"

"Business?" said Nevada. "I think it is." She grabbed the girl and pulled her away from him.

The man seized one of the girl's arms and tried to drag her back. That was when Nevada kicked him. She kicked him good and hard, aiming at the groin. He turned away just in time and she missed and caught him on the thigh instead, but it still must have hurt like hell.

The man let go of the girl and Nevada pushed her towards me.

I ended up holding the girl in my arms like someone trying to keep his drunken partner upright on the dance floor. Now that she was vertical—sort of—I realised she wasn't very tall at all. Petite, actually. Her head was tucked under my chin and my nose was in her hair, which smelled of a strange mixture of apple shampoo and puke. She wasn't heavy in my arms, but she was a limp, dragging sort of weight and I found myself shifting position to keep her upright. We were now like partners moving slowly around the dance floor.

Save the last one for me…

While I did this, I watched the guy in the leather jacket trying to defend himself. But he wasn't having much luck as he discovered, like others before him, that getting into a physical disagreement with my sweetheart was a very bad idea. She rained blows on him, using fists, elbows, knees and feet, with great energy and accuracy and resourcefulness. And she just didn't let up.

The guy dropped to the floor, holding his hands above his head in a defensive screen, and yelped, "Stop hitting me, stop hitting me, *stop hitting me*."

Nevada stopped. "Have you got her?" she said to me, without turning or taking her eyes off the man crouching on the floor.

"Yup," I said. My diminutive drunken dance partner flopped in my arms, following my lead.

"For Christ's sake…" said the man from his undignified position cowering on the floor.

"Where were you planning to take her?" said Nevada.

"Home!" said the man.

"Home?"

"She's my little sister and I was taking her home."

"Your little sister?"

"Yes! Look at her ID. Look at my ID…" He began to reach into his jacket and Nevada surged in towards him again. He froze and said, "Don't hit me." Begged, actually.

"Then use your left hand. And whatever you take out of your pocket, hold it between your thumb and forefinger."

"For Christ's sake…" But he obeyed, bringing out a wallet in the prescribed manner.

We compared his driving licence with a student travel card we'd found on the girl. They had the same surname: Butterworth. He was Abraham, she was Cayley. And it wasn't that common a surname. Then Abraham produced his phone and a wealth of photographs of the two of them together, from childhood onwards. Which rather settled it.

He put his phone and wallet away, his hands only trembling a little. You mess with Nevada Warren at your peril.

"I knew Cayley had come up here," he said. "With a lot of her friends, so-called friends. They're a bad lot. And when she didn't come home and didn't answer her phone, I got worried and I came up here looking for her."

"Very sensible," said Nevada. "Have you ever heard of Lambert Ramkin?"

"No."

"Or Imperium Dart?" I said.

"No, sorry." Abraham rubbed his shoulder. "I'm all-over bruises now," he said, a pitiful note creeping into his voice.

"Sorry about that. We thought you were abducting her."

"I suppose you can't be too careful," said Abraham. And then, rather surprisingly, "Thank you."

"You're welcome," said Nevada.

10: PRECISION AUDIO COMPONENTS

We were getting into our car, or rather Tinkler's car, and preparing to leave the hotel when something strange happened. The hotel car park was full of record dealers packing up and leaving in disgruntlement. Including one familiar-looking woman who came hurrying towards us, waving her phone in the air. She obviously didn't want us leaving before she spoke to us. "Who's that?" said Nevada.

By now I'd recognised her. "It's the dealer who sold me the Imperium Dart books at St Drogo's," I said, getting out of the car.

Nevada got out too.

"Ah," said the woman, somewhat winded. "Caught you. Good. Here, this is for you." She handed me the phone.

Nevada was as surprised as I was. But instead of asking the obvious question, it seemed easier to take the phone. "Hello?" I said, rather cautiously.

"Ah, there you are." It took me a moment to recognise the deep, rasping voice. But only a moment. Tabloid Tim.

"I was ringing Meredith to tell her that if anybody wanted their books signed, to give them my email address and I'd arrange to do it by post. Send them an autographed slip-in card, you know the kind of thing."

I didn't know, but it didn't matter.

"And she told me the show has been cancelled?"

"That's right," I said.

"Ah, shit. So I don't suppose there's any chance of you collaring Lambert?"

"No," I said. There didn't seem any point telling him about our near miss.

"All right, never mind. I'll suss out another place where you can nab the bastard. Don't worry."

He sounded like he was actually invested in our quest now. Or maybe he was just invested in the possibility of a payday. But he was definitely committed to the cause. We arranged a date and time to come and visit his house again. This seemed to be a vital part of his ritual. But he'd been right once—it certainly wasn't his fault the record fair had gone belly up—so I was willing to go along with it.

I was less happy with his proviso. "Make sure you bring your two lady friends along, too."

After giving Meredith back her phone and thanking her profusely, we got in the car and drove off, discussing what had just happened. "It's a relief he got in touch," said Nevada. "I was dreading contacting him because I thought he might try to charge us. After all, he was right about Lambert being here."

"Near misses don't count," I said.

"Oh, I agree," said Nevada. "But I thought he might not see it that way. Tabloid Tim strikes me as a man who could be very difficult."

"Apparently, so long as we keep on visiting him for tea with you and Agatha, he's fine."

"Fine but loathsome," said Nevada.

Since we'd come all the way to Wales, and so that it wouldn't be a complete bust, we decided to drive back via Llandrindod Wells and drop in on an old friend.

Hughie Mackinaw was affectionately nicknamed the Scottish Welshman—it was Tinkler who had done the nicknaming, of course. Hughie owned a high-end turntable factory just outside Llandrindod Wells. In his chequered past he had been a member of a motorcycle gang in Scotland. He'd been the guy who looked after their bikes and it was a safe bet that he did a fine job on them because Hughie was a great mechanic. These days he applied his skills to restoring vintage turntables and manufacturing his own.

He also had a thriving sideline in what you might call market gardening.

As we drove along the A44 through Ponterwyd, then Rhayader and Nantmel, Nevada made some phone calls, including one to Tinkler. She put him on speakerphone when she eventually got through. "How was the record fair?" he said.

"Complete bust," I said.

"I told you so."

"No, you didn't."

"As soon as you said 'Wales', I scented disaster."

"Anyway," I said, "we're making a detour on the way home to visit an old friend and we were wondering if you wanted any tomatoes?"

"Christ no… Wait, wait, I mean yes, yes please, I want as many 'tomatoes' as you can bring back with you. Do you want me to transfer you the money?"

"No," said Nevada. "We can settle up when we get back."

"Safe journey and godspeed," said Tinkler fervently.

Instead of just turning up and hoping for the best—two disappointments in one weekend would have been too much—we'd phoned ahead to make sure Hughie would actually be in and that the quote-unquote tomatoes would be available for purchase. Not only was it yes to both those questions, but he also sounded very pleased to hear from us.

As we drew near Hughie's factory, I found myself overcome by a strange mood. Nevada must have sensed this, or indeed maybe she was feeling the same thing. "I'm not sure I want to see this place," I said.

She put a hand on top of mine on the steering wheel.

"We should have arranged to meet him somewhere else," I said. "Anywhere else."

I glanced at Nevada, taking a quick look at her serious, level blue eyes and then back at the road.

"Because it brings back memories, coming here?"

"Yeah," I said. My throat was thick and I was finding it hard to talk.

"But everything turned out all right," she said. "Didn't it?"

"Yes." I could only manage about one syllable at a time. If I'd been capable of saying more, I would have tried to explain that somewhere, on some other timeline, there was another me it hadn't turned out all right for, one who had lost Nevada forever.

I remembered deep winter, a dog's claws clicking on frozen ground. A water tower with four steel legs that loomed against the night sky. Flames. Gunfire. The certainty she was dead...

My eyes swam with tears and I thought for a moment I would have to pull over and stop, but my vision cleared as we turned off the main road onto the access road that led to Hughie's factory, which was set deep in parkland. Suddenly, silhouetted against the hot blue sky above the trees was— not a water tower that stupidly contained fuel—but a line of wind turbines.

"Those are new," said Nevada.

We drove past the battered old brown two-storey factory building and turned into the yard behind it. Parked there was Hughie's equally battered old BMW. Beside it was a motorcycle that was anything but old and battered. Rather, gleaming and obviously well-maintained. Hughie the ex-biker apparently liked to keep his hand in.

Coming out of the back door of the factory was the man himself. "He's still got his afro," said Nevada. He did indeed, though it had gone entirely grey now, which made for quite an impressive sight. He was wearing a lurid orange Hawaiian shirt and cut-off jeans and sandals. This garb seemed immensely strange since the fixed vision of him in my memory was being dressed for the intense cold of that winter all those years ago.

He was still smoking a spliff, though. Smoke spilled out of his smiling mouth as he waved at us.

We got out of the car and he hugged and kissed Nevada, and thankfully just hugged me. "You got here, then?" he said. His Glaswegian accent had softened, or maybe he was just feeling mellow and it would come out more strongly if he got excited.

So many things seemed strange, and some of them were just making themselves known to me. "No dog?" I said, looking around.

"Oh, he's fine. He just stays home now. No dogs allowed at the factory these days. He's all right, though. Albina makes a fuss of him and he's getting fat." Albina was Hughie's wife.

"How is Boo?"

"She's going to be a teenager this year, if you can credit it."

Boo was Hughie and Albina's daughter, a sweet little girl. Or at least she was when last seen. "So, how's your turntable?" said Hughie. Having got family matters out of the way, we were now talking about something really important. "Still running the Garrard 301?"

"That's right," I said.

"Those things just keep going," said Hughie, a mixture of admiration and contempt in his voice. "Still using the Rega arm?"

"No, I put an SME on it," I said.

"Well, that will be a huge fucking improvement," said Hughie. "Good on you. Did you find it was a huge fucking improvement?"

"Absolutely," I said. "For a start, surface noise virtually ceases to be an issue. Not because it disappears but—"

"Because the music becomes so much more compelling," said Hughie. He wasn't wrong. "Which SME is it?"

"The M2-9R."

"With the P1 spacer?" said Hughie.

I shot Nevada an apologetic look for this tech talk. She just gave me an indulgent smile. Boys will be boys. Especially if they're somewhat on the spectrum. I nodded an affirmative about the P1 spacer to Hughie. "You'd need that with the Garrard," he said. "You were lucky to buy an SME. You must have got hold of that by skin of your teeth. You've heard what's happened to them now?" He shook his head sadly. "The end of an era."

"Now, about the tomatoes," said Nevada, firmly steering the conversation onto business. "I see you've still got your setup here."

Hughie's setup was a group of greenhouses made of heavy-duty transparent plastic in the shape of half cylinders that lay on the bare earth here in the courtyard of his factory. They were effectively giant poly tunnels and served the same purpose. A casual observer would only see the bright red tomatoes thriving inside. But anyone who was more sharp-eyed, or suspicious, would have soon realised these were merely a screen for the even more spectacularly thriving cannabis plantation.

These greenhouses were much as before, but something else was missing. "Where's the moat, Hughie?" I asked. The last time I'd been here—on that painfully memorable occasion—there had been trenches dug all around the greenhouses. These had been designed to be filled with water, the objective being to create a moat that the local rat population were reluctant to swim across. Otherwise, the rats were all too fond of eating the tomatoes and also gnawing through, much worse, the cannabinoid cash crop.

But these trenches had all now been filled in.

Hughie grinned at us. "We now have another method of rat control," he said. "And, as you may have noticed, another way of generating our electricity."

Cannabis growing required a lot of artificial light, even outdoors, if you weren't farming it in the tropics, and this kind of consumption of electricity created a telltale spike on the grid, which could lead to the embarrassment and inconvenience of being busted. Hughie had previously used a diesel generator, hence the fuel tank on legs which had once lived here.

"You're using wind power now?" said Nevada.

"Good guess," said Hughie.

"We saw the turbines when we were driving in," said Nevada. "Good choice."

"Right," said Hughie. "Nobody in their right mind would think of burning fossil fuels these days."

"Good for you," I said.

"And so what is the solution to the rat problem?" said Nevada.

By way of reply Hughie made a strange noise, half clucking, half whistling. And from around the corner of the factory promptly appeared a large ginger cat. When she saw us, she hesitated, then continued to approach Hughie, but with a measure of caution. He crouched down and smoothed the fur on her head. "Meet Candy," he said. "Her and her family live onsite now. They're terrific little hunters and the rats know better than to come around. Any that don't find out soon enough, all right." He grinned at us. "This is why the factory is off limits to dogs these days."

While Nevada made friends with Candy, Hughie set about packing our purchases for us. As was traditional, he placed the sealed bags of weed in a large cardboard box marked *Precision Audio Component, Handle With Care.* And he also spread a layer of tomatoes on top, as if that would fool anyone searching the box. "Is this for Tinkler, then?" he said.

"How did you know?"

"He rang me a few minutes ago, begging for me to give you my most high-grade weed."

"Did you?" said Nevada, casually, still scratching an ecstatic Candy behind the ear.

"Of course I did," said Hughie. "You're my friends, aren't you?"

"I hope so," said Nevada. "Because some of that is for me."

"Well I think you'll like it, love." Hughie looked at me. "You still don't partake yourself?"

"No," I said.

Hughie winked at Nevada. "He's a puritan."

"He likes to keep a clear head," she said, stroking the contented cat.

Hughie sealed our box with red-and-white tape, which read *Fragile*. "Now," he said. "What brings you to the wilds of Wales? You didn't come here just to see me."

"We would have done if we'd known about the cats," said Nevada.

"We're here on business," I said. "We were looking for someone."

"Who?" said Hughie.

"Do you know anything about electronic dance music?" I said. It didn't really seem like Hughie's genre, but he nodded decisively.

"Of course," said Hughie. "There are a lot of old ravers in Wales. When the police began their campaign of persecution, crushing the dance scene in London, busting the raves and smashing the sound systems, a lot of the partiers fled across the M25 and some of them didn't stop until they got here."

"Have you ever heard of Imperium Dart?" I said.

"That's who we're looking for," said Nevada, running her hand lightly across Candy's arched spine.

Hughie burst into laughter.

"What's so funny?" she said.

"You mean Lambert?" said Hughie.

"Yes," I said.

"You just missed him. He was here not two hours ago. Buying some plant matter. He got the good stuff, too."

11: THE SUMMONING

The day after our return to London I got a call from Poppy, who wanted to arrange a meeting. "In person, if you don't mind. And at Noise Floor if you don't mind."

It took me a split second to remember that Noise Floor was the name of their house, as well as the studio in the back garden.

"Also," she said, "could you please bring Agatha along? Again, if you don't mind."

We set a date and time.

As it transpired Agatha was working, so she couldn't come along. Surprisingly, despite this, Tinkler elected to join us. In fact, he drove us there. He wasn't the driver that Agatha was, by any stretch of the imagination, but the roads were clear and in a couple of hours we were admiring the hillside garden spread out around us, accompanied by Poppy as we walked up the steps to the big white house.

Garden admiring was curtailed, unfortunately, by the abrupt advent of Julian. "What are they doing here?" he said, looking at us.

"Are you going to join the family meeting?" said Poppy. It was gratifying that she parried his question with a question rather than giving him a straight answer—a straight answer being just one item on the long list of things Julian didn't deserve, in my view. It was remarkable how much you could dislike someone on such a short acquaintance.

"Family meeting?" said Julian in a tone of voice rich with sarcasm, which didn't bode well for his attendance at said meeting. "You aren't giving these losers any money, are you?" His gaze flickered across us.

"Come to the meeting and find out," said Poppy, remaining agreeably evasive.

Julian started to make his teeth-kissing noise but then, perhaps for variety's sake, opted for a straightforward snarl instead, and pushed past me and Tinkler, heading down the steps.

For a moment it looked like he was going to try to do the same with Nevada but he instead skirted her at a healthy distance, possibly sensing that pushing my darling around was an enterprise that wouldn't end well.

Which at least suggested that, despite everything else, Julian was possessed of some intelligence.

At his departure, descending towards the driveway, Poppy made a point of resuming our conversation about the surrounding garden as we walked up through it.

With its full glory revealed in daylight I could see Nevada was really impressed. "Look, they've got Thai purple sage like ours. But theirs is *huge*."

Also in her full glory was the Green Wellie Nympho, aka Selena. Also known as Julian's mother, which was a condition for which one could only feel a lively sympathy.

She watched as Poppy led us towards her, in a different part of the big front room to the one where we'd been interviewed that first night. There was no desk here, just a group of armchairs arranged in a loose circle, as if we were about to take part in a group-therapy session.

Selena wasn't wearing her green wellies this time. Instead she was barefoot. Perhaps she'd been for a drive. She was sitting with one leg hooked casually over the arm of her chair, the dirty sole of her foot aimed straight at us. The fact it was so dirty made it seem oddly childlike. That was the only childlike thing about her.

She locked eyes with Nevada as soon as we came into the room and didn't look away from her as we all sat down and exchanged greetings.

After the initial hellos and a very brief bit of small talk about how our drive down had been, silence fell over the big room like a cloud cutting off the sunlight, although the actual sun continued to shine, cheerfully lighting up the silent space. The silence seemed to mostly emanate from the barefoot and rather hostile Selena.

Then suddenly she spoke up. "Where's your friend?"

"Our friend?" said Nevada. It was very clear that Selena could only be referring to Agatha, since everyone else in our circle she might know was sitting right here in front of her. But Nevada wasn't going to make things easy for her.

"The one with the shaved head," said Selena.

"She couldn't make it."

"Why not?"

"She's busy."

"Doing what?"

"I don't know," said Nevada. "Possibly shaving her head."

"Oh well, if she's not going to be here, there's no point *me* being here," said Selena. She unhooked her leg from the arm of the chair and rose to her feet in a supple, sinuous movement then turned and strolled out at considerable speed, yet somehow at the same time giving the impression of being utterly unhurried.

She was a singularly unpleasant woman, but there was no denying the utter animal grace of her. Certainly Tinkler wouldn't have denied it, as he stared after her, clearly regretting her departure.

The front door slammed loudly behind her as Selena went out.

"Well, at least she didn't leave it open this time," said Nevada.

Poppy sighed. "Would it do any good at all if I apologised for Selena's dreadful manners?" she said.

"She doesn't have any manners," said Jacquetta. "What we should be apologising for is her spectacular rudeness. And, speaking of rudeness, I forgot to serve the coffee. I'm so sorry." She hurried out towards the kitchen.

After she went, Poppy looked at us as if she wasn't quite sure what to do with us.

"Perhaps you'd like a progress report?" said Nevada.

Poppy pounced on this suggestion. "Yes, please. That would be very good of you."

We outlined our recent adventures. When we got to Tim Purshouse and his place in these developments, Poppy immediately interrupted us. "Tabloid Timothy?" she said.

"I'm afraid so," I said. "We call him Tabloid Tim, but I'm afraid so."

"Well, that's actually quite a smart move," said Poppy.

"Calling him Tabloid Tim?" said Tinkler eagerly. "I thought of that."

"I actually meant getting in touch with him," said Poppy. "That is inspired. I wish we'd thought of it. As thoroughly detestable as Purshouse is as a human being—I suppose we have to concede he *is* a human being—he is likely to prove useful. If we want to track Lambert down, nobody knows more about him than he does."

Jacquetta came back with the coffee. "They've been receiving assistance from Tabloid Timothy," Poppy said, bringing her up to speed.

"Did you tell them about how he wouldn't stop trying to hit on us?" said Jacquetta.

"Oh god, yes. Back in the day. I'd forgotten that."

"How could you forget?"

"I've been trying to blot it out, I suppose," said Poppy.

"Well he did," said Jacquetta, turning to address us. "He wouldn't stop hitting on myself and Poppy and Selena. On the principle, I assume, that because we were involved in a somewhat unusual relationship with Lambert our morals must be so lax that we'd even stoop to sleeping with a vile little scribbler who scribbles for that vile jam rag of a newspaper."

"Showbiz journalist of the year five years running," I said. And everyone laughed.

We then continued to update Poppy and Jacquetta with an account of our attempt to find Lambert based on Tim's intel (credit where it's due), concluding with the memorable near miss at the Zobole Marine Hotel in Aberystwyth. We didn't mention the half-naked drunk girl we'd found abandoned on the bed. Not least because of the small but very real and very disturbing possibility it had been Lambert who'd abandoned her there like that.

"How frustrating to have come so close," was all that Poppy said about the matter. "You almost had him that time. You're getting nearer and nearer."

"Yes, we are," said Nevada confidently, although I didn't particularly share that confidence.

"We want him to come home to us," said Poppy. There was sudden raw emotion in her voice, a naked exposure of need that was rather uncomfortable to hear.

We all fell silent.

Finally, Poppy said, "I know what you're thinking. You're thinking we could just as easily have had this meeting online. Which is absolutely true. It was Selena who insisted you come down here in person. It was also her stipulation that Agatha should be here. And, unfortunately, that appears to have been a deal-breaker. Hence her flouncing out the door when it turned out Agatha hadn't come. I've no idea why. Why she flounced out, I mean. Or why she wanted Agatha here, for that matter."

"I do," said Nevada.

"Oh? Why?"

Nevada hesitated. "I don't want to tell tales out of school or get Selena into trouble."

I could detect a certain amount of insincerity in this latter clause, but it didn't matter because Poppy said, "Oh I suspect there's nothing you could tell us about Selena that would cause us so much as a raised eyebrow. And there isn't any kind of trouble which she hasn't already been in. Right up to her lovely neck."

Personally I didn't think her neck was that lovely, but I didn't feel it was my place to say so. After all, this woman had been involved with Selena in a rave star's orgy cult for decades, and who knew what sort of deep emotional attachment she might still have for Selena. And her neck.

Nevada explained about us—almost literally—running into Selena and Horatio the other night, and about Agatha's history with Horatio as her driving instructor.

"And now they've… renewed their acquaintance?" said Poppy.

"Looks like it," said Nevada.

Tinkler made an odd noise and we all turned to look at him. Perhaps to avoid scrutiny, he got up from his chair and wandered towards the window.

"Hence Selena wanted to confront her rival for Horatio's affections," said Jacquetta.

"She wanted to see Agatha at close quarters," said Poppy.

"Do you think they would have had a cat fight?" said Tinkler hopefully, turning from the window. He'd apparently regained his composure.

"That would have been fun," said Jacquetta. "Would anyone like more coffee?"

At the mention of coffee, Tinkler rejoined our group and sat down. "I don't suppose there's any chance of snacks?" he said. And then, before we could jump in with reprimands, he added, "We've got a visitor, by the way."

The front door opened and I looked towards it, fully anticipating the return of Selena. But instead, and very unexpectedly, it was Declan, our homicidal—not to mention suicidal—boy taxi driver. He was still wearing an Adidas tracksuit, but this time instead of pale blue it was bright orange.

He came into the room hesitantly, and moved towards us in a tentative and very un-Declan-like manner. As he drew nearer, I saw with a small shock that it wasn't Declan after all. But the resemblance was so pronounced that he had to be a close relative and the obvious bet was his brother.

"Hello, Dermot," said Poppy in a businesslike, don't-waste-our-time sort of way.

"Hello, Mrs Claypool," said Dermot cautiously.

"How is the clearing out of the studio going?" said Poppy. "It does seem to be taking some while."

"Well, it would go a lot quicker," said Dermot, showing a surprising flash of spirit, "if Julian would actually help with it instead of just giving everybody else orders."

"Unfortunately, not actually helping and giving everybody else orders is a pretty fair summation of Julian."

"Yes, Mrs Claypool. Anyway, Julian asked me to ask Mrs Witton…" at this point he turned to look at Jacquetta, "if we could have the sandwiches?"

"All right, Dermot," said Jacquetta. "The sandwiches are in the fridge wrapped in wax paper. Some of the wax-paper packets have little stars drawn on them. For god's sake don't let Julian eat any sandwiches in the wax paper with stars, because those sandwiches contain olives and, if he bites into a sandwich that contains olives, he'll have an epileptic fit."

"Literally?" said Dermot, his eyes wide.

"No," said Jacquetta. "Figuratively."

As she went into the kitchen to help Dermot collect the carefully labelled sandwiches and also, despite our protests, to fetch a snack for Tinkler, I wandered over to the window, attracted to the notion of seeing Julian clearing out the studio. Or giving orders to other people to clear out the studio.

Julian was standing on the lawn between the studio building and the flying saucer with two other young men. One was Declan, in his signature powder-blue Adidas sportswear. Another was a virtual clone of him, along the lines of Dermot, but wearing a matching tracksuit in red.

"Does Declan have *two* brothers?" I said.

"Two?" said Nevada, and she came to the window to join me.

"Yes," said Poppy, sounding rather weary. "There are three of them. Declan, Dermot and Darra. They're triplets." After a moment she added, "They're not identical."

"Well, thank god for that," said Nevada. And Poppy laughed.

Jacquetta and Dermot came back in from the kitchen, Dermot carrying a shopping bag that no doubt contained sandwiches wrapped in wax paper, some of them with little stars on them, Jacquetta with a plate crowded with what looked like sweet pastries. More specifically, delicious homemade sweet pastries which Tinkler in no way deserved.

"Thank you very much for these, Mrs Witton," said Dermot, and hurried out with the bag, politely closing the front door behind him in a manner that Selena could have profitably emulated.

"He's quite a nice boy," said Jacquetta.

"If only he wouldn't call us all 'missus'," said Poppy. "Did you really have to make them so many sandwiches?"

"I don't mind," said Jacquetta.

"I know you don't mind," said Poppy. "But you're much too generous. Julian takes advantage terribly."

"Oh, they're all growing boys and they'll need the calories. Julian is taking them for training after they clear out the studio."

"Training?" said Nevada.

"Yes," said Poppy. "They go for runs in the woods and do exercises together, things like that. Like boot camp. You know, basic training."

"Julian says it builds team spirit," said Jacquetta.

"And they go along with it?" said Nevada.

"They blindly do anything Julian tells them." Jacquetta smiled. "It's all a bit *Fight Club*."

"What sort of team are they building spirit for?" I asked.

"Julian fancies himself as a record producer along the old-school Svengali lines," said Poppy. "Like Phil Spector or Stock, Aitken and Waterman."

"He plans to turn the triplets into a boy band," said Jacquetta.

Just then, before this preposterous revelation had a chance to sink in, Julian himself arrived, leaving the front door open behind him in a manner that suggested it was an inheritable genetic disorder.

He stared at me and Nevada and Tinkler, and said, in an accusing voice, "You're still here."

"Yes, we're still here," said Nevada.

"Dermot said you were still here," said Julian.

"I think we've established that we're still here," said Nevada.

"Our guests," said Poppy, stressing the word, "are helping us to find your father."

"My father," said Julian.

And although I wasn't inclined to direct any admiration Julian's way, it was impossible not to admire the vast spectrum of emotion he managed to express in those two words.

And none of it positive emotion.

"They're in touch with Tabloid Timothy," said Jacquetta. "And they're making good progress."

At the mention of Tim's name, or nickname, Julian shot her a look, and then turned back to us. He looked angry. "You really upset Declan the other night," he said. Apparently he was angry on Declan's behalf.

"Declan really upset *us* the other night, by nearly getting us all killed," said Nevada.

"He said you made him a passenger in his own cab."

This was true. After our near-fatal collision, Agatha had insisted on him sitting in the back and doing the driving herself.

"That's all he's fit to be," said Nevada. "A passenger. Where did he get his driver's licence? In a raffle?" This last crack was borrowed from Agatha who'd used it in the heat of the moment the other night, but it was good enough to be worth repeating.

"You just watch yourself," said Julian in a low, dangerous voice that raised angry hackles on the back of my neck.

I'm not a violent man but I began to wonder if I could find something suitably blunt and heavy to hit him with.

No doubt sensing the way the discussion was heading, Nevada said, in her most polite voice, "Don't you have a training regime to get started on?"

Julian kissed his teeth, no snarl this time, and turned and stalked out, slamming the door behind him, *à la mama*.

Poppy took a deep breath that turned into a sigh and said, "It seems I'm always apologising for my family."

It was interesting that she counted Julian as a member of her family. I suppose he was, but if ever there was someone you should make an exception for, it was him.

We decided it was time to say our farewells and Jacquetta, despite protests from two of us, found a bag for Tinkler to put his pastries in. Then she and Poppy accompanied us down the steps through the glorious garden to the somewhat less glorious circular driveway. It was somewhat less glorious because Julian was there, pointedly ignoring us as he climbed into the Mini, then gunning the engine and screeching away as though he'd been taking lessons from Declan. Or possibly his mother.

"I thought he was going out training with the triplets," said Nevada.

"Oh, he doesn't actually go on the runs with them." said Poppy. "He's not crazy. He just monitors them intermittently with GPS, then gives them a stern pep talk when they get back."

"Why do they put up with it?" said Nevada.

Poppy shrugged. "He has charisma, like his dad."

This seemed like wishful thinking on her part. If Julian had anything resembling charisma, I, for one, was definitely immune to it. Poppy said goodbye and started back up the steps, probably eager to get back to her gardening. But Jacquetta lingered. "I hope your friend enjoys his Danishes," she said.

"Our friend is already enjoying his Danishes," said Nevada, nodding towards the little Volvo.

Tinkler had shut himself inside and was surreptitiously ransacking the bag he'd been given.

"Look," I said, "you really mustn't let him take advantage."

"Oh, he isn't taking advantage," said Jacquetta. "I like doing it. I miss cooking. There's no one to cook for these days."

"But you've got Poppy," said Nevada. And then added, with less enthusiasm, "And Selena and Julian."

"But we don't sit down to meals when Lamb isn't here. We're not a family without him. When he goes away, everything begins to fall apart." She looked around, a helpless expression on her face. "This isn't a home without him. Please find him and bring him home."

I realised, embarrassed but moved, that there were tears in her eyes.

"Please bring him home to us safely," she said.

As we drove away, she watched us go, not moving or waving, her shoulders drooped and weary.

12: A BEARD FOR THE BEER

Any tendency to feel that our trip to Noise Floor had been a waste of time was neatly avoided by combining it with a visit to the nearby hamlet of Nutalich, to follow up on our plans to turn that pretty little place—for one weekend only—into the Village of Vinyl.

"You're really going to go through with this?" said Tinkler.

"We think it's a great idea," said Nevada. "Don't you think it's a great idea?"

"Agatha came up with it, so of course I think it's a great idea," said Tinkler. "I would be untrue to my doomed passion if I thought anything else."

"Agatha came up with the basic concept," said Nevada. "We're the ones who decided to follow through on it, and site it in Nutalich."

"I still say that's a fucked-up name for a village," said Tinkler. "Even in Kent."

"It means 'flying bird' in Celtic," said Nevada primly.

"I know," said Tinkler. "Stop pretending you can speak Celtic. And it's still a fucked-up name."

"The roof of the church looks like a flying bird," I said.

"The roof of the church looks like a leftover pizza sagging on a shoebox," said Tinkler. Then he paused for a reflective moment. "Did I say sagging or shagging?"

"Sagging."

"Just checking."

"No, it doesn't," I said. "It looks like a bird taking flight."

"Now boys," said Nevada. "No bickering about church roofs. We can judge if it's a sagging pizza or a flying bird when we drive past it on our way out. Right now, everyone be on their best behaviour and get ready to meet the member of the clergy who's responsible for that very church."

A bit of online research had enabled us to reach out to the relevant person on the village council for our proposed project and this turned out to also be the local vicar, a certain Gerald Blanchflower DD (Doctor of Divinity).

Dr Blanchflower had proved refreshingly amenable, eager even. It seemed the council had been looking for something just like our brainchild to raise the profile of Nutalich and (although he didn't actually say this) bring the tourist dollars flooding in.

It has to be said, he sounded a little less enthusiastic when we rang him up again this morning to say we were in the neighbourhood and planned to drop in for a visit in person. "You don't think he's getting cold feet?" I said.

"He's definitely getting cold feet," said Tinkler.

"No he is not," said Nevada. "He's probably just shy. But he has nothing to be shy about. We'll charm his socks off. I assume the clergy wear socks?"

"With little crosses on," I said.

"He needs them for his cold feet," said Tinkler.

At this point we saw the sign announcing we were on the outskirts of Nutalich. We drove over the now-familiar stone bridge, which looked even more picturesque and cosily moss-covered in the light of day, past the Bird in Flight pub—still with a full car park, I noted, even at this early hour. I thought that boded well for our enterprise, and I said as much.

"Just so long as we have good weather for our weekend," said Nevada.

"It will probably rain," said Tinkler.

As we drove into Nutalich on this sunny summer morning it never occurred to us that this beautiful little village, with its single, narrow approach road and single, narrow exit road, was a perfect design for a death trap.

The vicar had told us that, instead of meeting at the church, we could talk to him by the duck pond in the centre of the village. I tried not to read anything ominous into him suggesting this encounter on what amounted to neutral territory.

We parked near one of the several pubs—the Green Man, with a monstrous figure painted on its sign that must have given many a local tot nightmares—and got out of the car. "I'm going to the comic shop," said Tinkler.

"I thought you'd overcome your childhood addiction to comics?" said Nevada.

"Adolescent addiction and recovery is a process, not an endpoint." He headed towards the shop, which had the rather odd name of MIWK 2.

"Sure you wouldn't rather meet a doctor of divinity?" called Nevada.

"Pretty damned sure," called Tinkler, and disappeared into the shop.

We found our doctor of divinity, as promised, by the duck pond, sitting right beside it on a bench, watching the birds frolic and splash with a fond, benign expression on his face.

It has to be said this was an expression that vanished as soon as he saw us coming. He rose from the bench and turned to meet us, putting his back to the pond.

Dr Blanchflower was clad in a traditional long, black cassock and a dog collar. But over the cassock he wore a rather well-cut tweed jacket in shades of rust and orange. On his feet, poking out from under the cassock, were what looked like a pair of oxblood Doc Marten boots. They were very muddy. And there was mud splashed on the hem of his cassock.

The Doc Martens, and indeed the mud, seemed to go with the fact that he was a trendy, youthful vicar. He hardly looked much older than we were, despite traces of grey in his neatly trimmed beard. His beard and shaggy but carefully shaped hair were approximately the same shade of red as his tweed jacket. His eyes were alert and perhaps a little alarmed behind the lenses of gold, wire-rimmed spectacles.

All in all, he looked oddly familiar.

As soon as we reached him, he gave a deep sigh—never a good sign—and said, "I'm afraid you've come here on a wild goose chase."

I thought for a moment that this was some kind of reference to the waterfowl in front of us. But only for a moment.

"What do you mean?" said Nevada, cutting to the chase.

"I don't think we are going to be able to proceed with your event," said the vicar, equally direct. It looked like Tinkler, ever the pessimist, had been right.

"But you said you'd just had something else fall through," said Nevada. "And you were looking for a replacement to schedule this summer."

"Yes, in a couple of weeks, in fact. But I'm afraid, on further consideration, I've decided that this idea of a record fair isn't really suitable." Dr Blanchflower shrugged his rusty tweed shoulders. "There's nothing inherently wrong with it," he said encouragingly. "It's just not for Nutalich." Then he fell silent for a moment, studying us with his high forehead creased in a frown. "Don't I know you from somewhere? Haven't I met you both before?"

"I've been thinking the same thing," said Nevada, clearly relieved to have got off the subject of our vinyl fair not being for them. She might even have been telling the truth.

Suddenly I made a connection somewhere deep in my memory and I said, "Did you used to have a church in Canterbury?"

He looked at me sharply. "Near Canterbury, yes."

"Valerian's grave," said Nevada. She hadn't been lying after all.

The vicar began to smile. It was a small, tentative smile, but it was the first time since we'd arrived that he didn't look as though he was attending a funeral. Which, come to think of it, as a vicar he probably had to do a lot. "We discussed films, didn't we, if I remember?"

"Stanley Kubrick," said Nevada.

"Ah yes." Dr Blanchflower was smiling a big, nostalgic smile now. He looked at Nevada more closely. "Are you familiar with the work of Christopher Nolan?"

"Sure," said Nevada.

"Because, personally, I regard him as the modern equivalent of Kubrick and his natural successor. He has the brilliant precision of Kubrick but without the rather uninviting coldness of the master."

"Really?" said Nevada. "I agree about precision, but I think he also shares exactly the coldness of Kubrick and that's his Achilles heel. I prefer David Fincher."

"Oh yes," said the vicar. "*Seven, Fight Club, The Game*…"

"*Gone Girl* was amazing," said Nevada fervently.

"Yes, yes, it absolutely was," said the vicar. He looked like he might be about to break into a happy little dance. "Have you seen *The Girl with the Dragon Tattoo*?"

"What about that ending?" said Nevada. "When she sees him with the other woman and throws his Christmas present in the rubbish?"

"It's so moving," agreed the vicar. "I'm getting goose bumps just thinking about it."

We'd gone from a wild goose chase to goose bumps, which could only be a good thing.

"Anyway," said Nevada. "I was going to say that, to my mind, David Fincher is the natural successor to Kubrick. He'll do literally hundreds of takes like Kubrick. But somehow Fincher doesn't squeeze the life out of a scene like Kubrick did."

"How very true."

"And there's a real passion and heat to Fincher's work that Kubrick never had," said Nevada.

The vicar was nodding happily. He suddenly seemed to realise we were all standing. "Won't you sit down?" he said.

We all sat on the bench, looking at the placidly splashing birds in the pond.

"Why did you suddenly go cold on our idea?" said Nevada. It was if they were old friends now, having bonded over modern cinema.

"Well," said the vicar, looking a bit embarrassed, "vinyl is a bit geeky and niche, isn't it?"

Nevada gave me a look as if to say, it's your turn, buster.

"Geeky, yes," I said. "Niche, not so much."

Although this was a business discussion, Nevada was happy to now sit back and let me do the talking. And I was quite eloquent, expounding on a subject I was passionate about. I told him that, while downloading and streaming dominated music, vinyl was still very much a contender and growing in sales every year. While the vile silver disc, or the CD as it was also known, was deservedly dwindling towards extinction, vinyl-pressing plants were working twenty-four hours a day trying to meet the demand for records. "And, actually," I said, "although it's true that you can call vinyl geeky, it's also cool and fashionable and trendy. If a young person is going to buy music in a physical format, it will be on vinyl."

"Well, that's true," said the vicar. "Both my nieces spend their pocket money on it. Have you heard of a singer called Self Esteem? She's really very good."

The mention of a music star gave me sudden inspiration. "And what's more," I said, "we might be able to get a local celebrity to open the fair."

"Really? Who?"

"Have you ever heard of Imperium Dart?" I said. This was a real leap of faith given that we hadn't even found this elusive personage yet, but frankly I would have said anything at this point to try and tip the scales in our favour. I could see Nevada giving me full marks for audacity. And possibly mendacity.

"Good lord, yes," said the vicar. "And I was aware he lived locally, but I don't think I've ever seen him in person, in the flesh, so to speak."

"He's a legend in the electronic dance music world," I said.

"Oh, you don't have to tell me that. I was really into Rotterdam hardcore in my wild youth."

"Well, anyway," I said, "we know his family quite well." By now this was true. "And we'll certainly do our best to get him to come along."

"Well…" said the vicar.

I could see him weakening. I looked at Nevada, giving her a non-verbal signal that it was time to move in for the kill.

"Look, Dr Blanchflower," she said.

"Call me Gerry."

"Look, Gerry. Just give us a chance and we'll deliver a wonderful weekend of vinyl that will bring in the customers from far and wide, and make every merchant here…" she gestured at the shops all around us. "We'll make them very happy indeed. And people will see how beautiful your village is, and they'll want to come back. We took one look at it and we wanted to come back, didn't we, darling?" She gazed at me with her big blue eyes.

"For once she's not lying," I said, and we all laughed. "Listen… Gerry," I said. It was a bit difficult to address a man in a clerical collar by his first name, but I managed it. "What was the festival that you said you had to cancel?"

"Oh," said Gerry. "Our annual beer carnival." He shook his head. "It's been a fixture for nearly a century, but these days the idea of encouraging people to drink, and indeed drink to excess, is rather frowned upon."

"So, it's definitely off," I said.

"Oh, yes."

"That seems a shame," said Nevada. Reassured that the beer festival was a dead duck, she obviously felt she could afford to play devil's advocate. "What with the pub and the pint being at the heart of English village life."

"Oh, don't worry," said Gerry. He glanced around a trifle furtively. "We firmly intend to sell just as much beer as ever. It's frankly too much of a money spinner to abandon. Last time we turned over a hundred grand."

I could see Nevada was impressed by this information. "Really?"

"Hard to say with any exactitude, since it's cash sales. It could be considerably more. Anyway, we intend to carry on with it. Only this year we won't be promoting the fact. We will, so to speak, be using your vinyl festival to conceal the activity."

"We'll be a beard for the beer," said Nevada.

"Ha ha. Yes. Exactly."

After a bit more small talk, we all shook hands and parted the best of friends, with our vinyl festival back on the table and a firm date booked for it. We went into the comic shop and fetched Tinkler, who was buying a stack of graphic novels. "Good job we got here when we did," said Nevada. "Before you emptied your bank account."

"Better to spend the money on these than drugs," said Tinkler. "Like I normally do." He winked at the girl behind the counter who winked cheekily back and offered him a bag for his purchases. He declined. "I'll be fondling these all the way back to London," he said, rubbing the covers of the graphic novels.

"In that case, I'll be driving," I said.

"You bet you will be," said Tinkler, waving goodbye to the girl, who seemed sorry to see him go.

We stepped out of the shop, with the door making a *Star Trek* swoosh as we exited, and emerged blinking into the sunshine.

"You fell off the wagon, eh, Tinkler?" said Nevada.

Tinkler hefted the books. "They had copies of Alan Moore's *Providence*."

"Oh good."

"In the limited edition hardcovers."

"Thank heavens for that."

We got into the car and drove out of the beautiful little village, with me at the wheel and Nevada beside me. Tinkler was, as promised, in the back seat fondling his purchases. But this didn't stop him saying, "Did the vicar have cold feet?"

"He did at first," said Nevada. "But we warmed them up for him nicely."

"Disgusting image," said Tinkler, leafing through one of his books.

"Are you referring to your reading matter?" said Nevada diffidently.

"No, what you just said."

As we approached the outskirts of Nutalich and the church with its extraordinary roof, Tinkler looked up and said, "Sagging pizza on a shoebox."

"Bird in flight," I said.

"In any case," said Nevada, "it must be easy to clean the gutters. You can just reach up to access them."

"Stop trying to make peace," said Tinkler. "Sagging pizza."

"Bird in flight," I said.

"Boys, boys, boys," said Nevada. And then she gave a contented little chuckle. "Village of Vinyl," she murmured.

"It'll probably rain," said Tinkler.

13: POSTCARD

Considering what had happened when we received that letter purporting to be from Poppy, we were naturally rather wary of the postcard from an anonymous sender that tumbled through our letterbox the next morning.

The image on the postcard was the same as the cover art of Imperium Dart's *The Magus* album, so at first I thought it was from Agatha. But it was unsigned. "And it's not her handwriting," said Nevada. "Could it be from Tinkler?"

"Can he even write?" I said. But, in fact, I could see it wasn't his handwriting either.

Other than our address, the only thing inscribed on the card was a phone number. A London landline number, in big bold numerals. It may seem overly cautious that I put it into a search engine before dialling, but that's what I did. No results. The number wasn't connected to any business, or any residential address, that the internet knew about.

There was nothing else for it. I dialled it.

My call was answered promptly—by a recording. A rather antiquated, somewhat sepulchral and very posh male voice immediately began to utter a sequence of numbers. These were repeated several times, and then the tape cut off and the call was dropped. I rang back again and got the same mechanical voice, intoning the same cryptic sequence (it did actually sound like it was being read in a crypt) and, this time, I recorded it.

Nevada was out of the house charity shopping just at the moment so, impatient to work out what the hell was going on and wanting to enlist another mind on the problem, even his mind, I got in touch with Tinkler and played it for him.

After listening for a while, he said, "Have you ever heard of EVP?"

"Who's she?" I said.

"Not Evie Pea, pea-brain, the letters of the alphabet E, V and P."

"Well, I've heard of the letters," I said. "But not that acronym."

"It stands for electronic voice phenomenon. Mysterious voices you pick up on a blank tape or when you're spinning the dial on your radio. Supposedly emanating from the spirit world."

"Uh huh," I said.

"Amazing how much scepticism you manage to pack into a single grunt, my friend. Or was that two grunts?"

"I would say scepticism is called for in a situation like this."

"I'm not saying I believe in this stuff," said Tinkler. "It's probably all just a massive hoax. Or aliens, of course. But this recording of yours sounds like EVP. It often involves just strings of numbers being read aloud."

"Okay, thanks," I said.

"Let's hear you say that again, and try for a little more sincerity this time."

"Thank you, Tinkler," I said.

"Always happy to help. Are we still on for dinner tonight?"

"Yes."

"Is Agatha coming?"

"Yes."

"Good. We can use the assembled might of our intellects to crack this code. My money is on aliens."

"See you later, Tinkler."

When Nevada got home, I asked her to listen to the recording. She jotted down the numbers, scrutinised them for a while, then started to smile. That smile told me she'd spotted something I hadn't.

"It's a map reference," she said. "Followed by a date and time."

"What date and time?"

"Good lord, tomorrow evening. That doesn't allow us a lot of wiggle room."

"Especially if that map reference turns out to be in Iceland," I said.

"No," said Nevada, busy on her phone. "It's for a location just outside London."

"Handy," I said.

"Assuming we're going to go," said Nevada. We looked at each other. I think, even then, there was no question of what we were going to do.

As promised, Tinkler and Agatha joined us for dinner that evening. And, as we poured them wine, we brought them up to speed on the meaning of the mystery message and showed them the postcard, which Agatha examined with approval.

"We thought it was from you," I said.

"No such luck," she said. And then she went and fetched her shoulder bag from the front hall, where she'd left it on arrival, and took out two paperbacks. They were both copies of *The Magus* by John Fowles. One was a chunky volume with cover art identical to that on the LP—and our postcard. The other was slimmer and had blue-stained page edges, and different but intriguingly similar art.

"That's the American edition," she said. "Using the wraparound Tom Adams cover painting from the hardback. Am I giving you too much information?"

"Not at all," said Tinkler. "You're merely being charmingly instructive. But, on the other hand, maybe you should check with someone who isn't hopelessly besotted with you."

"What I do think," said Agatha, "is that it's worth you guys hearing about what happens in *The Magus*. I'm assuming none of you have read it?"

We all confessed, somewhat shamefacedly, that we'd missed out on this modern classic, although Nevada hastily added that she had read Alain-Fournier's *Le Grand Meaulnes*, a 1928 French novel that was said to have inspired Fowles. In the original French, of course.

"Close but no cigar," said Tinkler.

We all settled down in the sitting room with wine and some music—Mal Waldron's classic *The Quest*. It wasn't the somewhat rare New Jazz original but instead a Dutch Artone pressing that used the original Van Gelder metalwork and was therefore the next best thing. Agatha said the music beautifully suited the mood of the book, which she proceeded to synopsise for us.

"It's set in the 1950s and it's about a young British teacher—he's a bit of a shit, really. But a handsome shit."

"The best kind," said Nevada.

"Anyway, he gets a job teaching at a private school on a small Greek island. And there he finds himself drawn into the circle of a mysterious millionaire—"

"The best kind," said Tinkler.

"Who then proceeds to blow the teacher's mind by playing what he calls 'the godgame' on him. Which essentially involves staging elaborate deceptions. For instance, he tells the teacher that the past can come to life and, the next thing he knows, the teacher sees this 'ghost', in heavy quotation marks, of a beautiful young woman."

"The best—"

"Shut up, Tinkler, and let her get on with it."

"A young woman in Edwardian dress. And that's just the start. The teacher knows the millionaire is staging these things for his benefit, and the millionaire knows that he knows. But that doesn't matter."

"Why is the millionaire doing it?" I said.

"It's all very enigmatic," said Agatha.

"Of course."

"But essentially the young teacher, who, like I said, is a bit of a shit, is being led towards enlightenment and becoming a better person. Or at least less of a shit."

"What a great summary," said Tinkler warmly. "Now I feel I have no need at all to read the book."

"You really should," said Agatha. "It's a masterpiece. But the point is, that elaborately staged deception at the gig in Brixton..." She was looking at me. "That reminded me of the kind of thing that goes on in this book. And, of course, we know that Imperium Dart, Mr Lambert Ramkin, has read *The Magus* and loves it enough to name one of his albums in honour of it, and to include a quote from it..."

"And you think he stole his modus operandi from this novel?" said Nevada.

"I think he was *inspired* by it."

"Well Poppy certainly said he was fond of these kind of pranks," I said. "Although she also said they're much too elaborate just to call them that."

"One other thing," said Agatha. "The games the millionaire plays, these masquerades he stages, they tend to have a definite erotic element."

I remembered the green-eyed siren, seaweed hair floating in the tidal surge of the strobe. I picked up the postcard and saw that, oddly, the woman painted on it had her hair floating just like that.

"In fact, the whole novel is quite erotic," said Agatha.

"Hang on, maybe I'll read it after all," said Tinkler.

At that point we moved to the table and sat down and ate dinner, and didn't talk business anymore. Assuming that was what we had been doing. When we were all finished and the plates had been cleared away, Agatha said, "So are you going to those map coordinates tomorrow night?"

Nevada frowned and turned the postcard over in her fingers. "I guess we owe it to our client," she said finally. Then she looked at me. "And this time both of us will go."

"And me," said Agatha. "Count me in."

"But we don't know what we're getting into," said Nevada.

"That's sort of the appeal. Anyway, you may need a good driver."

"I'll come too," said Tinkler. "Now I've heard about this erotic element."

"There wasn't anything very erotic about what happened last time," snapped Nevada.

"You only say that because he didn't tell you about the food wagon hottie," said Tinkler. "Whoops, sorry bro. I wasn't supposed to mention that, was I? What happens in Brixton stays in Brixton."

The following evening we gathered at our place, Agatha the last to arrive, with Tinkler's little Volvo DAF parked outside waiting to take us on our mystery tour. Agatha had elected to drive Tinkler's car on this odyssey, I suspect because we had no idea what was going to happen and she didn't want to risk damaging her own vehicle.

Plus she just enjoyed driving the DAF, with its unique Variomatic transmission.

We climbed into the car and set off as the summer-afternoon sun began to decline in the sky, and the hot air and light of the day started to cool and mellow. Our destination, as dictated by the disembodied voice on the phone, was near Swinley Forest in Berkshire. The fastest approach would have involved us dashing along the M4 motorway but we opted to take the scenic route. We drove along secondary roads through Richmond—very much our stamping ground—then Twickenham and Sunbury-on-Thames, before heading for Ascot, where we turned south towards the A322.

Agatha had been confident, despite us taking this winding and eccentric way, that we would be at our destination at the appointed time, which was just about nightfall.

We were in the midst of thickly forested woodland, driving towards the setting sun and ever-lengthening shadows, when Agatha suddenly said, "Did anyone happen to bring along an old-school paper map?"

"Sure," said Nevada. "Do you want me to get it out?"

"You'd better. The satnav on my phone just failed. In fact, my phone just failed."

"Here, use mine," said Nevada, taking out her phone. Then she fell silent. When she did speak, her voice was a careful monotone. "My phone isn't working either. Could you guys…"

Tinkler and I didn't even wait for her to finish the sentence. We immediately checked our phones. It was the same story for us. "No signal," I said.

"The same here," said Tinkler.

"Okay," said Nevada. "Now, I really don't like this one little bit."

"Could we have just driven into a dead zone?" said Agatha.

"In Berkshire?" said Nevada. "We're not exactly hundreds of miles from civilisation." Her voice was tightening with tension. "I would have thought the phone coverage out here would be fine."

"Maybe not," said Tinkler. "Maybe this is normal around here. I could check by looking it up for us… if only my phone was working."

"Okay," said Nevada decisively, "I don't like this and I think we should turn around and go home."

That was when the car's power failed.

As we drifted to a stop, Agatha carefully steered us off the road and onto the grassy verge. "What happened?" said Nevada. The tension was gone from her voice. Now things had become serious, she sounded entirely calm.

"I don't know," said Agatha. "The car just died on me." She experimented with various controls. "The lights are still working." Indeed, our headlights were shining on an impressive ancient oak tree, which towered over us. Each massive gnarled limb that stretched away from its trunk was as big as an ordinary tree. Pale green moss spreading across its bark gave it the unsettling look of scales, of the skin of a massive reptile.

"So, the battery is okay," said Agatha. "The engine just conked out." She switched off the headlights and the giant tree dropped into darkness. "Better conserve the battery," she said.

We sat there silently for a moment and then, as if by prearrangement, she and Tinkler opened the doors and got out. We tilted their seats forward and followed them.

It was cool outside, with the last of the evening's summer heat fading with the daylight. The sky above was dark indigo deepening into black. The air smelled wonderfully of the trees and plants all around us and, at any other time, this would have been a beautiful place to be. Just now, though, none of us could really appreciate it.

"Everybody's phone still works on flashlight mode, right?" said Agatha. "Then if you hold them up I'll open the bonnet and see if I can suss out what's wrong. Tinkler, can you hold mine for me?"

"Yes, ma'am."

Agatha handed him her phone and just then we heard a long, keening whistling, apparently coming from deep in the woods. We all froze. Was it animal or human in origin? Whatever it was, it was a deeply unnerving sound.

And then something moved in the air above us. We felt it rather than heard it—a big, shadowed shape, descending out of the night. "Look at that," murmured Nevada.

And we all looked up to see an enormous owl, its wings spread wide to create a shape as big as a man. It swept in silently to land high up in the oak tree, crouching in a notch between the main trunk and one of the huge limbs.

We stared up at the owl and it stared down at us, amber eyes glinting in its flat face, two tufts rising from its head like diabolical horns. Then it turned away from us, leaned in towards the trunk of the giant oak, pecked at something and then lifted its wings, falling forwards into the air and sweeping gracefully upwards, back into the night, out of sight.

I remember thinking that, whatever else happened, our trip had been worth it to witness this apparition.

But the night wasn't done with us yet.

"Holy… shit…" said Tinkler.

We all looked at him, and then turned and looked in the direction he was staring. A vehicle was approaching. We could hear its engine and then suddenly had to raise our hands to shield our eyes from its looming headlights. But we could see clearly enough what had caused Tinkler's consternation.

The vehicle was a Volkswagen camper van.

And, painted on the front of it, in luminous paint that glowed a ghostly milky green… was an *owl*.

As the camper van came abreast of us, it slowed down. And we could see there was also an owl painted on its side.

These owls were painted in an abstract, trippy style. Psychedelic. But there was no question they were owls. And that was rather an odd coincidence—wasn't it?

The van drifted to a stop beside us and the passenger window was wound down laboriously, allowing a young woman to lean out and look down at us. She had pale skin and long, blonde dreadlocks, and she was painfully thin. She smiled and said, "Broken down?"

"Looks like it," said Agatha. She was addressing the woman but she wasn't looking directly at her. Instead, she was peering intently up at something on the windscreen.

The woman leaned back inside the van and spoke in a muted voice to her companion at the wheel. Then she appeared at the window again. She lowered her voice conspiratorially, although we were the only people for miles around. "Are you heading for the rave?"

We all looked at each other.

"Yes," I said.

"Would you like a lift?"

"Yes," I said. "Please."

"Hop in, then," said the woman cheerfully.

We hauled open the big side door of the van and scrambled inside. As soon as we'd shut the door, the driver started the engine again and we were suddenly moving at speed through the darkening forest. I looked back at Tinkler's forlorn little car, abandoned, vanishing behind us, and I began to wonder if we'd made the right decision.

"I'm Lilith and this is Rodney," said the woman.

"Bad luck about your car," said Rodney. He was a skinny young guy with pale skin and long, blond dreadlocks, which matched Lilith's.

"And we can't get a signal on any of our phones," said Nevada. "Is this some kind of black spot for mobile signals?"

"Not that I know of," said Rodney. "Is it, Lil?"

"I don't think so, Rod," said Lilith.

"Here, try my phone," said Rodney, digging it out of his pocket while keeping his other hand thankfully on the steering wheel and passing it to Lilith, who passed it back to us. It was an ancient turquoise Nokia with a screen about the size of a postage stamp. And no signal on it when I tried.

"Any luck?" said Rodney.

"Nope."

"Pity," he said. "I don't know what's going on."

"Could be aliens," said Lilith.

"That's my theory," said Tinkler. "Nice phone, by the way." He took it from me and examined it. "It's a 3210?"

"That's right," said Rodney, and I sensed a boys' discussion of technology coming up.

"It was a classic," said Tinkler.

There was silence from the front of the van and then Rodney said, "What do you mean a classic?"

"What do you mean *was*?" said Lilith.

"Well, you know," said Tinkler, hastily handing the phone back to me. "It's old school but cool."

I handed the phone back to Lilith, who took it from me and held it protectively.

"Old school?" said Rodney. "It's the first one with an internal antenna, mate."

"That's right," said Tinkler. "It was."

"Why do you keep saying 'was'?" said Lilith. "We just bought it. It's the latest model."

I'd been aware for some time that Nevada and Agatha had been looking at something on the seat beside them, making discreet use of their phone lights. Now Nevada showed me what they were looking at. It was a newspaper. The headline read, *Crusading Russian Journalist Released*. Directly underneath that it said, *Military court frees Captain Grigory Pasko after 20 months' confinement on treason charges for reporting dumping of nuclear waste at sea.*

The date on the newspaper was 20 July… 1999.

"You have some nice newspapers and magazines back here," said Nevada, in a conversational voice.

"Feel free to have a read," said Lilith. "If you can manage in the dark. Can we switch the light on back there, Rod?"

"I'm driving, hon," said Rodney.

"Don't worry, we've got our phones," said Nevada.

"Your phones?" said Lilith, apparently deeply puzzled by this non sequitur.

"Sure," said Nevada, and showed Lilith her phone switched on in flashlight mode.

"What's that?" said Lilith, leaning over the back of her seat, staring in fascination. "A torch? It's flat. It's a flat torch."

"It's a phone," said Nevada drily, giving me a droll sidelong look as she passed it to Lilith, who accepted it gingerly like some sort of holy relic.

"Rod, look," she said.

"I'm driving, Lil," said Rodney tersely. "Don't shine that thing in my face."

"It's amazing, where did you get it?" said Lilith, looking back at us.

"It's my phone," said Nevada again.

"Your phone?" Lilith looked at us, all innocence. "But where are the numbers?" She caressed the smooth glass screen of the phone. "It doesn't have any buttons."

I couldn't quite give Lilith's Oscar-worthy performance the attention it deserved because I was looking at the pile of magazines and newspapers Agatha had passed to me. Highlights included a copy of *Jockey Slut* dated April—May 1999 and the *Face* dated August 1999. *Jockey Slut* featured Basement Jaxx on the cover (*"Garage punk's not dead!"*) along with Fatboy Slim, Space Raiders and an article entitled *Dance Porn!* Oh, and a free CD. The *Face* had a photo of three grinning young women I didn't recognise, but promised articles on Puff Daddy, Tom and Nicole, and *Porn Chic*.

Lilith was leaning over to our driver and saying in a small voice, "She says it's her phone, Rod." And Rodney said, "Then it would be very rude not to believe her, Lil."

"You have some great magazines here," I said. "Where did you get them?"

"WH Smith, I think," said Lilith, raising her voice back to conversational level.

"And I like your road tax on the windscreen," said Agatha.

"Always pay your road tax," said Rodney piously. "Keeps the cops off your back."

I thought if he wanted the cops off his back, not driving around in a van with a psychedelic glow-in-the-dark owl on it might also help, but it seemed ill-mannered to say as much.

"Congratulations on finding one for the correct year," said Agatha.

"What do you mean?" said Rodney, all innocence.

"Car tax discs for windscreens were phased out in 2014," said Agatha.

"Twenty-fourteen what?"

"The year twenty-fourteen," said Agatha. "Two thousand and fourteen."

There was a long silence in the front of the van and then Rodney said, "The year two thousand and fourteen?"

"Yes."

"Is that, uh… is that the year you guys think it is?"

"No," said Nevada patiently. "We think it's quite a few years after that."

"Is that where you come from?" said Lilith in an awed voice.

"Yes," said Nevada patiently.

Lilith leaned over to Rodney and spoke in a low voice. "They come from the future, Rod."

"Sure they do," said Rodney. He did not sound convinced.

"But they've got this… phone," said Lilith, examining Nevada's phone with fascinated awe.

"Which doesn't work," said Rodney.

"But our phones don't work either," said Lilith. "Fair is fair." And then she added thoughtfully, "Perhaps we've driven through a time warp."

"Just so long as the rave is still on," said the ever-practical Rodney.

"Can I have my phone back?" said my equally practical sweetheart.

"Oh yes, of course," said Lilith, and hastily handed the phone back to Nevada. She seemed simultaneously reluctant to let go of it and relieved to be rid of it.

Like I say, Oscar-worthy.

"So, you're from the future?" said Rodney finally.

"Yes," I said, both wearily and warily. If Lilith could simultaneously project two emotions, I felt that the least I could do was compete.

"You don't happen to have a list of Grand National winners, do you?" said Rodney. "Assuming you still have horse races in the future?"

"No, sorry," said Nevada.

"No horse races or no list?"

"No list," said Nevada.

"Of course not," said Rodney. "Pity, though." Then, with admirable tolerance, he added, "If you are from the future, you've come back in time for a great rave."

"Yes, you have," said Lilith eagerly.

"If my phone was working, I could give you a list of Grand National winners," said Tinkler.

"Of course you could, mate," said Rodney. "Well, let us know if you do get a signal."

"I will," said Tinkler helpfully. He sounded sincere and it was hard to say how much he was buying into this and how much was just playing along or perhaps even cruel mockery. "I'll tell you what I do have, though."

"Oh yeah?"

"I have some *drugs from the future*."

"Oh right, well now you're talking, mate," said Rodney. "What have you got?"

"Some rather neatly rolled spliffs," said Tinkler.

"So they still have weed in the twenty-first century?" said Rodney.

"They have much better, much stronger weed," said Tinkler.

"All right," said Rodney happily. "You get started on the spaceman's spliff, Lil."

"Not a spaceman," said Tinkler modestly. "Just a time traveller. A chrono-naut, if you will."

"You get started on the chrono-naut's spliff," said Rodney, "then pass it to me all right, love?"

"Yes, Rod. Can we have a bit of music?"

"Of course, love," said Rodney and turned the radio on. Britney Spears began to sing "… Baby One More Time". I was just relieved it wasn't Prince singing "1999".

"Can we have the windows open?" I said.

"Of course," said Rodney. As he and Lilith cranked their windows open, he said, "And you can open the sunroof in the back if you don't mind the draught."

"Don't mind my friend," said Tinkler, lighting his joint. "He's unusual in the future. Everyone else takes drugs. Lots of drugs."

"Nothing changes, then," said Rodney over the roar of air through the windows and the music on the radio.

Tinkler took a hit on his joint, offered it to both Agatha and Nevada, who declined, then he offered it to me satirically and finally passed it to Lilith, who said, "Thank you very much," and proceeded to suck on it enthusiastically. "This is really good puff, Rod," she said. "You should try it."

"I will if you'll leave any for me."

"Here you go." Lilith passed him the joint, which he took a mercifully brief hit from before passing it back. I prefer my drivers unstoned, given the choice.

The radio was now playing "Chocolate Salty Balls" by Chef from *South Park*, aka Isaac Hayes. This then gave way to a news bulletin of appropriate 1999 vintage. But unlike news bulletins in 1999, and indeed now, it wasn't being "broadcast" at the hour or half hour, but at a random time in between. However, it seemed churlish to point this out when someone had obviously gone to so much effort.

Maybe Rodney realised this because he abruptly turned the radio off.

"Why did you turn it off?" said Lilith. She didn't sound too bothered, though. I imagine after the amount of Tinkler's cannabis she'd inhaled that she wouldn't be too bothered about anything.

"Listen," said Rodney.

And then we heard it.

A powerful thumping in the distance.

"Here we go," he said.

14: RAVE

We turned off the main road onto a side road that led us onto a winding path through the forest. Then the trees on either side of us thinned out to be replaced by fields. All at once, we came around a curve and saw it: a gathering of cars and people in the field to our right. Numbers were hard to estimate with that milling mass in the darkness, revealed by random and dramatic spasms of coloured strobe lights, but my guess was at least a hundred ravers were present.

It had cost someone a great deal of exertion to set this up.

I wondered if everyone present would adamantly swear the year was 1999.

Besides the people and the cars, I saw some small tents, a bouncy castle… and a flying saucer.

It was either the same one from the back garden of Noise Floor or an identical model. And its presence here was somehow reassuring. We seemed to be making progress in our quest to find the wandering Lamb.

Music was blaring from two giant speakers and people were dancing all around, although they seemed to be mostly clustered in the area between and behind the speakers. And as we drew nearer, I saw there was a man standing there bent over turntables and other equipment set up on a folding table. He had long hair and was whipping it around, throwing his head back and forth and dancing like a dervish. It made my neck ache just to watch him. But watch him I did, because he looked startlingly familiar.

"He's here," said Rodney. He was trying for hushed awe in his voice, but the volume of the music meant he had to virtually shout. "He's here, Lil."

Lilith turned to us, beaming, and said, "It's Imperium Dart."

It certainly looked like Imperium Dart. But unfortunately not the Imperium Dart we were searching for, but rather the way he would have looked about a quarter of a century ago. Someone had gone to a lot of trouble to source a lookalike.

But then someone had gone to a lot of trouble all around.

Rodney drove into the field, carefully steering around some dancers who seemed oblivious of his approach, then slowed to a halt, cut the engine and headlights, and scrupulously applied the handbrake. He turned to look at us sitting in the back of his van. His excitement seemed unfeigned. "Welcome, visitors from the future," he said. "Come on, Lil."

They opened their doors and hopped out, running off hand in hand and leaving us visitors from the future sitting in the back of a Volkswagen camper van with luminous owls painted on it, in a dark field full of dancing strangers. It's true that we'd been in a lot worse situations over the years. Nevertheless, none of us were in a hurry to join the party.

"Well, shall we get out?" said Nevada.

"I wish I had some earplugs," said Agatha, as the music rattled the windows of our vehicle.

I was about to heartily endorse this sentiment when Tinkler cleared his throat in a meaningful way and held out three small transparent plastic packets, each containing a pair of bright yellow foam earplugs. He already had his own pair jutting out of his ears. We accepted them gratefully.

"And I'm supposed to be the stoned, irresponsible one," he said.

"No one ever said that," said Agatha.

"But you think it," said Tinkler.

"And you're reading our thoughts now," said Agatha.

"I come from the future," said Tinkler. "I have many special powers."

Tinkler actually did manifest an impressive power later on—the power of observation. But Agatha was the first to score points in this area. After we climbed out of the Volkswagen, she did a quick and thorough but impressively casual and innocent-seeming reconnaissance of the other vehicles parked around the field, and came back to give us a confidential report.

A confidential report under these circumstances—thunderous electronic music plus foam earplugs—consisted of shouting, but shouting in a private and intimate kind of way. "Everyone has got tax discs for the appropriate year."

"Full marks," said—or shouted—Nevada.

"Not quite. Virtually no one has got the corresponding licence number on them for their vehicle. Right year, wrong licence numbers."

It seems we'd discovered the time-warp ravers' Achilles heel. Agatha delivered her news with a kind of strange regret. Which I could fully understand because I was also oddly disappointed that we'd found them out.

I suppose this meant that, on some level, I actually wanted it all to be true.

I wanted magic to be real.

And I was the hardcore rationalist in our little group.

Tinkler's discovery came perhaps an hour later, by which time we'd all abandoned any pretence of trying to remain aloof or disinterestedly analyse the situation. In fact, we'd all started dancing. Imperium Dart's searing, high-speed techno certainly lent itself to this activity, pounding out in a rhythm considerably north of a hundred beats per minute. Despite thankfully not being dosed with psychedelics this time, I found it getting under my skin in a way the music at the Brixton gig hadn't. No disrespect to the Hartnoll brothers or Dominic Glynn. Maybe I was finding it more compelling because I *hadn't* been dosed with psychedelics.

Or maybe it was the sense of occasion. Being in the middle of a field, in the middle of a forest, in the middle of the night, at an illegal party with scores of happily hedonistic strangers, who seemed to be uninhibitedly and honestly having the time of their lives. We saw Lilith and Rodney throwing their dreadlocks around in a whirling, lashing frenzy that kept their fellow ravers at a wary distance—so as to avoid dreadlock flagellation injuries.

We were all dancing, too. I was dancing very badly, I suppose, but I didn't much care. Nevada's dancing was much better than mine, and Agatha's in turn was much better than hers. Indeed, she soon acquired a circle of admiring acolytes, and I don't think this was in any way a put-up job. As Nevada remarked, "That girl can dance." At the fringes of the admiring acolytes was the most ardently admiring one of all, Tinkler of course. Though he was doing a remarkably good job of not appearing to be fixated on Agatha, but rather seeming to be coolly doing his own thing. Which was dancing with such frenetic lack of inhibition— not to mention any discernible rhythm—plus such evident joy that he soon acquired a couple of acolytes of his own.

There was no denying it, it was an intoxicating experience.

And, underlying it all, there was the realisation that this whole enormous enterprise had been laid on purely for our benefit.

Or, at the very least, we were the guests of honour.

I tried to get a good look at our DJ, the guy who was pretending to be the young Lambert Ramkin. But I could only get near enough to confirm beyond doubt that it wasn't the *old* Lambert Ramkin in disguise. He not only would have had to shed an unfeasible quantity of middle-aged adipose tissue, he would have also required some considerable cosmetic surgery.

Because the guy operating the decks was incontrovertibly young.

What he *wasn't*, as Tinkler discovered, was actually operating the decks.

Tinkler came and found me, and wordlessly—which was much the best way to do anything under the current sound conditions—led me to look at something in the grass. The something was a group of dark cables that snaked away from the DJ's table towards the giant speakers, which stood like neolithic monoliths in this rural field, kicking out music that was anything but neolithic.

The speakers were as big as the horn-loaded specimen Tinkler had once bought and had delivered to our house. Indeed, bigger. And, as we approached them, the noise level became almost a physical force, like walking into a strong wind. We had to hold our hands cupped over our earplugs. Fortunately, what Tinkler wanted to show me wasn't in front of the speakers, in the blast zone, so to speak.

It was behind the speakers. Tinkler crouched there and silently—it was the only option—pointed to the cables we'd just traced from the DJ's table.

They ran all the way to the speakers, all right.

But they weren't connected.

Their copper terminators just gleamed there in the dark, dewy grass.

There were cables connected to the speakers, though. They snaked away in the darkness… towards the flying saucer. Tinkler was looking at me with a sardonic grin, and he nodded at me and I nodded back.

We walked, or rather danced, towards the flying saucer. But this was even more difficult to get close to than the

DJ table. There was a large group of dedicated dancers all around the legs of the saucer, and dancing under its elevated body. This was all understandable enough, because it was a very cool artefact, rendered even cooler by the dedicated light show someone had set up for it, which at times made it splendidly eerie and, yes, alien.

But I suspected that a lot of the surrounding crowd were there to make sure that certain people—like myself and my crew—didn't get too close. And, above all, didn't actually get inside the saucer. Indeed, there was a particularly hefty-looking bloke sitting on the bottom rung of the ladder that led up to the main body of the UFO, smoking a large joint. Despite the sitting and smoking, he looked for all the world like a bouncer who was there to keep unauthorised people out of the VIP area.

Or, in this case, out of the alien spaceship where the real Imperium Dart was actually playing the music.

We found Nevada and Agatha, and conveyed Tinkler's discovery to them. We stood there looking at the flying saucer, flickering and gleaming in its personalised light show on the other side of the field, and felt the frustration of being so close to our goal, but unable to get any closer.

And so we decided to bide our time. It didn't seem too much to ask for a crowd of blissed-out ravers high on a wide assortment of chemicals to have a moment of inattention. I had the strong feeling that, as dawn approached, the concentration of that crowd of dancers and even the bouncer at the foot of the ladder might lapse. And the latter person seemed to be the only one performing the function of sentinel. Surely at some point he would have to take a break, go to the loo…

I was confident we would get our chance. To invade the space invader.

But it was not to be.

About ninety minutes later, the music developed a sudden and dramatic new sound. But it wasn't coming from the direction of the speakers, it was coming from the road. And the light show was suddenly supplemented by flashing blue lights from the same direction.

That was when the penny dropped. Suddenly we could identify the new sound, buried under the music but getting inexorably louder, as a police siren.

Rodney and Lilith came running towards us, hand in hand, dreadlocks swinging frantically. "Come on, the cops!"

We could hear their voices clearly because the music had now suddenly ceased. The sirens were getting louder and people were scattering in all directions.

We turned and ran with Rod and Lil. By the time we got to the Volkswagen, many of the other vehicles were already on the move. We all jumped into the van and Rod started the motor. He was laughing happily, though, like a child playing a game.

Which I suppose was accurate. Not the bit about being a child. But it was all definitely a game. A fact that was reinforced when we drove off down the road at speed and didn't meet any police vehicles coming towards us. Nevada was looking at me with an ironic smile. She'd spotted this, too.

Amazing what you can do with some blue lights and a siren.

And a crowd of people cued to feign panic and flee. Stampedes are by definition infectious, and they'd actually done quite a brilliant job of fooling us.

And getting rid of us.

I wondered if, after we left, everyone else would go back and resume their partying. I hoped so. It seemed a waste not to.

And I had the strongest hunch that Imperium Dart himself would emerge from the saucer and take over the DJ table for real. I felt a pang of frustration and turned to look back at the field disappearing behind us. I thought I saw the light show starting again and heard the music begin. Nevada was looking back, too. She took my hand.

"We did what we could," she said in a low voice.

I took my earplugs out and felt that odd sensation of returning to the world again. I heard the sound of the motor and the buzz of our tyres on the road, the excited breathing of my companions, and Nevada saying, "We couldn't have done much more."

"Well," announced Rodney loudly from the front of the van, "that was fun while it lasted."

"It certainly was," said Nevada.

"Is it all right if we drop you off by your car?"

"Yes please."

By the time we reached the stretch of road where we'd left Tinkler's car, the sky was turning from black to dark blue and there was a faint mauve gleam in the east, which promised dawn. "Sorry we can't take you with us," said Rodney. "Isn't that right, Lil? Oh…" He dropped his voice. "Lil's gone to sleep."

"That's fine," said Nevada. "We'll be fine." She also dropped her voice in respect for the snoozing Lilith.

But, as soon as we stopped the vehicle, Lilith woke up, blinking but chipper, and said, "Are they off then, Rod?" She blinked at us. "Are you off then?"

"Yes, thank you for everything," said Agatha politely, as though we were leaving a dinner party.

"Give our regards to the twenty-first century," said Lilith.

"We will."

"Nice puff, spaceman," added Rodney.

"Always a pleasure," said Tinkler. "Drop by in a couple of decades and we'll do it again."

It was cold outside the van and we all shivered. We had the sweat from dancing and fleeing from imaginary police still on us to chill our skins. And there was that sudden drop of temperature you sometimes get just before sunrise.

But a lot of it was just seeing our ride drive away, Rodney and Lilith in their owl-painted van. It was a sight to make you feel cold and lonely, even with Lilith leaning out the window and waving until they disappeared around a bend.

"What now?" said Agatha, looking at the little red car.

"Well, how about that?" said Nevada, looking at her phone. "I've got a signal. I can call for a recovery vehicle."

"I've got a signal," said Tinkler. "I can call."

I looked at my phone. Of course, it was working too. As was Agatha's, which she was now inspecting with a rather cynical expression. "Don't anybody call for anything yet," she said firmly.

Then she got in the car and started the engine. She revved it and it roared happily and powerfully.

Agatha smiled at us. "To quote my friend," she said, "how about that?"

As we drove back to London, Nevada said, "If I wanted to stop some people using their mobile phones, there's plenty of tech to do it."

"Small enough to conceal in a car?" I said.

"Sure. The boot would have been the best place. When's the last time you looked in your boot, Tinkler?"

"Probably never," he said. "Should we look now?"

"No, I have a funny suspicion that anything that might once have been there will now be gone."

"A device in the car," I said, "and then one in Rodney and Lilith's van."

"I reckon so," said Nevada.

"And at the rave?" said Agatha. "I checked my phone a whole bunch of times and no dice."

"That would be the easiest of all. You'd be able to block the signals for everyone in a small area like that field with just a single device. Maybe the same one Rodney and Lilith were using."

"You know what?" said Tinkler. "I really don't like the word 'device'."

"It's a useful word, though, Tinkler," said Agatha. "I imagine it applies to whatever they put in your engine to cut the power. I'd love to know how they did that so suddenly. It just died on me. Maybe a combination of something electrical and something on the exhaust…"

"Somebody just pushed a button and made it happen," I said.

"That's right," said Nevada. "At a prearranged spot…"

"Where Rodney and Lilith could happen along, driving out of 1999 to rescue us," I said.

"And where a big fucking owl could come swooping down on us," said Tinkler.

"Yes," said Nevada. "That part is a bit strange."

"You think?"

"No sarcasm please, Tinkler. It's very late and we all need our sleep."

15: CURTAINS

Three days later we'd caught up on our sleep and got over what Tinkler had taken to calling our episode of temporal dislocation, and the four of us were meeting up again...

At Tabloid Tim's house.

This was the appointment we'd booked when we'd received his phone call in the parking lot of the Zobole Marine Hotel in Aberystwyth. Tim had seemed genuinely disappointed by our near miss with Lambert on that occasion, and quite determined to come good for us. He'd promised he'd come up with another lead.

And he'd characteristically insisted on another meeting in person, late this afternoon, at his house.

He'd also, of course, insisted on us bringing Agatha along, despite the charade we'd conducted last time—quite a convincing charade, I thought—of her being in a relationship with Tinkler. Of all people.

"Why does he always insist on us coming to his house?"

said Tinkler, who, like last time, was driving us down to Surrey to rendezvous with Agatha there.

"He thinks certain people will be impressed, go weak at the knees and tumble into bed with him," said Nevada.

"By certain people, you mean Agatha?" said Tinkler.

"And myself, of course," said Nevada. "My pretty little self."

"You'll tumble into bed with him because you see his *house*?" said Tinkler.

"It is a very nice house," said Nevada, giving me a mischievous look.

As before, Agatha was waiting for us when we drove up the low hill onto the concrete parking area. I hoped Tim wouldn't notice that the lovebirds kept arriving separately.

Actually, it didn't look like Tim could have noticed much at all today because the curtains were drawn in his glass house, turning it from a pair of transparent boxes into something that resembled a conventional domicile with opaque walls. "I hope he's at home," said Nevada, peering out the windscreen. The house looked empty and deserted. But then it had last time, too.

Reassuringly, as soon as we got out of the car, we heard music playing inside. "It's definitely Vivaldi this time," said Nevada. "Hello, Agatha."

"Hi," said Agatha. "Hello, lover."

This last was directed at Tinkler, who straightened up perceptibly at the words. "Greetings, darling," he said. "I hope Tabloid Tim takes his trousers off this time."

"Why?"

207

"Because then we can hold hands."

We walked across the cactus garden and the patio to the house which, as last time, featured a door that gaped wide open, although a curtain was now licking at the edge of it, dancing in and out with the wind.

As before, we paused on the threshold and shouted hellos, trying to make ourselves heard over the music. Also, as before, once a decent interval was deemed to have elapsed, we went inside.

But unlike before, we didn't find Tabloid Tim sitting at the table in the breakfast room. His chair was positioned at the table, but there were no tea things set out this time, and no sign of our host.

We called out again and waited for a moment. But waiting for a reply from Tim was a proven waste of time, so we walked through into the next room, which was the kitchen. This was modern and well-equipped, but devoid of human life. We hesitated a moment before going deeper into the house, but we'd come this far and there didn't seem anything else to do.

I think we all felt the transgressive thrill of prowling uninvited around someone's home, of exploring their private life, balanced by a wariness that he might be lurking in concealment somewhere and spring out at us at any moment.

It seemed like the sort of thing that might amuse Tim.

The next room was a sumptuous, you might say sybaritic, bathroom with a sunken bath and a large shower stall. Both seemed foolishly big for such a small man. When

I remarked on this, Agatha said, "They're probably built to be orgy-friendly."

"Do you think he's ever had any?" said Tinkler. "Friendly orgies?"

"I doubt it," said Nevada. "And you might like to keep your voice down. Because he could be in the next room."

"You're the one who said he hadn't had any orgies," said Tinkler. "You're the one who's dissing his orgy cred."

But Tim wasn't in the next room, which was the bedroom, and which was also orgy-friendly with a very large bed and a mirrored ceiling. In the next room, there was a rather anticlimactic—so to speak—utility area with a washer and dryer and a bicycle that looked as if it had never been used.

We had now come right through this wing of the house and arrived at the back door, which was open. But that didn't really signify anything, since the front door was also open. The back door led down some steps into a back yard somewhat smaller than the front. To our right was the garage, to our left another pebble-and-cactus garden. Directly ahead was a tiny patio area with some weight-lifting equipment on it and a canvas awning over it, for those occasions when you wanted to lift weights outdoors in the rain. It was sunny and drowsy and peacefully quiet except for birdsong that came from the trees of unseen neighbours, since there were no trees in Tim's own garden.

We went back inside the house, which was cool and silent. I realised the music had stopped. Presumably it had come to a natural conclusion, although I didn't rule out

Tim having snuck back in and switched it off. And I half expected him to be in the breakfast room waiting for us when we came back in.

But he wasn't.

"Now what do we do?" I said. I was on edge, suspended in a mood somewhere between irritation and anxiety.

"Give him ten minutes," suggested Nevada.

So we all took the chairs, which were once more ranked neatly against the wall, and grouped them around the table again, where we'd sat last time, as if this might ritually cause our host to appear.

It didn't.

After a couple of minutes Tinkler said, "Why don't we phone him?"

"Because that's his phone over there," said Nevada.

We all looked and, sure enough, on the ledge of the pass-through hatch into the kitchen, there was a mobile phone.

"Are you sure it's his?" said Tinkler.

"Looks like it," I said.

Tinkler rose from his chair and went to pick it up. "Don't touch it," said Nevada sharply. "Don't touch anything. Just sit down and wait. If you don't want to sit and wait in here, go outside and wait in the car."

"All right, all right. Don't be so grumpy," said Tinkler, sitting again. Nevada didn't say anything. We all felt the tension, though. And then we all felt the boredom.

In the end we gave him twenty minutes, sitting there, mostly in silence, and then decided to pack it in.

We went back out to our cars.

"Well, that was a royal waste of time," said Tinkler.

"Does anybody want a ride back with me?" said Agatha.

"Why would anybody choose your car over mine?" said Tinkler.

"My car wasn't recently riddled with sinister devices," said Agatha.

"That reminds me," said Nevada. "We never searched it."

"Yes we did," said Agatha. "After we dropped you off, post-rave. Tinkler and I had a look, and it was as clean as a whistle. In fact, rather too clean, considering it's Tinkler's car."

"I object to that insinuation," said Tinkler.

"Nothing under the bonnet or in the boot?" said Nevada.

"Nothing under the bonnet except a suspiciously clean engine," said Agatha.

"I clean my engine," said Tinkler. "Okay, I don't. Does anyone?"

"And nothing in the boot except a spare tyre that needs pumping up," said Agatha.

"That's all that's in there?" I said. "A spare tyre?"

"That needs pumping up… What is it?" Agatha was looking at me with some concern. So was everyone else.

I was looking at the back of Tinkler's car, where a small fold of transparent plastic was sticking out of the closed boot, as if a plastic bag had been put in there and the edge of it had got trapped when someone shut it.

Someone who wasn't Tinkler.

"There's something else in there now," I said.

I realised the others were standing beside me. We were all looking down at it. I knew I had to open the boot, and I did so slowly and carefully, as though it might explode.

It might as well have exploded.

I think we'd all been half expecting what we found. Somehow, sitting in that silent house, waiting for a person who didn't come, had planted the thought in our minds.

But that didn't diminish the horrid shock of it.

Stuffed into the small space in the boot of Tinkler's car, carefully wrapped in heavy plastic, was the body of Timothy Purshouse. He was clearly dead, his eyes open and looking blindly up at us. And in death he looked even smaller than he had in life. He was curled and crammed in an almost foetal position. It seemed cruel and disrespectful.

"Someone put him in there," said Tinkler. I don't think anyone was about to blame him for stating the obscenely obvious, in the trauma of the moment. But then he went on to say, "While we were in the house."

We looked at each other, everyone's face blank with shock, and realised he was right.

"What do we do?" said Tinkler. He sounded on the verge of tears. It was, after all, his car.

Nevada turned and walked away.

"Where's she going?" said Tinkler plaintively.

I had wondered that myself, for a fleeting instant before I'd put it together. "If someone put him in there," I said, "they might still be around."

"Oh, *shit*," said Tinkler, and he and Agatha instinctively moved closer together.

Nevada had disappeared around the side of the house. A moment later, she emerged again, circling around from the other side. "There was no one inside the house, right?" she said.

"There was no one inside the house," I agreed. The wing through which we'd entered was one large living room. Large and empty. And we had systematically searched the other wing from end to end.

"Well now I've looked outside too," said Nevada. "And there's no one outside. Not anymore. I looked in the garage as well."

I'd been trying not to turn my gaze on the thing in the boot, but I made myself do so. Timothy looked like a sad, lifeless animal. Crushed and abandoned. "He was dead when we arrived," I said.

"And someone put him in there while we were looking for him," said Agatha.

"Cool as a cucumber," said Nevada. She said it absently, as if deep in thought.

"Did they know we were coming?" said Agatha. "Were they expecting us?"

"Either that," I said, "or they got lucky."

"Lucky," said Tinkler with enormous distaste. Then he said, again, "What do we do?"

"There's only one thing we can do," said Agatha. She looked at us as if she was hoping she wouldn't have to say any more. But she did. "We have to call the police," she said.

I found I was nodding vigorously in response to this suggestion. "We have to get the police," I said.

"Look…" said Nevada.

"What do you mean, 'look'?" said Agatha.

"Let's call the police," said Tinkler, staring at the body.

"I really think we have to," I said.

"Listen to me," said Nevada. And she said it so fiercely we all fell silent and listened to her.

"We have to stop and think," she said. "Once we call the police, that is it. That is *it*. There's no going back. Our lives change forever."

We remained silent, staring at her. I'd seen Nevada in a lot of extreme situations, but I don't think I'd ever seen her radiating quite this level of serious intensity before.

"But we haven't done anything wrong," I said.

"The problem will be proving that, won't it? It's no accident that he's ended up in the back of our car. It's no accident that we're here. Someone is deliberately organising this. Someone has gone to a lot of trouble. They've given it a lot of thought."

Someone has gone to a lot of trouble. That sounded familiar.

I said, "And you think that calling the police…"

"Think about it. It's what we're most likely to do."

"That's because it's the smartest thing to do," said Agatha. "In fact, it's the only thing to do."

"It might also be exactly what they want us to do."

That gave us all pause.

"Someone's trying to set us up," said Nevada. She

nodded at poor Timothy Purshouse, lying there looking tiny and hunched in the boot of the car. "And that's just the bit we know about."

The skin on the back of my neck crawled when she said this.

"What are you suggesting we do, then?" said Agatha.

"Dump the body somewhere."

"*Dump it?*" said Agatha, her face twisted with disgust.

"Yes. Somewhere random, that has no connection with us."

Agatha's face had now set stubbornly. "That's a very bad idea."

"You don't have to be involved," said Nevada. "In fact, I strongly advise you not to be involved." She glanced at me. "The two of us can handle it."

Now Agatha really got angry. "We're supposed to be friends," she said.

"We are," said Nevada.

"I thought we were a team."

"We are."

"Then you're not doing this alone."

Nevada held her hands up, fingers spread out, in an I-give-up gesture. "All right, if you want to be in on this, you're in. But I don't advise it."

"Yes, I think you've got that across."

"Okay," said Nevada. "Tinkler, what about you?"

Tinkler looked at us. "Well, I'm sort of in it already. It's my car."

"I give up," said Nevada.

Agatha moved past her to look at Tim's body, curled in the boot, gift-wrapped in plastic. "Tinkler," she said, "where's your spare tyre?"

"Isn't it in there?"

"No. If it was, there wouldn't be room for him."

"They must have taken it out and dumped it," I said, looking around. "It could be around here…"

"We'll look for it," said Nevada decisively. "While we're doing that, if you two want to help, go into the house and find something to wrap him up in, for when we have to move him. A sheet or something. If it has his DNA on it, that's fine. But we don't want yours on it. So find some plastic shopping bags or bin bags or something, and put them over your hands like gloves or mittens when you handle the sheets. Can you do that for us, please?"

"Yes," said Agatha.

"Yes," said Tinkler.

"Thank you," said Nevada.

"You're welcome," said Agatha. Then she and Tinkler went into the house. I was oddly relieved that we were speaking politely to each other again.

Nevada closed the boot, hiding the body from view, and moved to open the door of the car. I turned and started off on a search of the garden.

"Where are you going?" she said instantly, from inside the car. She was bending forwards and leaning over the front seat.

"To look for the spare tyre."

"Fuck the spare tyre," she said. "Help me with this."

She had released the handbrake of the car and put the transmission in gear. Now she got me to help her push the car until it was at the point where the driveway began to descend. Then we both hopped inside. "Are you okay to drive?" she said.

"Yes," I said.

"Close the doors quietly."

We closed the doors quietly and sat in the car as it rolled downhill, powered only by gravity. A car with a corpse in the boot. It came to a stop as the driveway levelled out. "Okay, start the engine now and get the hell out of here."

I started the car and accelerated away from the house. My heart was beating fast and raggedly, and I was full of all sorts of emotions, not least a realisation that we'd just betrayed our closest friends.

I glanced over at Nevada, who was busy doing something on her phone. "You know that Agatha will be able to outrun us," I said. "She can certainly out-drive me. She will catch us."

"She will if she knows where we're going," said Nevada. "Does she know where we're going?"

"No." I didn't know where we're going.

"No," said Nevada. "Turn left here."

16: NIGHTFALL

We ended up driving into Kent, retracing our route of the other day, a million years ago, to the forest we'd seen outside of Nutalich. Something about its vast medieval darkness had impressed itself on our minds. It seemed so big and dense and wild.

Just the place to dispose of a body.

It was getting dark by the time we drove back to London. I was intensely glad it hadn't been dark earlier.

We hadn't buried him. The less we interacted with him the better.

Also, we weren't trying to avoid him being found. We just didn't want him found in our possession.

So we had simply carried him a certain distance into the woods and rolled him onto the ground. On our way there, we'd stopped at a chemists and bought some disposable latex gloves for cash then picked up a scrap of carpet we'd seen jutting out of a heap of junk in a skip—sadly such resources were all too readily available—and we'd used this to handle him, rolling him up in the carpet, in his plastic wrapper, taking care never to touch him directly, even with our gloves.

We brought the scrap of carpet back with us and detoured to the skip and put the carpet back exactly where we'd found it. This action had an oddly satisfying symmetry to it and, more importantly, it removed any chance of connecting the carpet with the body in the woods. As we drove back through London, we disposed of the disposable gloves in a random litter bin.

It was fully night by the time we were driving down familiar streets, approaching our home.

The usual glad warmth of homecoming that I should be feeling about now was utterly absent. I wondered if I would ever feel it again. Nevada and I had been driving in silence for a long time. That was very unlike us. I wondered if that was the way it was going to be from now on.

I parked under a streetlight outside our house in the little road that ran between our estate and the Abbey. I switched off the engine. And we sat there listening to the sound of it cooling, the hot metal clicking and shrinking, small random sounds that fell loudly into the gulf of silence between us. We were both too weary and too numb to want to move.

But we had to move.

And there was something I had to say. I turned to look at Nevada. She was looking at me, her beautiful face pale and silent.

"I can't bear to think of him lying out there," I said. I'd been thinking about this all the way back. It had got worse when night began to fall, the thought of him being all alone there in the dark woods, where we'd left him.

Nevada was looking at me gravely.

"I think we have to tell the police," I said.

"Let's go inside," she said, softly and gently. "And talk about it."

I knew that tone of voice. "You're not going to talk me out of this," I said.

"Love," she said, taking my hand. "It's what they want us to do."

"No," I said. "It's what I want us to do."

I pulled my hand free of hers.

We got out of the car and locked it, then walked the short distance to our garden gate and unlocked that. I went through the gate first, stopping myself just in time.

I didn't want to break the spider's web.

It was such a tiny thing, but somehow, right now, tiny things seemed terribly important.

Only the web was gone.

It had already been broken.

Nevada followed me through the gate and halted, her way blocked by me standing there motionless. I showed her what had happened. "We haven't had a storm, have we?" I said. "Up here in London while we were away?"

"Everything's dry," said Nevada, looking around. "There hasn't been any rain. And anyway, spiderwebs are made to withstand wind and rain." She stopped looking around the garden and looked at me. "What they're not made to withstand…"

"Is someone walking through them," I said.

In an ugly echo of what we'd done at Tim's, we searched our own little house from end to end. All we found was Turk asleep on our bed. Not only was there no intruder lurking, we couldn't even find our other cat.

"She's probably out and about," said Nevada. "Maybe she was in the garden…"

"When someone came in, and she got spooked and fled," I said.

"Maybe," said Nevada. "But I'm sure she'll be all right. She'll come back when she's ready. She's a sensible girl."

We walked back into our living room.

"But we're certain someone was in our garden," I said.

"Someone broke that spiderweb," said Nevada. "It's far too high up for a cat to have done it."

"I know," I said. "So, someone was in the garden, but they didn't get into our house."

"No," said Nevada. "I don't think they could. That's a very good lock on the door." She went and looked at the lock.

"What were they doing here?" I said.

"I don't know," said Nevada. She suddenly sounded very tired. "Maybe they were looking for us. Maybe they were casing the place for a future visit." Neither of these possibilities were very reassuring. "We need to get one of those doorbells with a camera on it," said Nevada, turning away from the door.

"For the back garden?" I said. "Nobody comes in that way." But even as I said it, I realised someone had tried, tonight. Nevada didn't bother to point this out to me.

"We need cameras on both the fucking doors," she said.

She sank down on the sofa and I sat beside her. I couldn't remember the last time I'd felt so exhausted. But no sooner had we sat down than there was an energetic scratching sound from beneath us. Nevada looked at me and chuckled. "I think we've found our missing pussycat."

There were some further scrabbling sounds and then Fanny emerged from beneath the sofa. She was doing her routine where she lay on her back under a piece of furniture and moved around by a kind of swimming motion, using her paws on the underside of it. Now her face appeared, gazing seriously up at us.

She gave a small, imperative cry.

"We can't play with you just now, honey," said Nevada.

Fanny disappeared under the sofa again, for all the world as if she was ticked off at this response. "At the risk of quoting Tinkler," I said, "what do we do now?"

Before Nevada could reply, Fanny appeared once more, crying out to us.

Nevada reached down to caress her, and Fanny emerged from under the sofa, slithered around so she was upright and sat there staring up at us and calling out. She dodged away from Nevada's hand.

"What's the matter, baby?" said Nevada.

Fanny regarded us in disgust for a moment, gave a final

small cry, and then trotted through the cat flap and out into the garden. "Well, now we've been told," said Nevada.

It was very dark in the room, but somehow finding Fanny had lifted our mood and it felt like life could go on. I got up, went to the big floor lamp and turned it on.

Nothing. The light didn't come on.

I sighed and reached into the lamp and screwed the loose bulb back in tight, and light flooded the room. The bulb started to grow warm under my hand. I was looking at Nevada sitting on the sofa, looking at me. I didn't move. I was thinking. The bulb was starting to get hot under my hand. But I was still thinking.

"What's the matter?" said Nevada.

I took my hand out of the lamp and went back to join her on the sofa. "The bulb was loose," I said.

"I know," she said. I could tell she wanted to say, *So what?* But she didn't. She was waiting for me to say something else.

"Something hit the leg of the lamp," I said.

"I know," she said. Now she was gazing up at me seriously.

"No one came in through the door," I said, looking at the door to the garden. The door with the cat flap in it. "But what if someone—or rather, something—came in through the cat flap?"

"And hit the leg of the lamp?" said Nevada.

"Right," I said. "Say that someone shoved something through the cat flap, pushing it into the room using…"

"A broom handle or something," said Nevada.

"Yes," I said, looking at the door and calculating angles. "Draw a straight line from the cat flap past the lamp and it ends up…"

We looked at each other and then we both bent forward and looked under the sofa. There in the darkness on the floor at the back, against the wall, was a large plastic bag. Full of something…

We dragged the bag out.

What it was full of was pills.

There were hundreds of them. They were all different colours and shapes and embossed with different designs. There were smiley faces and love hearts and pills in the shapes of Rolls-Royce radiator badges and Bugatti emblems and Judge Dredd badges. There were space invaders and cartoon ghost shapes and imitations of popular biscuits and dominoes. Mickey Mouse faces and diamond shapes and pineapples and Superman emblems and hand grenades and round pills stamped with robots and skulls and aliens and doves and dolphins and the Playboy bunny.

There were actually thousands of them, I realised.

"Ecstasy is still a Class A drug isn't it?" said Nevada.

"As far as I know."

"And someone has very carefully planted these on us."

She weighed the bag of pills in her hand. "If we were caught with this we'd go to prison for a long, long time."

That was when the doorbell rang.

17: DOORBELL

"Shit," said Nevada in a searing whisper.

The doorbell rang again, peremptory and impatient.

It was one of those sickening moments when you wished with ferocious desperation that you could turn back the clock. I was lost for an instant in just that dizzying, passionate and utterly futile desire to reverse time…

To somehow claw our way back to the instant when we'd found the bag. That was when we should have taken action. Done something about our treacherous find, instead of just casually talking about it, as if we had all the time in the world.

The seconds had been running out for us and we hadn't known it.

We should have taken action then. But we'd lost our chance.

It was too late now.

Nevada turned and disappeared down the hallway with the bag. I had no idea where she was going or what she was going to do with it.

I was too keenly aware that the doorbell was ringing, again and again.

I went into the kitchen and peered out the window.

The sense of relief I felt was indescribable.

"It's all right," I shouted. My voice was strained and shaking, but I didn't care. "It's Tinkler and Agatha."

Nevada came back and joined me. The bag was gone. She looked like she'd taken a shower. It was only then I realised I was soaked with sweat too, the fresh perspiration of panic on top of the stale sweat of body disposal. The aura of fear was heavy in the room, the primal bitter scent of it overwhelming the modern niceties of deodorant and soap.

Nevada looked at me and said, "I can't take much more of this." She collapsed into my arms.

Outside the door Agatha shouted, "We know you're in there. We can hear you." Fists pounded on the door.

Nevada and I clung to each other for a brief, endless moment, feeling our hearts thumping towards each other in our chests as if echoing the pounding on the door. And then we let go and went to the door and unlocked it.

Agatha and Tinkler were standing outside and, as soon as we opened up, Agatha strode in, walking furiously past us and then turning to look at us. Tinkler entered more tentatively.

"You ditched us," said Agatha.

"You were best off out of it," said Nevada.

"That was not your decision to make," said Agatha.

"Well, I made it."

There was a tense, angry pause and then Agatha said, "What did you do with him?"

Nevada took a weary breath. "You're best not knowing."

"You're very good at deciding what's best for me," said Agatha.

She was staring hard at Nevada. I could sense their friendship, all our friendships, being stress-tested in this moment.

Tinkler clearly felt it too. "We think you should have gone to the police," he said. He spoke quietly, reasonably, trying to lower the emotional temperature in the room.

"So did I," I said.

Agatha gave me a sharp, ironic look. "You say 'did', past tense. But then she got you to drink her Kool-Aid?"

"No," I said. "I was on the same side as you, until just now. Until we found something."

Nevada was already on her way out of the room. She was back in a moment. "Until we found this," she said, holding up the bag of pills.

"Whoa," said Tinkler.

Agatha didn't say anything for a moment, but her expression softened from anger to surprise and then, swiftly, understanding. She looked at me. "Someone put that in here?"

I nodded. "We found it hidden under the sofa."

"It's a good thing you found it," said Agatha.

"How did they put it there?" said Tinkler.

"Through the cat flap," said Nevada. "Shoved it in with some kind of extendable rod or something."

Agatha bent forward to examine the bag and its multitudinous contents. "My god, there's so many of them…"

"Enough to put us behind bars for years," said Nevada. "And years and years."

Agatha gazed at the bag and then straightened up, shaking her head. "You were right. Putting the body in Tinkler's car was just the part of the plan we knew about."

"Yes."

Agatha was still staring at the bag. "There was this, too," she said.

"When do you think they planted it here?" said Tinkler.

"Any time after they left Tim's house," I said. "We've been gone most of the day, so they would have had a free hand. They got over the garden wall, put this through the flap in the door and shot it under the sofa…"

"The cats couldn't tell us about what had happened," said Nevada, "though, in fairness, Fanny was doing her level best."

"So, if we had called the police…" said Tinkler.

"They would have found this little lot in our house." Nevada set the bag down. "And that would have been that."

"But would the police have searched your house?" said Agatha.

"Absolutely," said Tinkler. "When they found a bag of pills at Tim's."

"Tinkler's right," said Nevada. "What if they also planted drugs at Tim's? A lot of them. That would make sense." She frowned, thinking it through. "I bet they did."

"No, they did," said Tinkler.

"What?" said Agatha.

Tinkler pointed at the bag of pills. "There was one like that at Tim's. Not quite as big, but still pretty damned big. It was in a cupboard with sheets and pillows and quilts and things." He gave Nevada a droll look. "I was going through it with a bin liner on my hands because you'd sent us on a wild goose chase. In my case, a wild goose-down duvet chase."

"You didn't tell me about that," said Agatha.

"Just at the moment I found it, you spotted that they were gone." Tinkler looked at us. "There then ensued a great deal of cursing directed at you."

"I'm not surprised," said Nevada.

Tinkler turned to Agatha. "And so I got distracted and it didn't seem important anymore, so I ended up not saying anything about it. I'm sorry."

"No, it's fine," said Agatha. She looked at us. "So the police would have searched Tim's house and found a shitload of drugs and then they would have looked here…"

"And found even more of them," I said.

"From the same batch," said Tinkler.

"Right," said Nevada. "Tying it all together. And then the whole thing begins to look drugs related."

"Drug related," said Agatha.

"Like we killed Tim in a dispute," said Nevada. "A drug gang, falling out."

There was a long silence.

"I guess it's just as well we didn't call the police," said Agatha, finally.

"That's what I said all along," said Tinkler.

* * *

We went into the living room, four old friends, weary but relaxed and somehow at peace.

At least with each other.

"Does anyone want some food?" I said. I was suddenly ravenous.

"I'm starving, actually," said Agatha.

"Need you ask?" said Tinkler.

"You shouldn't have to cook, love," said Nevada.

I appreciated her having my back, as always. But I said, "It's okay. We've got some mango tabbouleh in the fridge."

I served it up and Nevada poured wine, and then we were eating and drinking together, and everything was definitely mended between us.

"Did you find Tinkler's spare tyre?" said Nevada, between mouthfuls.

"Eventually," said Agatha.

"I never would have found it without her," said Tinkler, busily feeding himself.

It had turned out we were all famished. Although, of course, with Tinkler this was a permanent condition. "I was going to give up," he said, between mouthfuls. "I assumed they'd taken it with them. But Agatha insisted we keep looking."

"And where was it?"

"They'd put it in his garage, with Tim's car and his car stuff, so it looked like it was *his* spare tyre. I would never have known the difference, but Agatha did."

"Ingenious."

"Fiendishly ingenious."

After we finished eating, our friends decided to take their leave. It was getting late and it had been a long day for all of us. We walked them to Agatha's car, pausing on the way to dump the bag of the pills in a roadside litter bin.

"You're not going to just leave them there, are you?" said Agatha.

"Absolutely not," said Nevada.

"But we don't want them under our roof while we sort it out," I said.

Nevada and I had agreed on this. We had at least learned something from that desperate wish to turn the clock back when the doorbell rang.

We said our goodbyes, exchanging kisses and hugs, and Tinkler left with Agatha, too drunk to drive himself home. And besides, it might be a while before he felt comfortable driving his car, after what had been in the boot.

As we walked back past the bin where we'd put the pills, concealed under a pizza box, Nevada said, "What are we going to do with those?"

"I know just the man," I said.

Normally it would take at least four hours to drive to our place from Wales, taking the motorway all the way. But, at this time of night, hurtling along on a motorcycle, often no doubt at highly illegal speeds, Hughie Mackinaw effortlessly halved that time.

We hardly seemed to have put the phone down when we heard the engine of his bike echoing to a stop outside and then Hughie was knocking on our door. Nevada and I put on sweaters against the night chill—Hughie was warm enough in his biker leathers—and took him out to the bin. We all sat on a bench nearby, Hughie's motorcycle helmet perched beside us, as he examined the bag and its contents in the quiet light of a streetlamp, in the nocturnal silence of our estate.

Meanwhile, we kept a vigilant, not to say paranoid, watch. But there was no one else around.

Hughie whistled as he inspected the vast bundle of pills. "You don't do things by half measures, do you?"

"We don't do this kind of thing at all," said Nevada. "Which is why we thought of you."

"Well, I'm your man." He put the bag in the pannier on the back of his bike and sealed it shut.

I was surprised at the sense of liberation I felt as soon as he did this. "One thing, Hughie," I said.

"Oh yeah?" he said, giving me a wary look.

"Before you sell those on, you need to do some testing," I said.

"We don't want to get anybody killed by bad drugs," said Nevada.

"Where did you get them, then?" said Hughie, looking at the closed pannier with a mixture of suspicion and affection.

We felt we owed him the truth. "Someone planted them on us," I said.

He glanced around sharply. "They wanted you to get busted?"

"Relax," said Nevada. "There were other moving parts to the conspiracy before that was going to happen, and we've disrupted those."

Hughie grinned. "Never put more moving parts in than you absolutely have to." He said this with the conviction of a man who'd spent his life dealing with mechanical contrivances.

"But anyway," I said, "what all this means is that we have no idea of what is in those pills. So they need to be checked out before there's any question of anybody taking them."

"The way to do it," said Nevada, "is to take one of each different type of pill and have it tested separately…"

"Really?" said Hughie with wide-eyed innocence. "Is that the way to do it?"

"All right, sorry," I said.

"No need for sarcasm," said Nevada as Hughie continued his wide-eyed stare to the point of idiocy.

"We didn't mean to teach our grandmother to suck eggs," I said, and Hughie abandoned his bug-eyed act. "But what we can tell you, which you might find helpful, is the contact details of someone who can do the analysis for you."

"Is his name Tetlock by any chance?" said Hughie.

Nevada and I were struck dumb for a moment. Then she said, "How did you know that?"

"You're pals with Erik Makeloud, right? Well, Mr Tetlock is pals with him too, isn't he? And I know all about Mr Tetlock. Now," he said, pulling on his motorcycle gloves, "if you're finished doing your due diligence, I'll make tracks."

"Okay, thanks for helping us out."

He opened the pannier again and peered inside, perhaps making sure the drugs hadn't done a disappearing act. Then he gave us a strange look. "Are you sure you don't want any money for these?"

I looked at Nevada. I could see her struggling with her entrepreneurial nature. Finally she said, "No."

Hughie shrugged. "Okay." He sealed the pannier again and picked up his helmet from the bench where he'd left it.

"Wait," said Nevada abruptly.

Hughie turned back to us with a cynical smile.

"Make a donation to a charity," said Nevada.

The cynical smile changed to a genuine smile. "All right. Which one?"

"Cats Protection."

His smile broadened. "How much?"

"Whatever you would have paid us for the pills."

"Right you are."

He put on his helmet and climbed on the bike.

"Ride carefully, Hughie," I said.

"Always."

We watched as he accelerated away into the night, the sound of the powerful engine echoing off the walls of the Abbey and our own small garden.

18: WHISKERY MISCREANTS

The pills—assuming they were kosher, and safe and saleable—represented a windfall for Hughie, so it was perhaps unsurprising he didn't ask himself the obvious question. If Nevada and I didn't want to profit from them, why hadn't we just thrown them away?

Even being scrupulously safe about this, avoiding them accidentally being stumbled upon by the wrong people, for example children, or ending up in the environment, say in the water supply, was quite easily achievable.

But Hughie didn't ask the obvious question and I left him alone for a few days before I followed up with the phone call we'd planned.

He answered immediately and sounded jubilant. I didn't have to ask him for the results of testing the pills. He instantly volunteered it.

"They're from a variety of sources, all high potency, but all sweet as a nut. Impressive purity, said Mr Tetlock. Whoever bought them was a bit of a connoisseur."

"So, they're from different sources?" I said, as if this had never occurred to me.

"Well, obviously. The people who make the pills with the dolphins on are different from the ones with the aliens on, and they're different from the ones with the skulls. Obviously."

I waited to make sure that Hughie had finished telling me how obvious all this was. But while Hughie may be arrogant, he wasn't slow. "Are you thinking of trying to work out who planted them on you?"

"Full marks, Hughie," I said.

"You want to know who tried to fuck you over?"

"It would be nice," I said, and he chuckled. "So," I said, "while loads of people will be customers for any of those pill-makers, how many people will be a customer for *all* of them?"

There was a pause and then Hughie said, approvingly, "Okay, that's sneaky. And whoever bought from all of those pill-makers, that's your man."

Or woman, I thought. But I said, "That's right. Even if we narrow the list down to a few buyers, that would still be okay."

"I don't know," said Hughie. I could feel him starting to resist. "We're talking about illicit deals here. Nobody's going to reveal who their customers are."

"They might to someone they trust," I said. "They might to you."

There was a sudden silence on the line.

"I don't know," said Hughie finally.

"Listen, Hughie," I said. "This could be life or death."

"Whose life or death?"

I thought of Timothy Purshouse lying in a forest in Kent, all his arrogance and confidence ended forever. Whoever was playing games with us, one thing was clear. They wouldn't hesitate to kill.

"Ours," I said.

"You and your lady?"

"Yes."

There was another long pause as Hughie struggled with himself. Then he said, "Okay, I'll see what I can do."

"Thank you."

For a few days at least, Nevada and I had decided we'd had enough of the search for Lambert Ramkin. We'd put that whole manifestly dangerous project on hold and tried to resume our normal life, for a therapeutic spell.

One aspect of that normal life was our new Village of Vinyl project. Nevada set about preparing a website for the event, only to discover that the vicar, Dr Gerald "Call me Gerry" Blanchflower, had already made a start on exactly this.

On the one hand, Nevada was delighted by his enthusiasm. On the other, she had lots of differences of opinion with him about the design of the site. I left them to argue about banners, click-throughs and JavaScript and concentrated on my own task of emailing record dealers who might want to attend.

I agonised over whether to invite the invidious Mindy's but, in the end, I decided they were too large to ignore. And, anyway, this was supposed to be about business. I made a note to let Nevada contact them. After all, I was blacklisted.

With our weekend festival in Nutalich starting to look rather healthy, we turned to other matters.

Nevada had a side hustle, or maybe by now it was her main hustle, of selling vintage clothes. She did this largely through her website, which was called Whiskery Miscreants. The title was a historical legacy. She'd originally set it up to feature photos and videos and prose accounts of our cats, thinking she might be able to somehow monetise their antics. When that didn't pan out—much to Tinkler's mockery—she'd transitioned it into her second-hand clothes-selling site, retaining the same URL and domain name to save on costs. Ever the practical one, my darling.

"And it's a distinctive trade name," she said.

It was. And it was through this website that Nevada received a message from an Italian graduate student who was going home and didn't want the hassle of taking all the contents of his wardrobe with him. He sent some photos of the kinds of items he had for sale, and Nevada began to get quite excited.

Apparently, the graduate student had superb taste, and these were all clothes he'd brought with him from his home country. The thought of Italian designer labels danced in my sweetheart's head.

What's more, the graduate student was selling some women's clothing left behind by an ex-girlfriend, also Italian.

"I'll have to make sure she really did abandon them and doesn't want them back," said Nevada. "And this isn't some kind of elaborate, invidious revenge scenario."

"Selling his ex's clothes without her knowledge or permission, to get back at her," I said.

"Right, exactly. I'm going to have to quiz him closely about that."

"When you say quiz him closely…" I said.

"We're meeting in town today, at Soho House." Nevada gave me a mischievous smile. "He's offered to buy me lunch."

"You're not going to eat with him," I said. It was somewhere between a question and a statement. An anxious question and an angry statement.

"Don't worry," said Nevada. "After the Füd Wagn incident, I'm not accepting food from anybody. Except you, of course. I've told Silvio to forget about lunch. We're just meeting for drinks and I'm not going to drink anything that doesn't come in a sealed bottle which I open myself. In fact, just to be on the safe side, I may not drink anything at all. But what I *will* do is go through the clothes he's bringing along and make an offer." She saw the worried look on my face and said, "Look, I'm sure he's on the up and up. And the clothes look great. But if you don't want me to go, I just won't go. We might miss out on some nice items, but it's no big deal."

"No," I said, "that's all right. You go."

"I asked Silvio if you could come along, too, but he went distinctly cold at the suggestion. I think maybe he was afraid I was going to try and sting him for two lunches."

"No, that's okay," I said. "I'll stay home." I wasn't entirely happy with this arrangement. But the truth was, if there was any kind of trouble, no one could handle it better than Nevada. And, if I was along for the ride, I was likely to just be a liability, to get underfoot, and generally make it harder for her to get back *out* of trouble.

So she kissed my worried face and promised to phone frequently, and set off out into the big wide world.

She'd been gone about an hour when the doorbell rang.

I opened it to find a petite young woman standing there.

Quite an arresting petite young woman. She was dressed in a black-leather miniskirt and a very striking scarlet denim jacket, which had been hacked in half so it barely came down to her midriff. She was emphatically braless under a tubular black top that left her shoulders bare and exposed her navel, into which was set a ruby, or at least a small, red gemstone. There was a matching, smaller, red gem in one side of her pert little nose.

Under honey-blonde hair, scraped back from her forehead, she gazed at me through a pair of bright red sunglasses—red seemed to be a theme—with dark blue lenses.

She smiled at me shyly and said, "Are you the Vinyl Detective?"

I couldn't think what to say, except, "Yes."

She reached into the pocket of her fashionably hacked scarlet jeans jacket and took out a business card, which I recognised. Where the hell had she got hold of that? Those things hadn't been in circulation for years.

"I would like to hire you," she said. "In fact, I desperately need to hire you." She hooked a finger into her sunglasses and pulled them down so she could gaze at me directly and imploringly.

Suddenly I recognised those eyes, though I'd hardly ever seen them open.

Indeed, I recognised her face now.

I probably would have even recognised her breasts, since I'd seen them recently in a hotel in Wales.

"My name is Fiona Taggert," said Cayley Butterworth.

The blonde hair had thrown me off, but either it was a wig or a supremely good dye job that concealed her natural carrot-coloured tresses. There was no mistaking her, though. I repressed the urge to ask how she was feeling after sleeping off her recent binge.

"I need your help," said "Fiona", aka Cayley.

"Listen," I said, trying to find the firmest and fastest—and I must admit, gentlest—way to shut her down. But she ploughed gamely ahead with her no doubt carefully prepared speech.

"I'm buying a rare record for my brother's birthday and I need your help." She had taken her sunglasses completely off now, the better to gaze at me with her entreating hazel eyes. Other adjectives to describe them would include insincere, dishonest and, more bluntly, lying.

"I really am very—" I began to say.

Cayley rushed on. "My brother is just mad about jazz, and we've found this record he's been after all his life. It's the record he wants most in the world."

It's shameful to admit, but I found myself asking, "Which record?"

"Well, it's by Hank Mobley. He's a saxophone player."

He certainly is, I thought.

"And it's on a label called Blue Note."

By this time, I discovered, to my appalled horror, that I was starting to find myself drawn into her little story.

"And it doesn't have a name," she said. "I mean the album doesn't have a title. It just has a number. And I keep forgetting the number…" She gave me an embarrassed little smile and an appealing flutter of the eyelashes.

To my eternal discredit, I actually did find it appealing, although one part of me was standing beside me, so to speak, shouting at me to snap out of it.

"It's fifteen something," said Cayley.

"Fifteen sixty-eight," I said. "Blue Note 1568."

"Yes!" Cayley looked at me as though I'd just saved a child from drowning. "That's right. I knew you'd know. You *are* the man we need for this job. You're the only one who can help us."

Her non-existent brother—I was quite sure that her serious-minded and now somewhat bruised *real* brother Abraham had nothing to do with this charming scheme; for a start, he would undoubtedly have told Cayley that, as far as I was concerned, her cover would be blown before she even began—anyway, her purely imaginary brother had great taste in valuable vintage jazz LPs.

Mobley 1568, as it was known to collectors, was the holy grail of the genre. To say that I wanted a copy myself would have been putting it mildly.

"Here it is," said Cayley, holding up her phone to show me a confirmatory picture of the cover with its black-and-white photograph of the tenor supremo looking strangely insectoid in dark glasses with his horn to his face.

I could almost feel the hook going in…

On the other hand, there was an element of overreach here. Someone could have, and probably had, just googled "rarest jazz album" and come up with this.

"Can we please go inside to discuss it?" said Cayley, glancing over my shoulder at the interior of our house. She gave a playful shiver. "I'm a bit cold standing out here like this."

This was probably true, given how she was dressed, or rather how little she was dressed.

A duplicitous, glamorous woman standing on my doorstep, holding my business card and trying to enlist my help in finding a record which didn't even exist…

I was beginning to experience a dizzying sense of déjà vu. Cayley and whoever had sent her couldn't have known it, but this situation was a virtual replica, you might even say parody, of how I'd first met Nevada.

Realising that, and thinking of Nevada, gave me the impetus to say, "Look, I'm really sorry, but I'm just too busy to take on any other work at the moment. I simply don't have the time to look for the record for you."

"Oh, you don't have to *look* for it for us," said Cayley quickly. "We've already *found* it. We just need you to authenticate it, make sure it's an original. If it's an original, then it will be a something-or-other version. Three initials…"

"RVG," I said. For Rudy Van Gelder, who had engineered the recording.

"That's right!" Now she was looking at me as though I'd saved a child from a burning building. "And then we need you to inspect it to make sure it's in good condition and worth the money they're asking." She gave me a little conspiratorial smile. "And perhaps you can beat them down a bit on their asking price. We'd like you to negotiate on our behalf. Of course, we'll be paying you a commission. We'll pay you whatever you want. May I come inside, please?"

I was beginning to feel like a punch-drunk boxer. How much longer could I stand up against this onslaught? They were pressing all my buttons.

Cayley was saying, "You see, it's my brother's twenty-first birthday coming up and the whole family has chipped in to buy him something really special that he really wants. But it amounts to thousands and thousands of pounds for this record, and we want to make sure it's the real thing." She said all this while looking at me with the utmost sincerity in her eyes. "You know, authentic."

The word "authentic" was a bad choice by her, as it helped break the spell. Because this young woman and her errand were anything but. Authentic, I mean.

Now Cayley looked past my ear at something and smiled. I didn't need to turn around to see what it was because, just then, behind me, Fanny made a small, puzzled sound: Why is the front door open? Who is this stranger? Why aren't I being fed, indeed overfed?

"What a beautiful cat," said Cayley, with evident sincerity. "May I come in and say hello to her?"

It was so hard to say no. Like the (no doubt imaginary) rare jazz record, using my cat was such an accurate targeting of my susceptibilities that I could hardly resist.

But I did, astonishing myself by saying, "Sorry, no."

The look of bewildered hurt on Cayley's face, possibly unfeigned, pinched my heart. I decided it was time to put our cards on the table.

"Actually, we've met before," I said.

She shook her head. "No, I'm sure I would have remembered." She was rallying again and managed a bright little smile.

You might have remembered, I thought, if you hadn't been hideously, drunkenly comatose. What I said—before she could launch another charm onslaught—was, "Listen, Cayley."

She blinked with shock at the sound of her real name.

"We met at the Zobole Hotel in Aberystwyth," I said. "We were the couple who tried to stop your brother taking you home because we thought he was kidnapping you." I emphasised the word "couple".

The change that came over Cayley was instantaneous and impressive. She blinked again, gave a businesslike little nod, as though confirming something, then without another word simply turned and began striding away at considerable speed.

"Say hi to Lambert," I called after her. And then I wished I hadn't because the words caused her shoulders to hunch as if I'd delivered a blow. I watched her hurrying away, making very good time for someone in high heels, and then I went out and closed the gate, which she had rather inconsiderately left open.

Going back inside, I closed the door firmly behind me, then fed Fanny, who seemed as bemused by our recent visitor as I was, but nevertheless dined with gusto as I tried to sort out my thoughts and feelings.

Some distant, treacherous corner of my mind was emanating regret that I hadn't invited Cayley in. But my main reaction, overwhelmingly, was relief. Coupled with an anxious realisation that, however much we might want to leave the Lambert Ramkin investigation alone, it wouldn't necessarily leave us alone.

My relief about sending Cayley packing—not admittedly unmixed with guilt and disappointment—was both profound and short-lived.

I had been thinking of what Agatha had said about the scenarios, which Lambert Ramkin stage-managed... "Particularly with an erotic element." And I don't believe I was just imagining things or indulging in reprehensible wishful thinking when I speculated on what might have happened had I allowed Cayley, the pint-sized seductress, through our front door and into our home...

To say that she had been provocatively dressed would have been to put it conservatively. And it didn't seem too far-fetched to describe what had just almost happened as a honeytrap.

A very carefully prepared honeytrap. I thought of the

business card she had been carrying, the choice of the Mobley album—they had done their homework.

And it had very nearly worked. If I hadn't recognised Cayley from our previous one-sided encounter, I dread to think what might have happened. Indeed, it had come dangerously close to happening anyway; I was amazed I'd managed to dodge the bullet.

I speculated on what someone else might have done in such a situation… and for some reason I thought of Tabloid Tim, licking his lips in his hairy little face.

His very dead little face.

And that was when the thought hit me with absolute icy force. What if sex hadn't been what they'd had in mind, whoever had organised that little encounter?

What if they'd planned something much more lethal for me?

Cayley the pint-sized assassin, rather than seductress?

On the face of it, it seemed absurd.

But there was the stone-hard fact that someone had killed Tim. And there was no way he wouldn't have invited Cayley, or someone like her, inside if she'd come knocking…

And then I spotted the obvious, crucial complication in all this. Whatever they'd had in mind for me, sex or death, for it to work I would have to be alone. There was no chance of success if Nevada was here with me..

Was it just blind luck that they'd happen to choose a time when she was safely—from their point of view—out of the house for a few hours?

Given the unerringly accuracy of the rest of their masquerade, that hardly seemed likely. Which meant they *knew* she was gone. But how could they know that? Yes, they could have us under surveillance, but I realised with a horrible sick certitude that there was a much better way to guarantee she was somewhere else.

I couldn't believe it had taken me this long to put it together.

I had my phone in my hand with no conscious memory of having picked it up and I was calling Nevada's number, consumed with cold, churning fear.

There was an endless minute or two while the phone rang and rang and rang. Then the call connected. "Almost home," said Nevada, before I could say anything.

"Is everything all right?"

"Better than all right. See you in a minute."

It was actually more like ten minutes, and I'm glad it wasn't any longer because my nerves were seriously frayed by the time I heard her key in the door. Nevada let herself in, slipped off her shoes, and came and gave me a hug.

She looked singularly pleased with herself and I had a terrible plunging realisation that there was a possible explanation for this, which arose logically from what had just happened, or almost happened, to me.

Why deploy just one honeytrap when you could go for a double?

So I sat Nevada down on the sofa in our living room and sat beside her and told her exactly what had happened with Cayley. The way she started to grin was a tremendous relief to me. "So, you sent her off with her tail between her legs, did you?"

"They're only short little legs," I said.

"What a boringly settled couple we are," said Nevada. And then she proceeded to give me her account of her close encounter with Silvio.

"He's Italian, at least that much was true. And devilishly handsome. A professional model."

"I thought he was a graduate student?" I said.

"He claimed he did modelling when he wasn't doing his studies. The modelling part was also true. He insisted on showing me pictures of his underwear shoot. Nice abs." Nevada was smiling and holding my hand as she talked. Which served to take the sting out of her story, or at least some of the sting.

"Now, Soho House is a *hotel* as well as a club," said Nevada. "And, of course, it just so happened that good old Silvio…"

"Not-so-good old Silvio," I said.

"…had booked a room upstairs. Which he invited me up to. Quite unambiguously to bounce around on the bed for a while."

"But you didn't go," I said.

"Oh no, I went upstairs with him."

"You went up to his room?" I said.

Nevada grinned. "It's all right. I made him sit on the other side of the room in a chair, where he sulked and nursed his thumb."

"His thumb?"

"He got a bit handsy in the lift, so I had to take measures. Establish boundaries. It saves confusion and embarrassment all round in the long run, although admittedly in the short run it hurts quite a lot. To have your thumb bent back, I mean. The way it isn't supposed to bend." Nevada paused thoughtfully. "Amazing how far it will bend in that direction if you apply sufficient force."

I must concede that I found the thought of Nevada applying sufficient force to handsy Silvio's thumb in the lift immensely cheering. I wondered if there had been any screaming but, before I asked about that, I had a more pressing question.

"What were you doing in Silvio's room while he was sulking over his maimed thumb?"

"It wasn't maimed. Just sore. I was going through the clothes, of course."

"There actually were some clothes?"

"Naturally," said Nevada.

Naturally. They'd had one of my old business cards, hadn't they? Providing convincing props was something these people apparently prided themselves on.

"And not just any old clothes," she said. "They were fabulous. And since Silvio was obviously a ringer, his ex-girlfriend was clearly imaginary, so I didn't have any scruples about making an offer for them, too. Her garments, I mean."

"You bought the clothes after all?"

"I didn't buy them. Silvio gave them to me."

"Gave them to you? For nothing?"

"He sulkily said I could take them for free, providing I just got out of there and left him alone."

"To nurse his thumb," I said.

"And to nurse his wounded pride."

"So you got the clothes?" I said. I was beginning to wish I'd got something out of my skirmish with Cayley. A copy of an original pressing of Mobley 1568, currently changing hands for about ten grand, would have been nice.

"Virtue should always be rewarded," said Nevada primly.

"Mine wasn't," I said and told her about the record. Which, in fairness, was unlikely to have even existed. They probably had a limit to their props budget.

"I'll reward you later," said Nevada, easing back into my arms and giving me a kiss.

"You got a professional underwear model," I said. "And I got drunken-hotel-vomit-girl."

"Oh, I'm sure she scrubbed up nicely," said Nevada, kissing me again.

"What happened to the clothes?" I said.

"They're in a duffel bag in the garden. Silvio generously threw in the duffel bag as part of the transaction. I suppose you'd call it a transaction. It really was very good of him. I hope his thumb isn't too sore."

"Why is a duffel bag full of clothing in the garden?"

Nevada swivelled around and I let go of her as she rose from the sofa. "Well, I got to thinking," she said. "If someone was really clever, that whole business with Silvio, including me turning him down flat—"

"Thank you for that, by the way," I said.

"You're very welcome. Thank you for turning down the midget strumpet. Anyway, I got to thinking that maybe their whole intention, their whole endgame, was actually to get me to take those clothes home with me. So I've left them outside until I can carefully go through them, and of course the duffel bag itself, to make very sure they don't contain any surprises. For instance, perhaps a small surveillance device they wanted to introduce into our household."

"You have a truly devious mind," I said with admiration.

"I certainly try," said Nevada.

19: OUT IN THE GARDEN

Out in the garden in the company of myself and one of our cats, Turk, Nevada proceeded to painstakingly check the clothes, and naturally the duffel bag itself, for anything untoward. "Clean as can be," she said finally, putting away our trusty Stone Circle 10 "bug buster" or electronic countermeasures device.

"They missed a trick there, then," I said.

"Looks like it."

Nevada went on to happily divide the clothes into three piles. For me, for her, and for sale. "Silvio is about your size," she said. "I knew that from his first email, when he sent details of the clothes." She paused. "I wonder if they took that factor into account?"

"It wouldn't surprise me," I said. "Frankly, by now, nothing would surprise me."

It would not be too long, however, before I would have to eat those words...

Right now, though, with the clothes sorted and stored

away, along with the duffel bag—"That will come in useful," said Nevada—we decided to go out and celebrate.

"Are we celebrating the triumph of virtue?" I said. "Or a really good clothes score?"

"Both, of course," said my eminently practical darling.

We left food for the cats and then walked to Albert's, our local, to have a meal and some wine. Both the meal and the wine were good, as we knew they would be. Plus, there was the opportunity to gossip about Agatha without Agatha herself, or Tinkler, present. In the very pub run by the guy who had, until recently, been going out with Agatha.

"Has she really ditched Albert?" I said, checking first to make sure he wasn't in earshot. But he was safely tucked away in the small kitchen at the back of the pub, exhausting the patience of the latest talented chef he'd hired. Albert ran a very good gastropub and had a knack for choosing high-calibre staff, whether it was to work behind the bar or in the kitchen. And then he'd proceed to screw things up with them. In the case of the chef, he could never resist interfering—Albert was a good cook himself, but he'd never learned the principle of hiring a dog and refraining from doing your own barking.

In the case of the barmaids, he invariably ended up sleeping with them. This latter scenario repeated itself with such reliability and regularity that Nevada, ever the cineaste, had dubbed it Barmaid Day, in homage to the film *Groundhog Day*. Which explained her next comment.

"Yes, it's a bit of a shame actually. Agatha had got him out of his Barmaid Day infinite loop. Now I suppose he'll revert to it."

"And is Agatha really seeing Horatio?" I said.

"Oh yes." Nevada smiled and winked. "It's going quite well, I understand."

"Poor old Tinkler," I said.

"Poor old Tinkler, nothing," said Nevada. "Didn't he recently have an affair with a gorgeous Swedish stripper?"

"Well, that's true," I said.

"And since then he's been shamelessly banging Stinky Stanmer's sister, hasn't he?"

"Well, now and then I suppose, apparently," I said.

"So poor old Tinkler, nothing," said Nevada. "He's having sex with more partners than you or me. Way more partners." She gave me a mischievous look. "Why so serious?"

"I was just thinking that maybe I didn't handle things so well with Cayley after all."

"What on earth do you mean?"

"Maybe I should have tried to get her to tell me where Lambert is."

Nevada shook her head. "No, she would never have told you. And I'm glad you didn't let her through the door." I felt her foot under the table seeking out mine. We kept talking while we shamelessly played footsy.

"What if the evil dwarf..." said Nevada, pausing for a moment so that giggles didn't send wine up her nose.

I recognised that poor old Cayley was being less and less generously described as time went on. Oh well, I had nothing good to say about Silvio the handsy underwear boy.

"What if she had tried unsuccessfully to vamp you," said Nevada, "and I'd come home all sweet and innocent, going on about how physically hideous Silvio had been. But suspiciously three hours late…?"

"And with a gift bag of Soho House-branded soap and shampoo," I said.

She laughed.

"Or turn it around," I said. "You come home having virtuously fended off Silvio's advances—"

"Which I did. I hope his thumb has recovered full function. Otherwise picking up small objects will remain a challenge for a while."

"And then you find I'm going on and on about what a boring afternoon I've had and how uneventful it had been."

"And yet, for some reason, you'd decided to have a shower in the middle of the day and change the sheets."

"Right."

"To remove the stink of the vertically challenged vamp they sent after you."

"Whom I didn't even allow through the door," I reminded her, because she was getting a little worked up. "It is 'whom' isn't it?"

She refilled my wine glass. "Yes, it is. You deserve credit on every front." Filling her own glass, she paused and said, "What is it? What are you worried about?"

Nevada's sensitivity to my moods, and ability to read my thoughts, was as impressive as ever. And one more reason why it was just as well I hadn't let Cayley and her jewelled navel into our house.

"I was thinking," I said, "that if they wanted to do something really insidious, they should have just set up a honeytrap for *one* of us. Lure you out of the house and then spring the trap."

"Spring the trap on whom?" said Nevada.

"Doesn't matter," I said.

She was silent for a moment then began to nod. "If one of us is honeytrapped… and actually goes for it, then…"

"It would be corrosive to our relationship," I said.

"But if we *don't* go for it…" I could see Nevada putting it together.

"Then that's the really sneaky part."

Nevada was nodding again. "Because, say I'm offered Silvio on a plate and turn him down, then I come home and find you acting like nothing has happened…"

"Because nothing *has* happened," I said.

"But I don't know that for sure. And, so, a seed of suspicion has been planted."

"Which is also corrosive to our relationship."

"It certainly would be," said Nevada.

"And it works the same way the other way around. If they honeytrap me, and I turn Cayley down."

"Which you did. Have I said thank you?"

"You have. And you're very welcome. But if I turn her down and then you come home, all innocence, because there's nothing to *not* be innocent about…"

"But you're wondering. If they set a honeytrap for you then maybe they set one for me. And maybe I fell for it."

"Exactly," I said. "If they wanted to split us apart, that would be an even more insidious way of doing it."

"But do you think that's what they were doing? Trying to split us apart?"

"No," I said. "I think Lambert was just having fun, creating generalised mischief."

"That's it exactly," said Nevada. "*Mischief*. Mischief but not malice. It's like he doesn't intend us any harm."

"Somebody certainly intended harm to Timothy," I reminded her.

That remark created a long silence between us as we thought back on everything that had happened. Meanwhile, all around us, happy pubgoers drank their drinks and ate their food in the carefree manner of people who had never had to dispose of a man's body in woodlands and then try and forget about it.

"Do we think it was Lambert who killed him?" said Nevada, keeping her voice low and conversational, and sipping her wine.

"We have to consider the possibility," I said.

"But why kill him?"

I shrugged. "Rave Star Orgy Cult," I said.

"You think that's grounds for murder?"

"It could be."

"But they've got that headline hanging up in full view where nobody can miss it when they visit the house."

"I think that's more about defiance than acceptance," I said.

"But that was all years ago," said Nevada. "Why kill him now?"

"Maybe bitterness has been brewing all those years… building up…"

Nevada shrugged. "Maybe. And maybe it wasn't Lambert at all."

I nodded. "Right. Maybe there's more than one person playing games with us."

Nevada looked at me, her eyes bright with wine but also with that keen, unsparing intellect of hers. "Lambert and somebody else."

"Right," I said. "Because it seems there's two kinds of weird shit happening. The kind where they intend to make mischief but don't really aim to cause harm…"

Nevada poured out the last of the wine, regretfully inspected the empty bottle, then set it aside. "Like making us think we'd gone back in time to 1999," she said.

"Or tempting us with extra-curricular activities," I said.

She smiled a wicked smile. "Nicely put. And then, on the other hand, there is the weird shit where there is a definite intent to cause harm. Like drugging you and leaving you to take a fall at the gig. Or killing poor Tim."

"And planting his body on us. And planting drugs on us," I said.

"So," said Nevada. "We're talking about two different groups?"

"At the moment," I said, "we're just talking. But if there *are* two different groups it would make sense that they have different casts of 'actors' which don't overlap."

"With Cayley and Silvio and the 1999 ravers in one," said Nevada. "For the sake of convenience let's call them 'Team Mischief'."

"And then," I said, thinking of the girl with green eyes, "there's Princess Seitan and unknown others operating in the second group."

"'Team Harm' shall we call them?" said Nevada.

"We shall," I said. "But that leaves us with all kinds of questions."

"For instance," said Nevada, "*why* are there two teams? And which team is Lambert running?"

I leaned closer to her and took her hand under the table. I was feeling the wine, but it seemed I was only feeling it physically, in my body. My hand was hot on hers. But my mind remained icy and lucid and clear. "Maybe Lambert is involved with neither."

Her wide blue eyes were looking into mine. "Okay…" she said, waiting for me to go on.

"We're having a lot of trouble finding Lambert," I said. "What if he isn't there to be found?"

There was a long silence in which we could listen to all the carefree people around us, in a pleasant pub on a summer London evening, who weren't giving a moment's thought to death. Nevada gently extracted her hand from mine. She folded her arms and leaned back in her seat, looking at me thoughtfully. "What are you thinking?"

I said, "What was the first thing that Poppy said? When we told her about those tickets to the Brixton gig and someone dosing me?"

Nevada began to nod slowly. "She said it was just like the sort of thing that Lambert would do."

"Right," I said.

"And, as a result, she was now certain he was alive."

"Right," I said.

"So, you think maybe Lambert is dead and someone doesn't want anybody to know that?" said Nevada. "And consequently they're playing these games to make it look like he's still alive?"

"If they are, it's certainly working," I said.

Nevada frowned. "But wait, people have *seen* Lambert. They've seen him alive and well."

"Just one person," I said. "Bronwen, our friendly neighbourhood concierge."

"My god," said Nevada. "You think she played us? You know what… it would be just like one of their games. She came up to us and introduced herself in the hotel lobby and struck up a conversation…"

"Which, to be fair," I said, "is what someone doing that job would do. But still…"

"We were the ones who brought up Lambert, weren't we?"

"We were," I said. "But if we hadn't, she could have easily steered the conversation in that direction. Talking about the noisy party occupying the suite on the top floor."

"Damn their eyes," said Nevada. "And I liked Bronwen."

"So did I. I still do."

"But you think she was part of their game?"

"I think I'd really like to find someone else at that hotel who saw Lambert there," I said. "Before I make up my mind."

"But Tabloid Tim sent us to the hotel in the first place, because he had reason to believe he'd be there."

"Tim was all about the money," I said. "What if he was helping someone try to convince us that Lambert is still alive?"

Nevada nodded, her eyes distant with thought. "And then he got greedy…"

"Right. He knew the truth."

"About Lambert being dead."

"Right," I said. "And he asked for too much money for his silence."

"But if all that's true, if Lambert is dead, then we don't have two teams, just one."

"Why?" I said. "There could be one group who are pulling these stunts to make it look like Lambert is still alive, and somebody else pulling them for another reason entirely."

"A reason that we don't know," said Nevada.

"That we don't know," I agreed.

"My head's starting to spin," said Nevada. "And I don't think it's the wine. Shall we head home? I could do with a walk in the fresh air."

But it would have taken more than fresh air to clear our heads tonight. As we walked back, we continued to talk. "Do you think we should run this possibility by Poppy?" I said.

"You mean the possibility that her husband, using the term loosely, may not be just missing but actually dead?"

"I'm afraid so," I said.

"Which would just upset her unnecessarily," said Nevada.

"Quite possibly," I said. "Alternatively, it might let her start bracing herself for the unpleasant truth."

I felt Nevada's hair brush my cheek as she shook her head. We were walking close, side by side, across the railway tracks on White Hart Lane. "I vote we stay silent about that particular possibility until we know for sure."

"I agree," I said. It would be a relief not to have that conversation. Purely conditional relief, though. "I have to say, I've got this bad feeling."

"You mean you're sure he's dead?"

"Yes."

"I have the same feeling," said Nevada quietly.

The sky was deep azure with the onset of summer night and the streetlights had come on. We walked past the pub by the bridge over Beverley Brook, past the old house with the sundial on it, and onto the Upper Richmond Road. We crossed the road and then we were back on our estate.

We were still quite a distance from our house, but apparently close enough for the keen hearing of a cat to detect our approach. Because, at this point, there began an unholy howling from Turk.

She'd made a racket like this before.

And it was because we so clearly remembered those other circumstances that we now broke into a run. We ran frantically, as fast as we could, and reached our back gate, breathless with hearts hammering. Turk was still howling but, as soon as we put our key in the lock, she fell silent.

We opened the gate and hurried inside—no spiderweb to worry about anymore—and stood in our dark, fragrant garden, illuminated by the three small lights which had come on at dusk. By their gleam we could see the bulky figure of a man sitting calmly on our outdoor sofa, and Turk watching him warily from the other side of the garden, crouched under the Japanese maple.

Our other cat, Fanny, however, was lolling contentedly in the man's lap.

The man was listening to music on his phone with earbuds, which he politely removed when he saw us come in.

The photographs we'd been using weren't massively up to date, but there was no question about it.

It was Lambert Ramkin.

"I hope you don't mind me making myself at home," he said.

20: ONE QUESTION

"As it happens," I said, "we were just talking about you."

"Really?" said Lambert Ramkin. "What were you saying?"

"That we were pretty sure you were dead," said Nevada.

Lambert chuckled. "Sorry to disappoint you."

"We're not disappointed," I said.

"Quite the opposite," said Nevada. "How did you get in here, by the way?"

"I climbed over the wall." He laughed again at the expressions on our faces. "All right, I know I may look a bit old and fat for larks like that, but I had some help. I was dropped off by a friend, or rather an associate. And they gave me a leg up before they left. Once I had a leg up, it wasn't that hard at all." There was a certain note of quiet pride in his voice.

Nevada and I drew up chairs near him and sat down. Turk emerged cautiously from the far shadows of the garden and sat down under my chair, not wanting to be left out of the party. Fanny continued to shamelessly lounge on the lap of our home invader.

"We met some of your associates," said Nevada. "Earlier today."

"So I understand," said Lambert. He grinned at us. He was as shameless as our treacherous cat. "I take it my associates weren't to your liking?"

"What wasn't to our liking was an attempt to disrupt a longstanding and rather valuable partnership," said Nevada. We were sitting on either side of our guest, too far apart to link hands, but she extended her foot, so it rested on mine.

Lambert shrugged. "It wouldn't necessarily have had to disrupt anything. But each to his own." He stroked Fanny, who sighed with contentment, quite unaware of the irony of her position. "I must admit, though," said Lambert. "It did make you seem quite interesting. To me." He looked at us, scanning slowly from one to the other, and smiled. "You both passed up the chance of guilt-free sex?"

"Who says it would have been guilt-free?" said Nevada.

He smiled. "I said 'the chance of'."

"Did we pass some kind of test?" I said. "When we turned them down?"

"Not really, not formally. I just thought you guys sounded like a nice couple. Like nice people."

"We are," said Nevada firmly.

"And I thought you might be more interesting to hang out with than the people I was currently hanging out with."

"For instance, Silvio and Cayley," said Nevada.

"Among others," he agreed. "I was getting a little tired of being on the road anyway. If you've seen one hotel, you've seen them all."

I thought if he left all his rooms the way he'd left the one in Wales, he'd never see the same hotel twice. Because they wouldn't let him back in.

But I said nothing and just watched as he tickled our furry traitor behind her ear, and she rolled her head to give him better access, purring enthusiastically all the while. Lambert looked down at her fondly and then up at us again. "Is it all right if I crash here for the night, at your place?"

"Of course," I said, looking at Nevada, who was nodding an eager affirmative. *Now we've got the fucker, let's not let him go*, was the subtext of that nod.

"Thank you," said Lambert. "Why did you think I was dead?"

"Because," I said, "these little shows you've been putting on for our benefit would have been a perfect way of making it look like you're still alive when you're not."

"My, oh my. That's an unnecessary elaboration, isn't it?" said Lambert. "Have you ever heard of Occam's razor?"

"Yes, we have," said Nevada patiently. "But what we haven't told you yet is that some of these shows don't seem to be your handiwork."

"What do you mean?"

"For instance, today," I said. "Cayley and good old Silvio. That was all your doing."

"I think I've kind of already said it was," said Lambert with friendly patience.

"And the great 1999 time-travel rave," said Nevada.

Lambert's face immediately split into a wide grin at the mention of this.

"That was your show," she said.

"Did you enjoy it?" he said eagerly.

After a pause, I said, "Yes, yes we did."

"Once it stopped freaking you out, you mean?"

"Once we were sure we weren't being set up in some kind of dangerous way," said Nevada.

"You guys are too untrusting and paranoid," said Lambert, caressing our cat. "You should learn to just relax and enjoy things. No wonder poor Cayley and Silvio didn't make any headway with you two. You're just too uptight."

"Uptight?" said Nevada, her voice sharpening and taking on a dangerous edge. "Untrusting?"

"You'll find your life much richer if you can just learn to take it easy and open up."

Nevada leaned forward, her teeth gleaming in the darkness with what I recognised as a savage smile. "Let's talk about taking it easy." She then embarked on a terse account of my experience at the Brixton gig, with unsparing emphasis on me being drugged involuntarily and almost seriously injured. The latter, of course, was speculation, but I certainly wasn't about to contradict her. Things hadn't turned out too well for Frank Zappa.

Lambert sat silent through the story, looking at us with at first puzzlement, then growing interest and finally— apparently sincere—concern.

"No," he said when she was finished. "That was nothing to do with me. I admit parts of it sound like the sort of caper I might pull…"

"That's exactly what Poppy said," I said.

"Really?" This seemed to make him proud. "How is Poppy?"

"Just fine," I said. "Concerned about you, though."

Nevada wasn't about to let us get distracted. "So you didn't send those tickets?" she said.

"Absolutely not."

"And you know nothing about the drugged food?"

"No, I'd never do anything like that… unless I was sure the person I was drugging was going to be okay."

This was a somewhat less than entirely satisfactory mission statement, but I let it go.

"And," he said, "that bit about you almost getting pushed off the edge by the crowd, I never would have sanctioned putting you in jeopardy like that." He paused. "You're sure it was deliberate?"

"Yes," said Nevada tersely. "But the point is that you knew nothing about any of this?"

"Correct."

"So someone else is also involved," said Nevada. "Imitating what you do."

"Stealing my schtick," said Lambert. "I'm not sure I like that. Although they do say imitation is the sincerest form of flattery." He looked at me. "I'm sorry you almost got hurt, but ultimately everything turned out okay. So, no harm done."

It was funny he should use the word "harm". Of course Team Harm had inflicted immense damage. They'd killed Tabloid Tim. But Nevada and I had both silently realised we couldn't tell Lambert anything about that, not without exposing ourselves to enormous risk.

We had gone to a lot of trouble so we wouldn't be connected with Tim's murder, and we weren't going to throw all that away now by telling Lambert about it. We had to stay silent and we couldn't share this vital fact with him, or get any potential help from him on identifying who had done it.

On the other hand, it was entirely possible that *he* had done it. That he knew all about it. That he was Team Harm.

"Is that it?" said Lambert.

"What do you mean, is that it?" said Nevada.

"That's all the examples you have of people imitating me?"

"Yes. Isn't it enough?"

"Sure." Lambert shrugged and grinned a lazy grin. "I just thought you mentioned some *shows* that didn't seem to be my handiwork. Shows, plural."

I realised that you couldn't afford to drop your guard with this guy. He was very alert and very sharp.

Fortunately, he didn't seem interested in pursuing this matter because he changed the subject. "Did you enjoy your country rave experience?"

"It was pretty amazing," said Nevada, as relieved at this new line of discussion as I was. "And Rodney and Lilith were brilliant. Where did you find them?"

Lambert smiled again and leaned forward, as much as a lazy cat draped across his lap would allow. "Now are you sure that's the question you want to ask? Because I'll give you a straight answer, to one question. Just one. You can ask me any question you like, but just one."

I assumed that any resemblance between him making this offer and a wise sage in a fairy tale was anything but coincidental.

"And you'll give us a straight answer?" I said.

"Assuming I can."

"Okay," I said, looking at Nevada to make sure she agreed with me. "Tell us about the owl."

Nevada nodded with approval and sat back in her chair, like a child waiting to be told a story.

"Ah, the owl," said Lambert. "Okay, so I know a chap who lives locally, near us in Kent. And he's done some work in films and he knows an animal trainer who also works in films. And…"

"The animal trainer has an owl?"

"Right. He has a Eurasian eagle-owl. Called Búho."

"Búho is the Spanish word for owl," said Nevada.

"Is it?" said Lambert. "Cool. Then we selected a suitable location, in this case that old oak tree… it's a beautiful tree, isn't it?"

"It certainly is."

"And the trainer habituated the owl to receiving snacks planted in the tree, when given a certain signal."

"The whistle we heard," I said.

"The whistle, right. It was fifty-fifty whether the owl would play ball what with you guys standing there. But we got lucky."

"You certainly did," said Nevada.

Lambert gave us a piercing look, perhaps not entirely unlike a Eurasian eagle-owl. "It's ruined the magic, hasn't it?" he said. "Now you know the secret behind it, it's spoiled it for you."

"Not at all," said Nevada. "We may know how you did it, but still we're amazed and proud that someone would go to those lengths just to give us such a wonderful experience."

Lambert relaxed and looked happy again. "That's a nice way of putting it," he said. "A wonderful experience..." He reached in his pocket and took out, inevitably, a joint. "Would you care to partake?" he said.

"No, thank you," I said.

"Maybe in a minute," said Nevada.

He grinned at her. "When we know each other a little better, eh?" He took out a lighter and ignited the joint, careful not to disturb Fanny who was spread like a little dead weight across his lap. "Now it's my turn," he said, puffing the joint to life. "I'd like to ask you a question."

"You can have two if you like," said Nevada.

"Assuming we can answer them," I said.

He chuckled and then said, very casually, "Cayley said you mentioned my name. In fact, she said you mentioned *her* name." He took a hit on the joint and looked at me through the smoke. "You really are a good detective. And I'd like to know how you found that out. I'm actually quite impressed."

"We're not so impressed," said Nevada.

"What do you mean?"

We told him about our visit to the Zobole Marine Hotel and finding Cayley comatose and half undressed in a pool of vomit. He looked shocked. "I knew she was paralytic," he said. "So we left her to sleep it off. And we left Silvio to take care of her."

"If, by taking care of her, you mean attempting to rape her and then abandoning her," said Nevada, "then he did a great job."

"The evil little shit," said Lambert.

"Quite," said Nevada.

"We won't be working with young Silvio again," said Lambert. He seemed genuinely angry. "Will you excuse me while I make some calls?"

We went inside while he used his phone, sitting out in our garden with Fanny still on his lap. His voice was indistinct, but the enraged rhythms of it were clear. He proceeded to call several people, apparently giving them varying degrees of hell, while Nevada and I sat in the living room, occasionally watching him through the window.

"I wish I'd bent Silvio's thumb back further," said Nevada. "A lot further."

"Assuming Lambert is telling us the truth," I said.

"He seems on the level. He certainly seems angry."

We put Lambert to bed on our sofa. He appeared perfectly happy there. Nevada crept out of our bedroom several times in the night to check on him and came back to report that he was sleeping peacefully, with Fanny crashed out on the big man's chest. She was asleep, too, and rising and falling with his breathing.

"They seem to have bonded," she said.

"I hope not," I said.

The next morning, we woke to the smell of cooking and discovered Lambert in the kitchen, making omelettes. "I found some mushrooms and cheese in the fridge," he said. "And eggs, of course." He looked at us, asking an unspoken question.

"That's fine," I said. "In fact, it smells good."

"The one thing I can cook," said Lambert contentedly. "Omelettes."

"What did you use for fat?" I said.

"Butter of course. What else?"

"Just checking," I said.

He tilted the pan carefully over the flame. "If I get these right, they should be runny in the centre. The French have a word for it."

"*Baveuse*," said Nevada. "Literally 'dribbling'."

"Here's to dribbling," said Lambert. "At least in omelettes. Looks like this one is ready. Who wants to go first?"

21: HOUSE GUEST

Perhaps surprisingly, given my last experience with a meal I hadn't cooked myself, I volunteered for the first omelette out of Lambert's pan and I was glad I had. It was tasty as hell, and it was a real pleasure to have someone else cook for us for a change.

Lambert even helped with the washing up afterwards and, when we were finished, he crouched by the wine rack in our kitchen—it is quite an interesting wine rack, in the shape of a rocket ship; not to mention its contents—and studied it with interest. Then he wandered into the sitting room. Nevada gave me a look that silently suggested I should go and keep our guest company.

And keep an eye on him.

I found him crouching in front of my rack of hi-fi equipment just the way he'd been crouching in front of the wine rack, inspecting it with the same keen interest.

"Is that a John Michell Iso?" Lambert had been looking

at the phono stage. Now he looked at me. One connoisseur recognising another.

"Yes, it is."

"With the Hera power supply?" he said.

"Circuit on the Iso designed by Tom Evans," I said.

Lambert nodded happily. "I was talking to Hughie—you know Hughie Mackinaw?"

"Yes, in fact we almost crossed paths at his factory after the collapse of the record fair."

"Oh really, were you there to buy 'Precision Audio Components'?" He pronounced the words with the droll mockery they deserved.

"Afraid so," I said.

"While I was there, Hughie and I had a chat about Tom Evans. Seems he knows him."

"They've both gone into exile in Wales," I said.

"Don't let the Welsh hear you say that," said Lambert. "Tom Evans is a genius at lowering the noise floor. That's his philosophy."

"That's right," I said. "He says it's all there on the original recording. You just reveal it by lowering the noise floor. You uncover the music, like draining a pool to reveal there was treasure at the bottom of it, all along."

He laughed. "Pirate treasure?"

"If you like."

"Are you sure you're not a stoner?" he said.

"Yup," I said.

"You talk like one."

"You're the one who suggested pirates," I said.

He laughed again. "You know, when I chose the name Noise Floor for my studio and for my house, I just chose it because it sounded cool. But then I learned what an important concept it is in recorded sound. Not to mention life itself."

"Life itself?"

He grinned. "Don't sound so cynical. It's a useful principle to live by. Remove what is irrelevant and distracting and you come to the truth of things."

Any danger of this turning into a deep philosophical discussion was averted because he suddenly spotted his record *The Magus*, which was in the front of my pile of recently acquired vinyl. "Hey," he said softly, picking it up. He turned it over in his big hands, beaming. He seemed delighted to discover I had a copy of a something by him.

"Is this the limited edition?" he said.

"Yes," I said, trying not to flush with foolish record-collecting pride.

"Even I don't have a copy of this." He looked at me eagerly. As with his evident delight, there was something touching, even childlike in his eagerness. "Would you consider selling it?"

I didn't tell him that was the only reason I'd bought it, because that might have seemed rude.

We put the record on in the background, probably more quietly than he would have liked, and sat down on the sofa and haggled.

Realising what we were doing—she can detect the sound of financial negotiations with superhuman acuity—

Nevada came in and watched us happily for a moment or two before going out again and leaving us to it. Where vinyl was concerned, she left the bargaining to me. And, in the end, Lambert offered more than I'd hoped to get for the album at auction. I felt a bit bad about extracting such a high price from him, but any guilt was offset by his obvious pleasure in obtaining the record.

That and the fact he was very wealthy indeed.

When I told Nevada about the deal, there was plenty of obvious pleasure on her part, too. "Aren't you glad we asked him to stay?" she said.

I admitted I was.

In fact, Lambert Ramkin proved to be the ideal house guest. Courteous, considerate and, above all, low maintenance. He had a bath—Fanny had to be banned from accompanying him into the bathroom; she really seemed to have formed an attachment—and then spent the rest of the morning sunning himself in the garden, listening to music on his phone and smoking the occasional joint. Nevada joined him in at least one of these and then went about her business humming merry tuneless little tunes to herself.

Since Lambert said he only cooked one dish, it fell to me to make lunch. As he had raved—apt word in his case—about the cheddar he'd found in our fridge (Waitrose Davidstow Cornish Vintage, strength 7), I decided to use some more of it, and cooked the macaroni and cheese that Tinkler had recently lobbied for.

Lambert watched in fascination. "I might actually be able to learn to cook this," he said.

"Then you'll have two dishes in your repertoire," said Nevada. "Think how the girls will swoon."

Lambert laughed. "And you don't need to make a sauce at all?" he said.

"It makes its own sauce, with the starch from the pasta," I said. "You cook it all in one pot."

"It's a one-pot wonder," said Nevada proudly.

"Tell me how to do it again." Lambert took out his phone to make notes.

"Six hundred millilitres of milk," I said, "three hundred of water, three hundred grams of macaroni, sixty-five of butter…"

"You understand that all of these ingredients have to be of the highest quality?" said Nevada.

"Of course," said Lambert.

"Except the water," I said. "Which comes out of the tap and is provided by a corrupt monopoly who are poisoning our rivers while asset-stripping a public utility and ripping off everybody except their shareholders."

"Don't get him started," said Nevada.

"No, I'm down with him," said Lambert fervently. "Some of my best friends are surfers. And they don't like surfing through sewage. Anyway, so you put it all in the same pot…"

"Not with any sewage," said Nevada.

"Not with any sewage," said Lambert.

"Right," I said. "Milk, water, butter, macaroni. Cook gently, stirring so it doesn't stick, until it begins to simmer. Then lower the heat and cook for ten minutes. Add three hundred and fifty grams of cheddar, grated."

"Of very good cheddar," said Nevada. "Grated."

"Of course," said Lambert.

"And seventy-five millilitres of double cream," I said.

"Ditto," said Nevada.

"Ditto," said Lambert.

"Then turn off the heat, cover the pan and leave it for a while to set. And then eat it at any time."

"Even I can cook that," said Lambert happily, making notes on his phone.

We ate the mac and cheese with a green salad and a couple of bottles of red wine—Jaboulet Parallèle 45 organic Côtes du Rhône. Lambert also raved about the wine, and made a note about that on his phone, too.

When we finished eating, we all went and sat outside in the garden, Fanny in her now traditional position of lying on Lambert's lap, and Turk watching with contempt and scepticism from the shadowy concealment of the undergrowth.

"Well," said Lambert finally. "I guess it's about time I was getting home."

"By home," said Nevada, "do you mean…?"

"Noise Floor."

Nevada flashed me a look of triumphant delight. "I'll book us a ride," I said. "When would you like to go?"

"Soon… this evening…" said Lambert, stroking the cat, who was now apparently permanently resident in his lap. "No hurry."

I went inside and phoned Agatha, and booked her to drive us down to Noise Floor. Then I rang Poppy and gave her the good news. It's not often you get a chance to make someone happy, or at least as I happy as I made her.

I hung up with a glow of good cheer and satisfaction at a job well done.

I didn't have long to rejoice in it, though, because my phone rang almost instantly. It was Hughie. And, as soon as I heard his voice, I knew something was wrong.

"I've been thinking about what you asked."

"Okay," I said.

"About tracing the pills… and I just can't do it."

"Okay," I said.

"I'm sorry pal, but I just can't do it. I have contacts with these people, I know a lot of them. Some of those MDMA factories are right here in Wales. As a matter of fact, there's one just up the road…"

I sensed a "but" coming, and I wasn't disappointed.

"But what you want me to do is to ask for a list of virtually everyone they've sold to. There's no way they'd give me that, and there's no way I'd ask for it."

"Fair enough, Hughie," I said.

"Sorry, pal."

"There is another possible approach," I said. I'd actually been giving this some thought. "This will only involve you only having to ask about one person."

"I still can't do that. Why would they tell me someone's a customer of theirs? It would be breaking client confidentially."

"How about this, Hughie," I said, thinking furiously. "Tell them that someone is selling dodgy pills that look like their pills. Counterfeits."

There was a pause. "But what if people aren't selling counterfeits and they know it?"

"They can't be sure. And it doesn't even have to be true."

"What do you mean?"

"I mean you don't even have to pretend to be certain about it. You just tell them there's a rumour going around to that effect. And there is now. We've just created that rumour."

"Okay… And then what?"

"And then you say that you've got some of their pills, which is true. And you want to confirm they're the real thing and not the dodgy counterfeits."

"Why won't they just tell me to get them tested?"

"Do they know you know Mr Tetlock? Or anyone else who can test them?"

"Probably not. But what if they just tell me to wait for a festival where they're doing pill testing and take them there?

"Are they likely to think you have enough impulse control to wait that long?"

"No, all right, you're right. They'd probably think that I want to start throwing them down my neck immediately."

"Right," I said.

"But what if they offer to test them for me?"

"Why would they go to all that bother when they can just reassure you that the pills are kosher by confirming they sold some of their stock to the person you bought them from?"

There was a long silence at the other end, so long that I thought the connection might have dropped. But then Hughie said, "Okay, that might work. Who is this person I say I bought them from?"

I looked out the window at the garden where our house guest was sitting with our cat in his lap, Nevada at his side, sharing a joint and laughing.

"Lambert Ramkin," I said.

The odd thing was, we were all sort of sorry to see him go.

Certainly Fanny was.

But any regret about losing our visitor was immediately effaced by Poppy's joyous reaction to the news that we'd found him, and we were bringing him home. "It's so heart-warming," said Nevada. "Plus, now we can bill them for successful completion of our job." She commenced humming a merry little tuneless tune again.

There was a pleasing sensation of closing a circle in the fact we had enlisted Agatha to drive us back to Kent again, returning the wandering Lamb to his fold. We drove down through rich golden sunlight, gradually sinking and lengthening the shadows, and reached our destination at dusk.

"I'll stay with the car," said Agatha.

"We won't be long," I said.

"Probably a good idea, staying with the car," murmured Nevada as we climbed the steps.

Lambert was forging ahead of us eagerly. For a man who'd spent so long trying to avoid being found, he seemed very enthusiastic about coming home.

"Yes," I said, "she doesn't want to run into Selena."

We thought our conversation was inaudible, but Lambert turned and said, "Why, is there bad blood between Agatha and Selena?" He clearly had extremely keen hearing, a truly remarkable attribute after decades of raving.

Nevada and I didn't know how to answer his question. We might not be particularly fond of the Green Wellie Nympho, but it was hardly our place to rat her out concerning her affair with Horatio.

Lambert seemed amused by our discomfiture. "Is there a man involved?" he said.

We didn't say anything. What could we say? He laughed into our silent faces. "Don't worry about it. I'm sure Selena will be only too eager to tell me all about it herself. And if she doesn't, Poppy or Jac will be happy to."

They were all waiting for him on the lawn in front of the house. Poppy and Jacquetta and Selena. And even Julian, although he was exuding his trademark sullenness.

Poppy and Jacquetta flung themselves on Lambert. Indeed, he flung himself on them. It was a mutual flinging thing, with much hugging and kissing.

Selena and Julian remained outside the happy little group. Then Selena, having proved her point, sauntered forwards and joined the hugging and kissing.

Which just left Julian. He watched in disgust for a moment or two, and then turned and walked away.

Soon after that, we took our leave, too.

But first I took Poppy aside for a quiet word.

"We didn't really find him," I said.

"What do you mean?" said Poppy. She glanced at Lambert, as if expecting him to ripple like a mirage and vanish.

"I mean we didn't *find* him. He came to us. He just gave himself up." Nevada and I had discussed this, and she agreed we'd have to tell Poppy what happened. Nevada wasn't pleased because, if we hadn't actually found Lambert, we didn't necessarily qualify for our full fee. But since it appeared inevitable that Poppy would find out what had really happened, it seemed best for us to be upfront and come clean about it.

But we needn't have worried.

"Yes, he came to you," said Poppy. "He came to *you*. Because he likes you guys. It doesn't matter that you didn't track him down to some hidden lair. This is just as good." She looked over at Lambert and Jacquetta. Even Selena was smiling, something I didn't think I'd ever seen before. "He wouldn't have come to you if I hadn't hired you. Hiring you was the smartest thing I could have done."

We started to say our goodbyes and then I remembered I had Lambert's record under my arm, packed in a sturdy cardboard mailer, of course, and I gave it to him. He stopped hugging the women in his life for a moment and hugged me instead. Then he hugged Nevada.

And that was that.

I felt an odd, intense melancholy as we drove away.

Lambert was gone and even his record was gone.

Now there was virtually no trace of him in our lives. It seemed unreasonably sad.

But then Agatha took a new route back to London, taking us past exactly the stretch of woods where we'd abandoned Tabloid Tim's body.

And I realised we were lucky to be leaving Lambert Ramkin and his complicated life behind.

22: INVITATION

With our grand weekend festival of the Village of Vinyl fast drawing near, Nevada was pestering me to record a video clip to promote it. She even went so far as to enlist Tinkler to help with the sound and camera. Which involved using a Zoom H1n audio recorder attached to an iPhone via a specially designed frame.

Tinkler, and indeed the rest of us, had learned about this setup from Alicia Foxcroft, a professional sound artist he'd once failed to sleep with. Perhaps more than once.

Tinkler, although it was easy to forget this, was actually very adept with tech. So he was a good choice. I just wasn't so sure *I* was a good choice.

"Why don't you do it?" I said to Nevada. "You'll be better on camera."

"That's true," said Tinkler. "People would rather look at a gorgeous woman than… well… him."

"What's wrong with him?" said Nevada.

"Nothing," said Tinkler. "If we shoot him from the correct angle with the right lighting and lots of coaching, he probably won't look like a hillbilly necrophile guiltily interrupted in the middle of a nocturnal endeavour. At least not too much. But whatever we do with him, people would rather look at you."

"But we need to build the brand. And I'm not the Vinyl Detective."

"No, but you'd look a lot better in a bikini."

"Tinkler…"

"I'm just saying you're a more appealing visual."

"I second that," I said.

"Tell you what," said Nevada. "We'll both do a version. And then we can choose which one we think works best. But don't worry, you'll only have to appear on camera at the beginning and then it's voiceover."

I agreed Nevada and I would both do a version, and then we'd let Gerry—Gerald Blanchflower, Doctor of Divinity—decide between us. "Never trust a priest," said Tinkler.

But we ignored him and went ahead with the recording, starting with me reading from the script we'd cooked up.

"Why should booklovers have all the fun?" went my spiel. "We got to thinking—or rather, our friend got to thinking…" At which point we'd edit in a quick shot of Agatha and provide a URL for *Clean Head's Crime Scene*, her blog, "… why not create a village like Hay-on-Wye, but instead of devoting it to books, we'll devote it to *vinyl*." (Emphasis indicated in the script.) "And, for one weekend only, in the beautiful Kentish hamlet of Nutalich." By this time it would be, as Nevada indicated, thankfully just a voiceover, with my words accompanying travelogue shots of Nutalich, emphasising its rural splendour. Which wasn't difficult.

We got my version out of the way after mercifully few takes.

"You did fantastically," said Nevada, and kissed me.

"She's such a convincing liar," said Tinkler.

"Isn't she just?" I said.

Then we did Nevada's version, and then we sent them both to our friendly neighbourhood vicar to adjudicate.

After Tinkler packed up and went home, we were surprised and rather touched to get a message from Lambert Ramkin, via Poppy.

"They want to say thank you to us for the fantastic job we did," said Nevada.

"He handed himself in," I reminded her.

"Yes, but he handed himself in to *us*," said Nevada. "Like Poppy said, he wouldn't have handed himself in to just anyone. And they're so pleased that they have not only already paid us our full fee, they're also inviting us to Noise Floor for a grand thank-you dinner and homecoming celebration."

"Did we say yes?" I said.

"We said yes please."

When the big night arrived, I was looking my best, all dressed up in finery that Nevada had picked up for me for a song, for various songs, in assorted charity shops. She had helped me choose what to wear, which is to say she went through my wardrobe and selected items for me, brooking no argument.

I was allowed to choose my own shoes.

Nevada was wearing the sky-blue leather jacket we'd found at a *secondhand-butik*, as they were called in Sweden, on top of a black silk dress that managed to be simultaneously chic and sufficiently revealing to cause Tinkler's eyes to bug out when he turned up unannounced.

"Are you guys going out?" he said.

"Yup," said Nevada, tying around her throat a pale-blue-and-black art deco silk scarf which neatly unified the two colours of her ensemble. "Good to see your drug intake hasn't prevented you making basic inferences from available data."

"What's the occasion?"

"We're celebrating reuniting the long-lost Lambert Ramkin with his family."

"He wasn't lost that long. Where are you going and can I come along?"

"Noise Floor and no," said Nevada. "Because you weren't invited."

"Noise Floor is Imperium Dart's orgy pad?"

"If you must."

"I must. Will you be getting a home-cooked meal there?"

"I expect so," said Nevada with a little smile.

"You lucky bastards. That Jacquetta is my new favourite cook. No offence," he said, looking at me. And then adding, with just a trace of a whine in his voice, "So I've come around here for nothing?"

"That's the downside of dropping in at random," said Nevada.

"How are you going to get there?"

"That's the upside of dropping in at random," I said. "Go into the sitting room and find out."

Tinkler, who'd immediately worked out what this meant, hurried through to see Agatha sitting on our sofa with both of our cats curled indolently beside her. "You're in on this, too?" he said.

"I'm driving them down to Kent, and picking them up again afterwards and driving them home. It's all part of the deal."

This was true. Poppy was generously going to pick up the bill for chauffeuring us to dinner and back. Which was nice because it meant we didn't have to worry about drinking and driving, or rather not drinking and driving. Plus, it provided a paying job for a friend.

"But you're not going to join them for the meal?" said Tinkler.

"No. I wasn't invited," said Agatha.

"Just like me," said Tinkler, always eager to form a bond with Agatha, even on the flimsiest of pretexts.

"I suppose so," she said, toying with Turk's whiskers.

Turk was enjoying this attention so much that Fanny got annoyed and came over to demand some too.

"Don't you feel left out?" said Tinkler.

"Nope."

"I feel left out," he said.

"You can come with us for the ride if you like."

"I don't feel *that* left out."

In the end it was agreed that Tinkler would stay at our place to keep the cats company and listen to my record collection while Agatha drove us to our destination. "I'll also be raiding your refrigerator," said Tinkler, although this pretty much went without saying. "What's on offer tonight?"

"There's some of that beetroot salad," I said.

"The one with the walnuts?"

"Pecans," I corrected him.

"Then my visit won't be a waste after all. Have fun and think of me."

By the time we reached Noise Floor, night was falling over the countryside and Agatha had just switched on her headlights, which gleamed on the big gates as they opened for us. We drove through and Agatha said, "Oh look, a welcoming committee. Lucky you."

She pulled up on the circular driveway next to another car—not one I recognised—and stopped.

The putative welcoming committee standing outside the garage consisted of Julian and Declan and one of the other triplets. And, far from welcoming us, they hardly noticed Nevada and I as we got out of the car, embroiled as they were in what appeared to be a heated argument that had been going on for some time.

As she pulled away and started for the gate, Agatha buzzed down her window. "Hello, Declan," she called chirpily and, when he looked at her, she blew him a kiss.

"Fuck off fuck-head baldie," screamed Declan, with more gusto than lucidity, but Agatha was already gone. This brief encounter had not improved Declan's temper, however. He turned back to Julian. "Who died and made you god?"

"I'm no god," said Julian with commendable modesty. "But I am your manager. That means I'm in charge."

The other brother—we couldn't immediately tell if it was Darra or Dermot—was watching, anxiously silent, clearly unhappy about being caught up in this squabble.

"We need money," said Declan.

"I'll get us money," said Julian.

"Get it? You threw it away."

"I'll get it," said Julian stubbornly.

"How? Are you going to pull it out of your arse? Are you going to pull it out of your dad's arse? Maybe you should. Because I understand he's back. Back home, for a change."

"You know what your trouble is, Declan?" said Julian. "You don't know who your friends are." Then he looked pointedly at us. "And you don't know who your enemies are." He turned away and walked up the steps, self-consciously making an exit. He wasn't quite as good at this as his mum. He probably just hadn't had enough practice.

Not one to be outdone on the dramatic exit front, Declan turned and ran to the car parked by the garage, jumped in, gunned the engine and screeched away, barely clearing the gates in his trademark style. And incidentally leaving his startled brother stranded with us. "Bang goes my lift," he said, staring sadly after the car.

"Where's the London taxi?" said Nevada.

"That belongs to our dad. He only lets Declan drive it and only when there's a paying job."

"Are you Darra or Dermot?" I said.

"I'm Darra," he said, clearly offended. "We're not identical, you know."

"No, but there are so many of you," said Nevada, soothingly.

"I suppose so. But nobody has any trouble remembering who Declan is."

"That's because he's so rude and horrible."

"I suppose so." He looked at us as if searching for friendship and understanding, or at least support. "I wish they wouldn't fight, Declan and Julian. Julian's a really good manager and we won't get anywhere if we fight among ourselves. We've got to stick together and work hard if we're going to be a success. That's what Julian always says, and Julian's right. But Declan hates taking orders. From anyone."

"There's a surprise," said Nevada.

"He's always been like that, ever since we were little," said Darra. "But the band is our big chance and he mustn't spoil it."

"What's your band called?" said Nevada.

"The Trippy-Lits. Because our music is all trippy and lit up." He paused for a moment as if trying to remember something. "Oh, and because we're triplets." He looked at us beseechingly. "Do you think it's a good name?"

Before the ensuing silence grew too agonisingly long, I managed to say, "It's at least as good as Boyzone."

Darra's face lit up. "Do you really think so? They're the second most popular boy band after Take That and the twenty-ninth bestselling singles artists of all time in the UK. If we could be that successful, it would be amazing."

I agreed that it would indeed be amazing, but not out loud. Poor Darra. He looked around as if searching for something and then said, "I suppose I'll have to walk home."

"Can't you get a ride?" I said.

"It's all right. It's not far. I should have brought my bicycle."

Leaving Darra to his regrets, we started up the hillside steps, following in the wake of Julian, although I think we'll be forgiven for saying we were relieved there was no sign of him.

Instead, there was a young couple, or in any case two young people standing side by side, waiting for us halfway up, whom we didn't recognise. Or at least we didn't recognise them as members of the Noise Floor household.

But as we grew closer, we realised we did indeed know them. That it took us a moment or two to grasp this was not least down to the fact they were currently dressed like a butler and a maid from a 1920s English country manor house.

The guy I was startled to recognise as Rodney, our driver on the night of the rural rave. But now mysteriously minus his long, blond dreadlocks. The girl was none other than Cayley. She was minus the ruby in her nose. I didn't allow myself to speculate about her navel.

She was holding a tray on which there were drinks. He was holding a tray with canapés. "Good evening, sir and madam," they both said in unison.

"Hello Cayley, hello Rodney."

"It's Gordon actually, sir," said the "butler". As well as his dreadlocks, he had also lost his geezer accent and now sounded like someone in a Noël Coward play. "Please have an appetiser." He lifted the tray. "Homemade biscuits with bitter chocolate and brandy cream topping."

Enough said. We were both reaching for these when a voice above us shouted, "Wait."

It was a familiar, steely shouting of that word and we looked up to see Jacquetta hurrying down towards us. She looked a little odd in a pearl-grey evening dress and white high heels. She came tottering towards us, arriving somewhat out of breath. "Sorry," she said. "I'm not used to these heels and I have to be careful not to break my neck coming down those steps. But I'm glad I got here in time. I forgot to ask Gordon to warn you about the biscuits."

"Warn us?" I said.

"They contain hash oil," said Jacquetta, smiling proudly.

"Thank you for the heads up," I said. "I'll pass."

"Can I have two?" said Nevada. Jacquetta chuckled indulgently.

"Of course," she said. "But no more than two or you won't enjoy your dinner." She sounded for all the world like a fussing mother.

"Any reason I shouldn't have one of these?" I said, indicating the tray of drinks Cayley was patiently holding.

"Poppy is handling the drinks," said Jacquetta, "but I think I can safely say you will be all right. Now, if you'll excuse me, I'd better go back to keep an eye on dinner." She hurried back up the hill.

"Don't trip," called Nevada after her.

"I won't," she called back, then adding half-cryptically, "at least not on these steps." Then she laughed and disappeared into the darkness above.

"There you go, sir, madam," said Cayley as Nevada and I lifted the long-stemmed glasses from the tray. She did a nice but quite unnecessary little bobbing curtsy as we took our drinks. It was a good performance, but I sensed more than a little iciness radiating from Nevada towards her.

The drinks were fizzy and pink, with a blackberry bobbing in each of them. We sipped appreciatively as we started up the steps. The party had started. I glanced back at Cayley and Rodney, or rather Gordon. They were watching us and, when we reached a certain point, they began to follow us up. I assumed this was because, as good domestic servants, they weren't supposed to come too closely behind the guests.

Poppy was waiting for us at the top. She was wearing a loose-fitting dress that looked like something you might find on a South Pacific isle. It had a red-and-white floral pattern which verged on the psychedelic. "How are the drinks?" she said.

"Delicious," said Nevada, truthfully. "Champagne and crème de cassis?"

"Yes," said Poppy approvingly. "A Kir Royale."

"It's lovely," said Nevada. "But I hope you didn't use your best champagne."

"It's actually a supermarket champagne but, as it happens, it is a very good one, probably a little too good to mix. You're quite right."

"Is it the Co-op Les Pionniers?" said Nevada.

"Yes."

"The non-vintage?"

"Yes." Poppy was seriously impressed, but she hadn't heard anything yet.

"Did you know it's actually made for them by Piper-Heidsieck?" said Nevada.

"I did *not* know that," said Poppy, leaning closer towards her in fascination as she led us towards the house.

23: DESSERT

We were dining in the kitchen. I had not been in here before and I discovered it was a big, open space, only slightly smaller than the huge front room, and ran most of the length of the back of the house. Its rear wall was all glass, tall windows looking out on the back garden with a glass door set in the middle. The garden looked rather beautiful and moody and mysterious: dark green vegetation, with the swimming pool and the flying saucer brightly illuminated.

About half of this big room was the kitchen proper, equipped with the usual—or rather, very high-end—cooker and refrigerator, and counters and cupboards. The other half contained a large circular dining table, which was atmospherically lit by spotlights recessed in the ceiling above. The kitchen area was all in shadow to provide, as we were to discover, a sense of secrecy and surprise about the various dishes emanating from it.

The dining table really was large and could have seated considerably more than the seven people arrayed around it tonight. There was no tablecloth, revealing the natural wood surface, which was very handsome. Apparently, Poppy wanted to keep it that way because there were placemats and drinks coasters all over it—although Selena seemed to feel herself exempt from using these latter, as would become annoyingly clear as the evening wore on.

When Poppy brought us in, everyone else was already seated at the table. It was a little surprising to see Lambert there, looking natty in a moss-green cashmere hoodie and black cords. I'd half expected him to take off again and leave us all without the benefit of his company. It was even more surprising to see Julian at the table. After his shouting match with Declan, I was certain he'd be sulking in his bedroom, teenage-style. But here he was, sitting between Poppy and his mother.

This evening, Selena, rather impressively, was neither barefoot nor wearing green wellies. Like Jacquetta, she was in high heels. And an unbiased observer might have been forced to admit she had outgunned Nevada in the slinky little black dress department. Luckily for me, I was a biased observer.

Selena had a bottle of expensive-looking tequila at her elbow and made frequent use of it to provide refills for the large chunky glass in front of her, carefully positioned on the table so it fell neatly between the various coasters provided for her use. She struck me as being drunk but very much still in control.

As soon as we sat down, our butler and maid friends Gordon and Cayley bustled in and prepared to serve everyone. They'd obviously been lurking in wait for this moment.

"Lambert tells us you know your wines," said Jacquetta, leaning across the table towards Nevada.

"Well…" said Nevada modestly.

"She correctly identified the champagne in the cocktails," said Poppy.

Jacquetta made suitably impressed noises. While Poppy showed Nevada the various wines they'd sourced for our pleasure tonight, Jacquetta supervised the putative maid and butler in bringing the food dramatically out of the shadows in the kitchen. And Selena silently sipped her tequila.

It was clear Poppy was in charge of the drinks and Jacquetta was in charge of the food. Selena was in charge of the sullenness.

Dinner was outstanding. We started with a blue cheese and broccoli soup of velvety texture served with garlic rye bread croutons, homemade of course, and a swirl of lemon-infused olive oil floating on it. Accompanying this were more fresh-baked rolls, sourdough rather than ciabatta this time, served warm from a basket with a cloth over them, and supplemented by sweet white Italian butter.

"Don't fill up on the bread," said Nevada, cutting one of the rolls open and spreading butter on it. "No matter how good it is."

"Rookie error," I agreed.

The main course was salmon Wellington—fillets of salmon baked in a golden pastry shell with a soft melted filling of spinach and mozzarella—served on a bed of wild rice, mushrooms, purple chillies and pickled segments of blood orange. By the time we reached the third and fourth courses, an elaborate tropical fruit salad and a bafflingly big and varied selection of cheeses, all at the perfect point of ripeness, I was very glad indeed I hadn't filled up on the bread.

We only discussed business at one point during the meal, when we broached the subject of Lambert appearing as a celebrity guest at the Village of Vinyl festival in Nutalich.

"Is there any money in it?" said Lambert. "Not for me. I mean for the village."

"The vicar reckons they turned over more than a hundred grand cash last year, in beer sales alone," said Nevada.

Lambert whistled. Even Julian, listening in surly silence in the background, seemed impressed. In a surly, silent sort of way.

"Sure," said Lambert.

"Sure, meaning yes you'll take part as our guest of honour?" said Nevada eagerly.

Lambert chuckled. "Meaning exactly that. And gratis, of course. I don't need to be paid to support our local community." He looked at me. "And my friends."

"Well, here's to friendship," said Nevada, raising her glass. And we all toasted to that. Several times.

As Cayley and Gordon cleared away the plates and we braced ourselves for the onslaught of dessert, Lambert took out a small pipe and a lighter. The pipe was like an elegant, elongated golden teardrop. He slid its lid smoothly open with his thumb and said, "I hope nobody minds if I have a little smoke at this point."

"May I please be excused?" said Julian, rising from his chair. I thought it was astonishing he had asked permission and

I assumed this was a ritual hangover from childhood. Indeed, he sounded like a little boy rotely uttering a polite formula.

"No, you may not," snapped Selena. "Shut up and sit down."

Even more astonishingly, Julian obeyed.

Dessert was served, a rich but remarkably light lemon cream sprinkled with tiny lavender biscuits. And then we all sighed with relief.

Jacquetta rose from her chair and headed for the kitchen area. Cayley and Gordon moved to help her, but she waved them back. A moment later she emerged from the shadows wheeling a trolley. Oh shit, I thought. Not more food.

It wasn't just more food. It was more sweets. The trolley was big and it had two shelves on it, and both were crowded with pies, golden brown and covered with soft snow-white topping. I could smell their warm spiciness, but I really couldn't face another bite. And there on the trolley I could count no less than a dozen of these jokers.

"Pumpkin pie," announced Jacquetta.

"Oh, I'm sorry," said Nevada. "But I don't think I could eat another morsel."

I was relieved that she was taking one for the team, getting in first and sparing me the effort of declining.

"Oh, don't worry dear," said Jacquetta. "These aren't for you. They're for Poppy and me. And Selena."

Indeed, for the first time in the evening Selena seemed to have perked up and be taking a keen interest in proceedings. Julian rose from his seat now and left the kitchen without anyone saying anything or even looking at him.

We were all looking at the pies.

"Nice, soft pumpkin pies with lots of whipped cream in nice, soft foil pie plates," said Jacquetta. She looked around proudly.

It seemed odd about the foil pie plates, both the fact of their existence in this otherwise posh meal, and also the fact she'd bother to mention them. "For Selena and Poppy and me. And for Cayley."

Cayley, who had begun to collect the dirty dishes with Gordon now paused at the mention of her name and looked up. She was puzzled. And so was Gordon. And Nevada and I, for that matter.

Everybody else seemed to be in on some private joke.

"She's very pretty, isn't she?" said Jacquetta, looking at Cayley.

"She's *very* pretty," agreed Poppy.

"No I'm not," said Cayley, clearly embarrassed.

"She's very *young*," said Serena. "You're what, twelve years old?"

"No."

"No, not that old," agreed Selena. "Seven? Six?"

"I'm twenty-two," said Cayley, clearly stung.

"A lovely age," said Jacquetta. "Don't you agree, Poppy?"

"I do agree. I do."

Lambert was watching this situation, whatever it was, unfold with an immense benign detachment, as if none of it was anything to do with him.

"She's awfully pretty," said Jacquetta.

"Lambert does like them pretty," said Poppy, as though making the most commonplace of observations.

"And young," hissed Selena.

"She's going out with me," said Gordon hastily, stepping forward like an actor suddenly realising he's missed his cue. "Cayley is going out with me."

I noticed he didn't move towards her, though. And she didn't move towards him.

"He just told you to say that," said Poppy. She said it in a playful you're-a-naughty-boy kind of way.

"If you're going out with her, what's her birthday?" said Jacquetta. She sounded a lot less playful.

"I don't know," said Gordon. He looked helpless and out of his depth as the women began to throw questions at him.

"You don't know?" said Jacquetta.

"We've just started going out!"

"What's her middle name?" said Selena.

"Her middle name?"

"What colour are her eyes?" said Poppy. "No looking!"

Many a young man genuinely involved in a legit relationship might have had difficulty in answering some or all of these questions. Certainly Gordon would have been hard pressed to check his alleged girlfriend's eye colour because she had turned her back and was trying to quietly sneak out towards the living room.

Jacquetta had observed this and she said, "Cayley?" She said it in such a normal, sensible, conversational tone of voice that Cayley paused and turned around. As she did this, Jacquetta stepped to the trolley, picked up a pie and *threw* it.

She threw it with impressive accuracy, only missing catching Cayley full in the face because the girl jerked to the side at the last moment. Nevertheless, her cheek and ear and hair were spattered with cream and pumpkin-pie filling.

Not surprisingly, she turned and fled through the door to the sitting room.

Jacquetta grabbed two more pies and, one in each hand, went after her. Cayley was considerably younger and lighter on her feet, but Jacquetta was off in pursuit at an impressive clip.

"Mind you don't get any on the carpet," Poppy yelled after her as she went.

Selena rose from her chair, swiftly and gracefully and with remarkable steadiness for someone who'd put away as much tequila as she had. She went to the trolly and selected a pie and advanced towards us, holding it.

"As for you, you beautiful blue-eyed bitch…" she said, looking at Nevada. "You're next."

Now if this had been a threat of serious physical violence, I would have just stood clear and left Nevada to defend herself. No one could do it better. But in this case, since it was merely pie-related mayhem, I felt I had to intervene.

As Selena advanced with the pie, I moved between her and Nevada. "Out of the way," she snarled.

"No," I said.

"Now, Selena," said Poppy.

"She's next," announced Selena to the room at large, indicating Nevada with a grand and rather unsteady wave of the hand that wasn't holding the pie. It looked like the impact of the tequila was making itself felt after all. It has to be said, though, that the other hand—the one holding the pie—was rock-steady.

Both Nevada and Lambert, who were after all the real focal point of this confrontation, were watching with detached interest. In fact, Lambert refilled Nevada's wine glass.

"He'll be fucking her next," said Selena.

"Now, Selena," repeated Poppy.

"No, he won't," I said. "She's with me."

Selena stared at me for a long moment. Perhaps she saw something in my eyes or heard something in my voice, because she lowered the pie and turned away in disgust, kissing her teeth as she returned it to the trolley.

"Well, I think I'll join Jacquetta in the hunt," said Poppy, selecting one of the pies for herself. I realised that she must have been aware of what was brewing up with Selena and had stayed around until it looked like Nevada was safe; and I appreciated that.

Now, though, she hurried out into the sitting room with a pie of her own, to join the pursuit of Cayley. The pumpkin-pie pursuit.

Selena, for her part, returned to her seat and her tequila and her sullenness, which now manifested itself in silently glaring at Nevada. Finally, this must have become boring, even for someone who could single-mindedly bear a grudge like Selena. Because she suddenly spotted movement beyond the big windows at the back of the kitchen and said, "They're in the garden."

Evidently the thought of an outdoor pie hunt appealed to her more than an indoor one, because she now leapt to her feet again, retrieved her pie, kicked off her shoes and ran, barefoot and fleet as a deer, out the back door. Not bothering to close it behind her, of course.

Gordon watched her go. "They're not going to come after me with pies, are they?" he said.

"No," said Lambert. "You're a bloke and luckily I've never swung that way. Luckily for you, I mean. Why don't you help yourself to a drink, old chap?"

Gordon sank wearily and gratefully into the chair just vacated by Selena—apparently we weren't pretending to be domestic servants any more—and poured himself a large shot of her tequila. I had intended to ask him if he really was going out with Cayley but, judging by his utter lack of concern about her becoming pumpkin-pie prey, I already had my answer.

"Actually," said Lambert, "if you wouldn't mind terribly, Gordon, could you take that drink somewhere else?"

"Of course," said Gordon, rising politely from the table.

"I'd like to have a little chat with my friends here," said Lambert.

"Of course," repeated Gordon. He went out towards the sitting room with his tequila.

Lambert gave him a moment or two to make sure he was out of earshot and then he turned to us and smiled. "Thank you for coming here tonight."

"Our pleasure," said Nevada.

"The girls wanted to say thank you for everything you've done for us. And so did I."

"You're very welcome. I'm a little sad this job is over, though," said Nevada, apparently not ironically, as screaming and shouting came from the garden where the pie hunt continued.

"Oh, it isn't over," said Lambert. "In fact, I had another reason for inviting you here tonight," said Lambert. "I have a new job for you guys."

"Really?" said Nevada, perking up at the thought of further paid employment. "What's that?"

"Someone's trying to kill me and it would be really great if you could stop them."

24: DEATH THREAT

We heard the sound of the hunters coming back indoors; apparently they hadn't found Cayley outside and were going to search the house again. Lambert led us out into the garden to continue our conversation free of distractions. And pies.

We went out the back door of the kitchen, down some steps and onto the wide, dark lawn, heading towards the flying saucer, which was illuminated dramatically by the garden lights, though not as dramatically as the one we'd seen in the rave field.

I wondered if it was the same saucer or whether Lambert had two of them. Or perhaps more. But we'd already asked the one question we were allowed.

And right now there was something much more important for us to talk about.

"So, you know who Timothy Purshouse is?" said Lambert, pausing and turning back to look at me.

Immediately I was on full alert. I quickly reviewed my

options, working out what would be safe for me to know, and to tell him.

And what might be the opposite of safe.

"Sure," I said. "Showbiz journalist of the year." It felt strange to say this phrase because it had become a running gag. But now it was no longer funny. It would have been strange of me not to say it, though, if I thought Tim was still alive and well. Which is what I had to pretend. "He wrote a book about you."

"He certainly did," said Lambert.

"And he was helping us find you," said Nevada.

"I know, said Lambert.

There was a pause while this sank in and then I said, "So that's how you knew about us?"

Nevada had seen it, too. "He was feeding us information about you, and feeding you information about *us*?"

"Yes." Lambert smiled a tight little smile. "And he was getting paid by both sides—I assume you were paying him?"

"Oh yes," said Nevada.

"He tipped you off about us coming to the hotel in Wales?" I said.

Lambert shook his head. "No. He told me who you guys were, and that you were looking for me. Enough information so that I began to get interested in you, and decided to find out more about you. But he didn't warn me you were going to be in Aberystwyth."

"Why not?" said Nevada. And then she answered her own question. "Because if we caught up with you, we were going to pay him a finder's fee."

"Yes, that sounds like Tim," said Lambert.

"So," I said, choosing my words carefully, like a man treading through a minefield, "he was helping us to try and find you. And then suddenly he went silent."

"Yes, he would have done."

We had paused halfway towards the flying saucer while Lambert lit his pipe. He offered it to Nevada, but she shook her head. Lambert took a pull on it, as if for sustenance, then said, "Timothy Purshouse is dead."

Nevada and I didn't have to feign our shocked silence, because we didn't think anybody else knew this.

Anyone except the killer, of course.

I felt I had to ask the obvious question. "Why do you think that?"

"Because they found his body. Not far from here. In fact, it was Julian's friends who found him. You know, the boy band? The triplets?"

"We know them," said Nevada.

"They were out in the woods for a run and they stumbled across him. Apparently, somebody killed him and left him there."

It's hard to describe the sense of relief I felt, both that Tim's body had been found and that he had been identified. I don't know what else we could have done in the circumstances, but it had still been wrong of us to abandon him there in the woods like a piece of discarded furniture. I have no spiritual beliefs, but in some sense he now seemed more likely to be at rest.

All of which flashed through my mind as we stood

there, chatting with Lambert Ramkin. And all of which had to be concealed from him, at all costs.

On the other hand, this approach had to be balanced against the possibility that he was playing an elaborate game with us.

He might know all about us putting Tim in the woods.

He might have been responsible for planting the body in Tinkler's car.

And killing him, of course.

"Is that why you think your life is in danger?" said Nevada. "Because someone killed Tim Purshouse?"

"No, that just made it seem more immediate. Made me feel like I might be next. But I've been worried for quite a while. I've known that someone had it in for me. That's one reason I took off this time. Why I pulled a vanishing act. I didn't want to put my family in danger."

I noticed it was only one reason.

"How do you know someone has it in for you?" said Nevada.

"Because I've been receiving messages. Death threats."

"What form do these threats take?" said Nevada.

"Pretty nasty, explicit statements that the world would be a better place without me, and it was time I was dead and that they were going to do something about it."

"No, sorry," said Nevada, "I meant how were these messages sent?"

"Oh, sorry. They were emails."

"Do you have copies of them?"

"No," said Lambert. "I deleted them, though I suppose there's ways of un-deleting them."

"That's right. We have a colleague who can help with that," said Nevada.

This was true, though calling Tinkler a colleague made him sound a bit grand.

"I don't suppose you were able to trace the sender of the emails?" I said.

"Oh sure," said Lambert. His pipe glowed in the dark. "We traced them back to the website for my fan club."

"How many people have access to that?"

"It doesn't matter," said Lambert, "because it wasn't any of them. Someone hacked the website so they could relay their emails through it and we wouldn't be able to trace them back to their true source. Which means that all we know is that it's not someone at my fan club."

"Not necessarily," said Nevada. "It could be someone there, who did the hack to throw you off the scent."

Lambert chuckled. "Smart thinking. Twisted, but smart. I'm glad I hired you guys."

I wanted to say that he hadn't hired us yet, but I knew Nevada wouldn't approve, so instead I said, "You need to go to the police with this." I must admit I felt like an enormous hypocrite hearing these words come out of my mouth, considering everything that had happened when we found Tim's body.

"And how much of their resources do you think the police will be able to bring to bear on my little problem?" said Lambert.

Our silence indicated he had a point there.

"I want you guys to help me," he said.

Once again, I went through my set speech about not being a real detective, but this left Lambert as unmoved as my suggestion about the police. "You know me and you know my world," he said.

"We only met you the other day," I said.

"But you've been immersed in my world for quite a while, haven't you? And you're already involved with these other people."

"Which other people?" said Nevada.

Lambert nodded at me. "The ones who set him up at the Brixton concert."

"You think these are the same people who are threatening to kill you?"

"Yes. And who killed Tim. That's what I do think," said Lambert.

"But you have no way of knowing if that's the case," said Nevada.

"No, I don't," said Lambert. "But do you have any better candidates?"

"No," I said. I didn't add that we'd come to pretty much exactly the same conclusion ourselves.

Lambert sucked on his pipe, discovered it was dead and set about efficiently cleaning it, refilling it and finally relighting it. "Another thing," he said, starting to walk slowly as he worked on his pipe.

We followed him.

"Since, like I said, you're already involved with these people," said Lambert, "they might be a threat to you as well."

"They might well be," said Nevada.

"So it would also be to your advantage to identify them."

"Okay," I said. "You don't need to sell us on the job. We'll do everything we can to help."

He smiled at me as he got his pipe going and exhaled smoke. "Looks like you are a detective after all."

"I don't know about that but, if your life is in danger, Nevada can help you."

"Help me how?"

"By providing security," said Nevada.

"Really?" Lambert sounded intrigued and pleased rather than sceptical.

"She's had special forces training," I said. This was something I'd only found out relatively recently myself and I was still absurdly proud of the fact.

"Informal training," said Nevada modestly. "By someone who was ex-SAS."

We had stopped walking and were now standing under the flying saucer.

Lambert nodded at the house. "Sorry about the pie hunt, by the way," he said.

"Nothing to apologise for," said Nevada. "Once Selena was dissuaded from chucking one at me, I was able to relax and enjoy it. It's a fine spectator sport."

"It's something Jac invented," said Lambert. "It's an outlet, a way of dealing with aggression and hostility and negative feelings. Like she said when she dreamed it up, 'Men throw punches, women throw pies.'" His voice grew warm and fond. "I think Jacquetta's a genius. An intuitive genius. We're so lucky to have her creative spirit. You need strategies like that in a big family. The cathartic custard cream."

Nevada, who likes a bit of alliteration, said, "Or, in this case, the purifying pumpkin pie."

Lambert nodded, grinning. "It's sort of non-violent violence. Nobody gets hurt and afterwards everybody feels better."

"Except perhaps Cayley," I said.

"It's very unfair on Cayley," agreed Lambert. "Since, despite what the women think, there's absolutely nothing between us."

"Really?" said Nevada, in an uninflected way that spoke volumes.

"Yes, really," said Lambert.

And oddly enough, I believed him.

"But there's nothing between her and Gordon either," said Nevada.

"No." Lambert sighed. "I asked him to enact that pretence to stave off trouble. Because I saw it coming. But he didn't do a very good job of pretending to be her boyfriend."

"No, he didn't," I said. He'd been a lot more convincing with Lilith. Maybe he liked her better than Cayley. Maybe she really was his girlfriend.

"A very unconvincing performance," said Lambert. "Hard to believe he was trained at RADA."

"Seriously?" said Nevada.

"Oh yes," said Lambert, puffing on his pipe. "Whereas Cayley is just a natural talent."

Since we'd moved on from talking about matters of life and death, I felt I could ask him. "Do you have more than one of these?" I said. I was leaning on the ladder attached to the alien space vehicle and looking up at its bulk looming above us.

"Just this one and one other," said Lambert.

"The one that was in the rave in the field," said Nevada.

Lambert didn't say yes, but he didn't say no, either.

"Were you inside that one?" she said. "Playing the music?"

He smiled at us. "What do you think?"

"Could we have a look inside this one?" said Nevada.

Lambert glanced around at the big dark garden and then at the brightly lit house. Somewhere in there his three women were on the hunt for someone who was supposedly his fourth, and therefore surplus to requirements. "I'd rather you didn't just at the moment. You see, people get used to this being purely decorative and tend to forget that someone can go inside... and hide." He winked at us. "In fact, it might be a thought to move away from here before anyone sees us and suddenly gets a bright idea."

I walked with him over towards the swimming pool. Nevada followed us a moment or two later after apparently making a phone call while standing under the UFO. In any case, I heard her voice, briefly and quietly, in the night.

There were wicker chairs on the tiled fringe of the pool and we all sat down in them. Lambert told us how he'd passed his time while he'd been on the run—"on the Lamb", as Nevada would later put it. He spoke about this in a fond nostalgic way, as if it had all been a long time ago.

Essentially, when he wasn't avidly crate digging (an activity I could sympathise with), he'd been partying and crashing with old friends. "And some new ones," he said. As well as playing private gigs in a well-established network of underground clubs.

"And some new ones," said Lambert again. "I actually opened some new clubs. The culture is starting to thrive again, like the heyday of Spiral Tribe. Back then, if you wanted to set up a rave club, all you needed was a basement, some black paint, some ultraviolet paint and a strobe. And a rig, of course. That's the sound system. Oh, and lots of drugs."

And thus we passed the time, chatting casually while we waited for our ride to take us home.

"Fun evening?" said Agatha, as we climbed into the back of her car.

"We couldn't begin to tell you," I said.

"I told you they'd be enlisted in an orgy," said Tinkler, who had come along for the ride and was sitting in the front with Agatha.

"He did tell me that," said Agatha. "And wasted a considerable portion of his youth trying to work out how many possibilities that would make on the erotic Rubik's cube." She started the engine and released the handbrake.

"Hang on a moment," said Nevada.

"What?" said Agatha.

"Just wait here for a second." Nevada opened her window and whistled.

In this case the whistle didn't summon a gigantic owl, but a figure did emerge from the shadows of the garage and ran towards us. The satanic red glow of our tail lights revealed it to be Cayley.

Nevada opened the door and she scrambled in beside us, bringing a smell of cinnamon and other pumpkin-pie spices into the car with her.

"Extra passenger," said Nevada.

"No problem," said a bemused Agatha.

"Thank you," said Cayley.

"I'm Jordon and this is Agatha," said Tinkler.

"Hello Jordon, hello Agatha," said Cayley.

"Here," said Nevada, handing her a damp hand towel, pinched from our hosts' bathroom, which we would have to remember to return. As Nevada helped Cayley clean her hair with it, I felt a perfectly understandable tingle of déjà vu.

We drove through the gates and headed home.

This time Agatha didn't drive us past the woods, but it didn't matter anyway, because Tim Purshouse was no longer lying there, abandoned and alone.

25: COMMAND AND CONTROL

"Okay," said Tinkler. "What we're talking about is called a command and control attack, also known as a C&C or C2 attack."

He was being a little didactic, but I suppose that was inevitable if you give someone control of the screen during a meeting and they start showing you diagrams.

Plus, computers were Tinkler's special area of interest. After vinyl and drugs and pornography. And Agatha.

The diagram he was currently showing us had three headings: *Phishing*, *Social Engineering* and *Malvertising*.

"Malvertising," said Nevada. "Is that really a word?"

"Afraid so," said Tinkler.

"Christ, I'd only just resigned myself to phishing spelled with a 'p' and an 'h'."

"Anyway," said Tinkler, "the upshot is, someone got into the machine or the network at the Imperium Dart website and effectively made it their zombie. That way they could, for example, send messages—in this case, death threats to Lambert—and they could only be traced back there. Cute, huh?"

"Is there any way you can trace the real culprits?" said Nevada.

"No, sorry," said Tinkler. "But what we can do is find out what other activity they might have used the zombie system for. They will have left footprints there."

We'd already put Tinkler in touch with the people at Lambert's website, so we left him to look for footprints and get back to us.

That night we had Agatha over for dinner but, for once, Tinkler didn't join us. This was understandable enough because Agatha had a date for the evening.

And it was Horatio, his bête noire.

Horatio was a big guy, affable but quiet with long curly hair and a flourishing, curly beard. He was wearing jeans and a leather jacket that he kept on during our meal, which was a bit weird. He was also wearing rather a lot of aftershave. Rather too much for me. And also for Nevada, judging by the quick, sardonic look she shot me, accompanied by a wry wrinkling of her nose.

But he did manage to carry off that beard with conviction and panache, which would have flummoxed most men.

Horatio declined any wine when we poured it out. But since he was driving, this was a point in his favour. Agatha was able to drink as much as she liked, which was unusual, and she became notably animated and talkative. And she could hardly keep her eyes off Horatio.

She was clearly smitten, and it was kind of sweet.

But Tinkler might have been pleased to know that he featured heavily in our conversation that evening. "After I dropped you guys off," said Agatha, "I gave him and Cayley rides home."

"That was nice of you," said Nevada.

"Oh, Lambert's paying for it all," said Agatha, apparently eager to disavow any suggestion of altruism. "But the point is Tinkler rode in the back with Cayley."

"Really?" said Nevada.

"Yes, he moved to the back seat when you guys got out and they started chatting. She seemed quite charmed by the attention."

"You're sure this is Tinkler we're talking about here?"

"Yes. And what's more, he got Cayley's phone number."

"He was probably just attracted by the whipped cream in her hair," said Nevada.

"The fatal allure of pumpkin pie," I said.

"The fatal allure of pumpkin-pie residue," said Nevada. "But you say she actually gave him her number?"

"Yup," said Agatha.

"Well, she probably wasn't thinking clearly," said Nevada. "After all, she was in an emotionally fragile state. She was on pie-fight rebound."

We all laughed, Horatio included. He was doing his best to join in. But it was such a forced and phony laugh that it made us realise this couldn't be easy for the poor guy, trying to fit in with a trio of old friends who had their long-established rituals and jokes and codes and signals.

So we made more of an effort to include him.

Unfortunately, the only topic of conversation that seemed to spark any enthusiasm in good old Horatio was cars. And although Agatha shared his passion in this area, she was considerate enough to know that it bored us silly. So she steered the conversation, as it were, on to other topics.

Without much success, it must be said.

For a while it looked like films and film-making might be a fruitful area. After all, Horatio had worked on a lot of movies, including ones we would have been eager to hear about. From the horse's mouth, in this case.

But he wasn't very forthcoming.

It wasn't that he'd signed a non-disclosure agreement or anything like that, it was just that Horatio clearly took no interest in the directors, the cast or the scenarios of these films. All he had to offer was gossip concerning the stunt teams—rather a niche topic if you didn't know any of the personalities involved—and strong and detailed opinions about his particular passion: the relative merits of the catering on the various projects.

You might have hoped that the car chase filmed in Birmingham for Spielberg's *Ready Player One* would have yielded a more interesting focus for anecdotes than the pasta salad on offer at the craft service table.

But you would have hoped in vain.

Things really took a wrong turn, though, when we got onto the subject of the Village of Vinyl weekend in Nutalich, which was looming imminently. Suddenly Horatio began to take an animated interest in the conversation.

"You mean Stinky Stanmer's Village of Vinyl?" he said.

If Horatio was surprised by the sudden and total silence that now fell on our conversation, he gamely tried not to show it.

Choosing her words carefully, Nevada said, "Stinky Stanmer is doing a Village of Vinyl event?"

"Yes," said Horatio cheerfully. It was clear that to him this was a good thing.

"Where is he doing it?" said Nevada.

"I told you," said Horatio, exuding good-natured patience. "Nutalich."

"*When* is he doing it?" said Nevada.

"That weekend you're talking about," said Horatio. "Here, look." He showed us his phone.

It was our website, or what had been our website, to promote the event. Except now all the Vinyl Detective branding was gone and had been replaced by, yes, Stinky Stanmer. We played the promotional video and now, instead of the one featuring me, which had been on there earlier, or the one Nevada had recorded as an alternative, here was a clip featuring Stinky, exuding smarm and speaking in his most matey voice.

"Why should booklovers have all the fun?" said Stinky. "I got to thinking…" and then he proceeded with the spiel we had written, naturally minus Agatha and her URL.

"Isn't he great?" said Horatio, apparently unaware of the appalled expressions on the faces of the other three people in the room.

* * *

I went out into the garden with my own phone and, once I stopped trembling with rage, I phoned up Gerald Blanchflower, everybody's favourite vicar. At least until recently. "I'm so sorry," he said when I got through to him. "I meant to forewarn you. I didn't think the new website had gone live yet."

"Well, it has," I said.

"I hope you understand," he said. "Stinky Stanmer is such a big name. We consider ourselves very lucky to have him associated with our event. We feel he'll really bring in the punters and raise our profile." He went on like this for a while, but I had stopped taking it in.

Luckily Nevada came out and joined me at that point, took one look at my face and then took the phone from me. She finished talking with Dr Blanchflower, and was at her most friendly and charming. There was very little charming and friendly about the expression on her face when she hung up, though.

"That vile fucker," she said.

"Stinky or the vicar?"

"Both of them. No, I don't mean that. It's not really Gerry's fault. He's just been used by Stinky like so many others in the past. And it makes sense from his point of view. Stinky Stanmer being such a big name, as he said about seven times." Nevada looked at me. "Are you thinking about cancelling the weekend?"

"We can't cancel it, it's out of our hands."

"I mean us not attending," said Nevada. "You and me."

"I must admit that was my first thought," I said. "But it would just be childish. We've gone to all this trouble to set things up. Walking away would be like handing a total victory to Stinky."

"And we wouldn't be able to make any sales," said Nevada.

"No," I said. "And it looks like people will be selling a lot of vinyl that weekend. I'd just be cutting off my nose to spite my face."

"And it's such a nice nose," said Nevada, kissing me. "And such a nice face."

I sighed, a man defeated but counting his blessings, including the woman in my arms. "Who knows, we might even sell more vinyl because of Stinky's participation," I said.

"Don't be too angry at Gerry," said Nevada.

"I'm not," I said. "He doesn't know anything about our long history with Mr Stanmer."

When we went back inside, we discovered that Agatha had been filling Horatio in on exactly that history. "And Stinky keeps stealing his ideas," she concluded, nodding at me.

"That's terrible," said Horatio, in the voice of a man who clearly didn't believe a word of it, but wasn't very good at lying. Reading between the lines, he was a huge Stinky Stanmer fan and didn't think his hero needed to steal ideas from anybody.

Least of all me.

Not too surprisingly, our little party broke up soon after that. We walked Agatha and Horatio out to her car. Agatha was constantly changing cars and this sporty little green one was new, or at least new to her. Different from last time, anyway.

After we said our goodbyes and they drove off, Nevada, who had been briefed by Agatha, told me it was a Renault Clio Sport 200. "A classic 'hot hatch' beloved of guess who?"

"Who?" I said.

"Stunt drivers in the movies. Apparently the six-speed manual transmission makes for an excellent throttle response."

"I'd like to throttle Stinky," I said. "And see what his response is."

Nevada took my arm. "Of course you would. But let's not talk about that anymore. Don't let Stinky Stanmer blight any more of our evening than he already has."

"Okay."

"Now, do you see what I'm getting at with the hot hatch? I just love that expression, by the way."

I said, "If I was Tinkler, I'd say that Agatha was using her hot hatch to please Horatio."

"Well done," said Nevada. "It's almost like he's here. And yes, full marks. She's deliberately acquired a car which is a favourite for movie stunt drivers. It's obvious she got it to impress him."

"A fact he doesn't seem to have even registered," I said.

"Well, I don't think old Horatio is the sharpest tool in the box where women are concerned," said Nevada.

"Witness the fact that he was dating the Green Wellie Nympho," I said.

"It looks as if our Agatha has well and truly put the kibosh on that, though," said Nevada, with some satisfaction. "Hurray for the home team."

It was a beautiful evening, but it was starting to get cold, so we went back inside.

We might have been forgiven for thinking we'd reached peak bad news that evening with the revelation of Stinky's takeover of the Village of Vinyl. But we were hardly back in the door when the phone rang.

It was Tinkler.

"Okay," he said. "I've made some progress and I've found out what else the bad guys were using the Imperium Dart system for."

"All right," I said.

"You won't like it."

"Okay tell us." I held the phone so Nevada could also hear.

"They've been shopping on the dark web," said Tinkler.

"For drugs?" I said.

"No."

"Malware?" said Nevada.

"No."

"What then?"

"Automatic weapons," said Tinkler.

26: VILLAGE OF VINYL

Tinkler's news about the guns changed everything. We arranged a video call with Lambert to discuss it. Nevada said, "What we're talking about here are ex-Soviet military assault rifles which can shoot a hundred rounds a minute. With firepower like that the threat has just escalated exponentially. I can't guarantee your safety. I'm not sure the army, navy and air force could guarantee your safety."

"So, what do I do?" said Lambert.

"Like I told you, get out of the country. Book a holiday. Or rather, don't book it. Stick a pin in a map, choose a tropical paradise, don't tell anyone where you're going and just go."

"And never come back?" Lambert's eyebrows were raised in polite but sarcastic enquiry.

"Of course not. Just stay away until we can properly assess the threat and hopefully get a handle on who is behind it. But the possibility of those weapons changes the whole equation. The safest and smartest thing is for you to just leave for parts unknown."

Lambert took a deep breath. "Okay," he said. "If you say so."

"I say so."

"I'll do it. But it's going to take a while for Jacquetta and Poppy and Selena to clear the decks and be ready to go with me."

"Well, then don't take them with you. Leave and have them follow when ready."

Lambert gave a humourless little chuckle. "No chance. If I did that, they'd all just think I'd taken off again. You know, flown the coop. And I've only just come home."

"Explain the situation to them."

"I have, or at least I've tried. But no one entirely believes me. They think I'm either dramatising to get attention or laying the groundwork for another disappearing act. In short, they don't really trust me, and I must confess I can't entirely blame them, based on my behaviour in the past." He looked at Nevada. "And the fact that I've hired you as my personal bodyguard has already not gone down very well."

"Why not?

"Because of the way you look," said Lambert.

"What do you want me to do?" said Nevada. "Put a paper bag over my head? Listen, you are entirely at liberty to hire someone else. In fact, I strongly urge you to do so."

"No," said Lambert. "I'm happy with you guys. And I'll do what you say. I just need a little time."

"Okay," said Nevada. She didn't sound entirely satisfied with this promise.

"How many assault rifles, by the way?" said Lambert. "When they were shopping on the dark web, how many guns were they shopping for?"

"Six."

"Then at least we know there's six of them," said Lambert.

"Not necessarily," said Nevada. "Tinkler says there was a special deal if you bought six. Substantial savings to be had."

Lambert laughed. "So not only are these people prospective killers, but they're thrifty."

"I'm glad you think this is funny."

"What else can I do but laugh?"

"Get the hell out of Dodge," said Nevada. She was starting to become seriously angry.

"I will," said Lambert. He had picked up on Nevada's anger and he seemed genuinely chastened. "Just as soon as I can. Just give me a few days…"

A few days, however, would put us on the other side of the Village of Vinyl.

"So Lambert's going to attend?" I said.

"Yes," said Nevada. "At least he can still be guest of honour."

"I thought that was Stinky," I said. "Or at least, Stinky will think that's Stinky." I looked at her. "Listen," I said. "I really don't like this."

She shrugged. "Lambert is taking the threat seriously and he's moving as fast as he can, by Lambert standards.

Give him just a bit of time, like he says, and then he'll be flying off into the sunset and won't be our problem anymore." She could see I still looked sceptical. "Love," she said, "we only need to get through the next few days. And whenever Lambert's conceivably at risk, I'll stick to him like glue."

"Don't stick so close that you get between him and any gunfire," I said. "You don't have to take a bullet for him. You're not the secret service and he's not the president."

She took my hand. "With a bit of luck there won't even be any gunfire."

"With a bit of luck?"

"Tinkler can't even confirm they actually bought the weapons. They might just have been…"

"Window shopping?"

"Yes."

When Saturday morning dawned on the big weekend, Agatha arrived bright and early to drive us down to Nutalich, the Village of Vinyl.

"No Tinkler?" she said.

"He can't come, he's working."

"Uh huh," said Agatha, expressionless.

"In fact, he's doing some very important work for us," said Nevada. While all this was true enough, Tinkler could easily have found time to join us at the Village of Vinyl. The fact that he didn't want to was entirely down to the presence of Horatio.

Tinkler had never previously been particularly bothered by Agatha's boyfriends. Indeed, he'd regarded Albert the gastropub guy, for example, with something approaching affectionate contempt.

But Horatio, and Agatha's feelings for him, were clearly different. And even Tinkler sensed this. Or, to be more accurate, especially Tinkler sensed this.

I'd tried to talk him into coming and he'd said, "Look, I know she's with him, but I don't have to *see* her with him." And that, it seems, was that.

But right now, Agatha appeared uncharacteristically hesitant, apologetic even, concerning Horatio. "He's going to be coming to Kent with us," she said, in the manner of someone getting a piece of bad news out of the way.

"No problem," said Nevada.

"I thought we were going to meet him down there," said Agatha. "But, you see, he stayed overnight with me last night."

"Wait," said Nevada. "You guys aren't having sex outside of wedlock, are you? I'm afraid our friendship is at an end."

Agatha relaxed a bit and smiled. "I was just concerned because there won't be as much room in the car for all those lovely boxes of vinyl."

It was true that with Horatio in the car it was a tight fit for my crates of records. But a richer potential source of trouble grew evident when we came out of the house and found Horatio had moved over from the passenger seat to the driver's seat. Of Agatha's car.

Agatha wasn't happy about this, and she tried to get him

out by asking him to help load the boxes of records. But Horatio wasn't going to be tricked so easily into surrendering his position. He just smiled a lazy smile and stayed where he was, saying, "I'll unload everything when we get there."

In the end Agatha reluctantly yielded and took the passenger seat beside him after we'd packed the car, filling the small boot to capacity and ending up with just two crates in the back seat lodged between Nevada and myself.

It was very odd to be in a vehicle with Agatha and have somebody else at the steering wheel.

We made record time down to Kent, though.

Horatio drove more aggressively than Agatha, and faster. Indeed, a little faster than I was entirely comfortable with. But he clearly knew what he was doing and I never felt unsafe. Also, he was remarkably aftershave-free, which, on a fairly long journey in a fairly small car, was thankful. We suspected Agatha had had a word with him on the fragrance front, and we were duly grateful.

Our first stop was to drop Nevada at Noise Floor. She would then accompany Lambert to Nutalich in her capacity as his personal security adviser, aka bodyguard. Parking for cars in Nutalich would be at a premium this weekend with the—hopefully—massive crowd of cashed-up visitors arriving, so the original plan had been for bodyguard and client to book a ride to bring them to us. But Agatha had talked Nevada out of this.

"For Christ's sake, don't do that. You might get Declan. I'll come back and collect you after I drop off the boys and the records."

So that was the plan. Which meant at least Nevada wasn't there to witness my first humiliation of the day. It had been agreed I would have a table to sell my wares in the village hall, which was a prime location thanks to the presence of other high-profile sellers there, and its proximity to several pubs. All in all, the village hall was virtually guaranteed to provide a torrential flow of customers.

When Agatha and Horatio and I arrived in Nutalich, Horatio still at the wheel, of course, we pulled up outside the hall and prepared to unload. But I had hardly climbed out of the car when an all-too-familiar voice hailed me. "Hey, cuz, what's going on?"

What he actually said was more like, "Ay, cuz, wagwan?" Not that this made it any more palatable.

I braced myself and turned to see Stinky Stanmer standing there. His dirty blond hair was disarrayed and spiky in the way that only a very expensive haircut could achieve. His bulging eyes gleamed with simple-minded malice and his smile—a sincere enough smile, given he was indulging in the aforementioned simple-minded malice—revealed perfect teeth.

He was wearing a black blazer with flowers embroidered on the lapels in silver thread, over a T-shirt that featured an Andy Warhol Campbell's soup tin. His jeans were very baggy and ripped at the knees, and his Timberland boots had the laces untied and flopping around as he walked. Possibly he had yet to master the art of tying them.

Stinky approached me, beaming.

"Nebraska not with you, then? Finally left you, has she? Never mind, bruv. Bound to happen with a good-ass peng baby-gal like that. Be sure and give her my phone number."

"Nevada," I said patiently, "is on her way. She's escorting Imperium Dart."

"Oh yeah! Dart. He and me are collaborating on a project."

"You know him, do you?" I said.

"Never met him, fam, never met him. But we'll be spending the day together." He nodded towards the village hall. "And it will be our chance to bond." Then he turned to the car where Agatha and Horatio were standing, watching our conversation with two rather different kinds of bemusement. "Wagwan, Clean Head?" said Stinky.

"Still using up good air, then, Stinky?" said Agatha.

"Ha ha, yes, nice one," said Stinky. Then, to Horatio, "Yes, mate?"

Horatio, it's horrible to report, was rather starstruck. He held out his phone and asked, shyly, "Could I get a selfie please, Mr Stanmer?"

"A selfie with Stinky? Why yes, mate. And for any friend of my friends here, no charge."

"Thank you," said Horatio, with fervent sincerity. I turned away from the dispiriting spectacle and caught Agatha looking at me with a what-can-you-do expression of shared despair and disgust.

We opened the hatchback and were about to unload the crates of records when the Reverend Gerald Blanchflower came hurrying over to us.

"I'm so glad I caught you," said Gerry. "There's been a slight change of plan."

I immediately scented catastrophe. "How slight?" I said.

"I'm afraid you no longer have a table at the village hall."

"Why not?" I said, trying my best to keep my cool because I didn't want to start screaming at a member of the clergy in the presence of one of my oldest friends and her new boyfriend, even if he was preoccupied with getting his picture taken with my personal nemesis.

"Well," said Gerry, glancing in the direction of that nemesis, "Stinky Stanmer, you see…"

"I do see," I said.

"He needs a table to sign his autographs."

"Of course he does."

"And it was decided that the village hall…"

"Naturally," I said.

"But we have found a location for you somewhere else," said Gerry eagerly.

"Oh good, where?"

"You're in the duck shed."

"The what?"

"The little shed by the duck pond. It's very nice, and very central. You'll get lots of customers there."

Gerry then proceeded to give directions to Horatio, who had finished having his selfies taken and was now profusely thanking Stinky and putting his phone away like a sacred artefact.

Stinky stood there watching us, grinning and waving, as we drove away.

Towards the duck shed.

I leaned back in my seat, my arm draped over a crate of vinyl that I probably wouldn't be able to sell, and wondered why I'd bothered to get out of bed this morning. "Stinky planned this," I said. And then immediately wished I hadn't because I caught starstruck Horatio giving Agatha a just-humour-the-paranoid-nutcase look.

The little shed by the duck pond was apparently where you stored all the necessities for duck pond maintenance. What exactly these were was hard to say because someone had thoughtfully cleared them out to make room for me. It was a concrete-floored, wood-sided rectangle painted blue. with a window and door in the rear and large, vertically folding wooden doors at the front like an old-fashioned garage. The front doors faced the road, presumably to allow easy loading of supplies, and the back door faced the village green with the pond in it. There was a long fluorescent tube hanging from the ceiling which would have provided ample light if we'd needed it. But on this bright, sunny summer morning there was plenty of daylight coming in from the window at the back of the shed and the half-open folding doors at the front.

Besides being well lit, the place was clean and apparently recently swept, and whatever thoughtful person—I suspected a contrite Gerry or a minion of his—had cleaned it for me and had also provided two folding tables and half a dozen folding chairs. My spirits lifted a little as I looked around; I could work with this.

Horatio was as good as his word. He unloaded my crates from the car swiftly and efficiently, lifting them with the casualness of a man who took his considerable strength for granted. He set them on the pavement beside the parked car and then, after I set up the tables, transferred them inside and put each crate where I directed him, waiting patiently and holding them instead of setting them down while I made up my mind. One of the tables had a wonky leg, promising potential collapse, so crates had to be positioned on it carefully. But otherwise, everything was fine.

And, not to be outdone in the macho crate-carrying stakes, I brought some in myself. With Agatha helping too, we were finished in very few minutes indeed.

Then Agatha climbed into the driver's seat of her little green Clio Sport 200, back in control at last and giving Horatio a dirty look which merely seemed to amuse him, and sped off to collect Nevada and our client.

"If you don't need me for anything else," said Horatio, "I'll go and have a wander around."

"No, that's fine," I said.

"See you later."

I'd hardly finished setting up when I got my first customer of the day—a soft-spoken, middle-aged fellow who clearly knew his jazz. I sold him a slew of British Decca and RCA issues of classic US hard bop of the 1950s. He was delighted with his haul, and well he should have been. They were immaculate pressings of great music. They were not, however, the American originals, which had been issued on labels like Atlantic. I was in the process of acquiring those and getting rid of these—I'd fallen under the sway of Tinkler's doctrine of the original pressing.

The simple truth was that these always sounded better.

But my buyer was very happy, filling two sturdy Vinyl Detective-branded tote bags (ordered by my true love for just this occasion) with his purchases and handing over a hefty sum in cash. I also had a gadget for swiping credit cards, but it would turn out today that everybody was carrying, and spending, cash, having been encouraged to do so by the village council and their army of beer vendors, who were apparently allergic to paying income tax.

Having made my first sale of the day, and a substantial one at that, my mood was on an upwards trajectory. Things improved still further when the phone rang and I saw it was Nevada. "We heard about the backstabbing concerning the village hall," she said. "I'm so sorry, love."

"No actually, it's fine here," I said, sitting behind my table full of vinyl and inspecting my small domain. "And I've already made a good sale."

"Brilliant," said Nevada. "Well, we'll come down and join you as soon as Lambert and I are finished here. He's absolutely pulverising Stinky in terms of autograph sales, by the way." My darling was nothing if not competitive.

"Sales?" I said. "I thought Lambert was appearing free of charge."

"All proceeds go to an environmental charity," said Nevada. "Unlike Stinky, where all the proceeds go to Stinky."

"Has Stinky tried to ingratiate himself with Lambert yet?"

"It was wonderful. When he introduced himself, Lambert pretended he'd never heard of him. In fact, it turned out he wasn't pretending. He really had never heard of him. Stinky was crushed."

"Has he brought Röd and Röd with him?" I said. Röd and Röd were Stinky's own bodyguards, a matched pair of Swedish paramilitary types.

"He's given them the weekend off. He surmised the poor blokes would be bored silly in a little Kentish village."

"So, not only did he draw a blank with Lambert, now he's got bodyguard envy," I said, with some satisfaction.

"Ha! Yes," said Nevada. "See you soon."

She blew me a kiss and I put my phone away, as some more customers appeared through the duck shed door. While they were digging through my crates, Agatha came in.

"Mind if I join you?"

"No," I said. I was pleased to see her. "Pull up a chair. You don't want to hang out with Horatio?"

"Nope." She didn't say any more on that subject and I didn't ask any further questions. "I had to park on the other side of the green," she said, pointing in the direction of the back door of the duck shed. "But I'll move around to this side later in the day, when there's room to park. So we don't have too far to carry your crates."

"With a bit of luck," I said, "later in the day most of these crates will be empty."

Then, as if to support this happy theory, we proceeded to get quite busy. And Agatha proved more than useful, taking cash and making change. We enjoyed surge after surge of customers, and my crates began to empty. I rotated some stock off the floor and onto the tables with Agatha's help.

"Careful with that table, it's got a dodgy leg. Put the crates at the other end."

"Right you are," said Agatha.

After a while Horatio came in and joined us. He didn't take part in any of the selling, which was fine with me, and just sat quietly looking at his phone. Which seemed fine with Agatha. We stayed busy and I congratulated myself on being a grown-up and not bailing on this event just because Stinky had hijacked it.

Indeed, if other people were enjoying sales like mine, it was going to a very lucrative weekend of vinyl retail. Not to mention all the beer peddling we were providing a cover for.

Then Nevada and Lambert turned up, both looking cheerful and lively. The autograph session had finished and I realised it was late afternoon already. There's nothing like being busy selling vinyl to make the time fly.

"You've done well," said Nevada, inspecting our much-diminished stock.

"You're just in time to help swap the table crates with the one from the floor," said Agatha, my trusty sidekick and by now seasoned vinyl retailer. "Careful with that table, it's got a dodgy leg. Put the crates at the other end."

"Roger that," said Nevada cheerfully.

Meanwhile Lambert had taken a chair beside Horatio. They seemed to know each other and were soon chatting congenially. Perhaps they had a lot in common. For instance, Selena.

More customers arrived and Nevada contentedly counted our take while Agatha and I sold records. It was one of those low-key happy moments that life sometimes provides, here on a fine summer day selling vinyl like crazy in the company of people dear to me. I was just sorry Tinkler wasn't here.

That was when the first of the strange things started to happen.

The peaceful air was split by the wild, angry blaring of car horns. It was a sound more suited to central London in rush hour than this sleepy village on a Saturday afternoon. And it went on for a ridiculous length of time before giving way to a somehow tense silence.

Then we heard, of all things, a chainsaw. It was coming from a different direction to the car horns, the other side of the village.

It was a savage, aggressive sound. And again, inimical to our surroundings.

By this time, we were all exchanging quizzical looks.

Then the chainsaw stopped and was replaced by more car horns, coming from the same direction.

"I'm going to see what the hell's happening," said Agatha.

"Me too," said Horatio, clearly happy to have something to do. He was the kind of guy who needed to be doing something. They both went out of the duck shed towards the bright daylight.

"I kind of fancy going to take a look myself," said Lambert.

"No," said Nevada. "You stay in here with me."

"Fair enough," said Lambert.

Customers had stopped coming in and, after those odd bursts of clamour, silence seemed to have fallen over the village. Time passed. I began to feel a certain irrational tension and even what might be described as fear. "How long has Agatha been gone?" I said.

"You're right," said Nevada. "Let's give her a call." She took out her phone but, before she could use it, my own phone rang.

It wasn't Agatha. It was Hughie.

"Hello," he said. "Well, I made the enquiries you wanted. It wasn't easy, but I worked out who bought all those pills that were planted on you."

I was staring at Lambert Ramkin, sitting against the wall of the duck shed, looking back at me with benign bemusement in his eyes. My chest was suddenly hollow. "Who was it?" I said, dreading the answer.

"Well, you were close. It wasn't Lambert, but it was his son Julian. Hello? Are you there?"

"Yes, yes," I said. "Thank you. I can't talk now, but thanks."

"No problem. Be well." He hung up.

"Was that Agatha?" said Nevada.

"No, Hughie."

Nevada cursed and took out her phone again.

But just then Agatha came back into the shed, followed a moment later by Horatio, who said, "Some idiot's jammed a van in the middle of the bridge. No one can get in or out that way." He was relaxed, jovial, full of contempt for the sort of idiot who could get his van stuck in the middle of a bridge.

Agatha was far from relaxed or jovial, especially after she heard what Horatio had to say. "The road's blocked the other way, too," she said.

"What?" said Nevada.

"Somebody's taken a big lorry and just parked it head-on in the road between the church and the stables. It's completely blocked."

"There couldn't be two accidents," said Nevada.

"Well, possibly there could," said Agatha. "But I don't think any accident would explain someone cutting the gate off the stables with a chainsaw and stacking it in front of the lorry, to help barricade the road."

She showed us a picture on her phone, revealing the massive wooden slab of the stable gate leaning at an angle against the blunt face of the lorry.

"So, we're cut off," I said.

"By road, at least," said Agatha. "No one can get in or out."

"All right," said Nevada. "We need to get out of here now."

"But the road's blocked," said Horatio. "Both ways."

"We get out on foot," said Nevada. She nodded to the back door of the shed. "Through there and then away from the roads and into the forest as quick as we can. We may have to cut through people's gardens, but—"

That was when someone came in through the front door of the shed.

It wasn't a customer, though.

It was a woman dressed all in black—boots, leggings, leather jacket. Her face was covered with a red-and-white

Chinese opera mask, but it did nothing to disguise her identity, at least from me, because of the unforgettable green eyes staring out of the holes in the mask.

She had a rucksack slung over one shoulder and she was carrying a large gun which required both her hands.

I don't know anything about weapons. but I was pretty sure it was an ex-Soviet military assault rifle.

27: NOW LEAVING

"All right," said Princess Seitan, pointing the assault rifle at us, "everyone stay calm. This is a robbery. All we want is money. Give us the cash and we will go away and no one gets hurt." She managed to keep the gun pointing at us while she reached into the pocket of her jacket and threw something on the table. It landed softly and silently.

It was, oddly enough, a sock. A woolly grey sock, rolled up in a ball.

"Take out all your cash and put it in that."

"Do it, love," said Nevada, immediately and without hesitation. Perhaps I looked a little surprised because she said, "It's only money. It's not worth dying for."

"Exactly right," said Princess Seitan. "Very sensible."

Nevada was looking at her with interest. She said, conversationally, "Money isn't worth dying for. But it also isn't worth killing for, considering the consequences." She even smiled, as if this was a casual chat they were having.

"I'll definitely avoid killing anyone if I can," said Princess Seitan. "But if you give me any shit, I'll blast those boxes of records and I wouldn't be surprised, what with fragments flying everywhere, if someone doesn't get hurt. A splinter of vinyl in the eye, maybe, eh?" She sounded amused underneath her mask. But that amusement ceased as she suddenly swung her gun to point it at Horatio. I realised that he'd made a tiny movement.

"All right, hero," she said. "Here's what happens if you try something. I'll shoot, but I'll shoot at your feet. Best case scenario, you'll always walk with a walking stick or two. Worst case, you end up in a wheelchair or—who knows—maybe they can give you those springy steel prosthetic feet. Amazing what they can do these days."

Horatio stayed very, very still.

Princess Seitan glanced at a large wristwatch she was wearing on the outside of the sleeve of her jacket. "Now stop wasting time. Give me the money. And as soon as you do, I suggest you make yourself scarce. Go and lie low somewhere and hide until this is all over. Which will be in about four minutes." She glanced at her watch again. "Three and a half now."

I put all the cash into the sock she'd given us. I'd thought about hiding some of it, holding it back, but Nevada had picked up on this and had decisively shaken her head. So I put it all in the sock, everything we'd made today, plus the float we'd brought with us. It made me feel angry, and a little sick and defeated.

"Very good," said Princess Seitan. "Now roll it up in a ball again and throw it gently on the floor here, right by my feet."

I did what she said and she crouched down, scooped it up and transferred it to her rucksack in a swift, economical sequence of movements. We got a glimpse of the inside of the rucksack, which was full of plump rolled-up socks. I realised this operation was all very well planned and thought out.

"Okay," she said. "Now remember what I said about making yourself scarce."

She started for the door then stopped and stepped back as two men came into the shed. They weren't customers, either. They were dressed all in black, wore Chinese opera masks and carried assault rifles.

"Oh well," said Princess Seitan, addressing us. "Too late now. You shouldn't have wasted my time."

"Too late for what?" said the taller of the men. Even without knowing what Hughie had just told me, I doubt I would have had any trouble identifying the person under the mask as Julian.

Certainly Lambert didn't, judging by his reaction.

"Listen, Number One," said Princess Seitan, "I've got all their cash, let's just get out of here." She glanced at her watch. "We're running out of time and there's still plenty of money to be had."

"We're here for other things than money," said the other man. It was pitifully easy to identify him, from his voice and manner, as none other than our old friend Declan. Now menacing people with a gun instead of his driving skills.

"Stay out of this, Number Two," said Princess Seitan.

Number Two, I thought, Declan won't like that.

"She's right, Number Two, you stay out of it." Julian turned to Princess Seitan. "But you stay out of it as well, Number Zero. This is my show."

"Watch the young buck with the beard," said Princess Seitan, nodding at Horatio. "He's itching to do something heroic."

"We don't need your advice," said Declan.

Princess Seitan shrugged. "Number Zero over and out," she said and left.

"She's got all the money," said Declan.

"If you're worried about it, go with her," said Julian.

"I'm not the one who's worried," said Declan.

"Julian…" said Lambert. The two men, masked and dressed in black, carrying automatic weapons and in the middle of a very serious crime, both froze like guilty schoolboys.

"Julian, what are you doing?" said Lambert. He was a man stricken.

"He's rumbled you," said Declan. "You've got to do it now."

"Do what, Declan?" said Lambert. "What does he have to do?"

"He's rumbled us both," said Declan. "He's got to go." He swung his gun so it passed over all of us, and my stomach froze and shrivelled. "They've all got to go. They can identify us."

"Julian, what in god's name are you doing?" said Lambert.

"He's here to put things right," said Declan. "Put years of wrong things right. Years and years of wrong things."

"Shut up, Number Two," said Julian.

"Oh, fuck Number Two and Number One," said Declan. "They know who we are. Just do it."

"Listen, Julian," said Lambert. He was calm now and at his most persuasive. "You're in quite serious trouble but we can put it right. We can start putting it right immediately. But you have to stop what you're doing."

"Shut up, old man," said Declan. "That's what he's come here to do. That's what he's going to do. Put things right." He grasped Julian by the shoulder and shoved him towards his father. "*Do it*," he hissed.

Julian raised his gun and aimed it at Lambert.

"Julian, please," said Lambert. "Don't point that at me."

"Don't listen to him, Julian," said Declan. "You've been listening to him all your life."

"You made my mother one of three," said Julian. His voice was trembling. So was the gun in his hands. But it was still aimed squarely at Lambert.

"What?" said Lambert.

"You made her one of three," said Julian. "She never meant anything to you. I never meant anything to you."

"Julian, that's not true." Lambert's own voice was trembling with emotion. "Look, we should talk about this. We need to talk about it. We must. But not like this."

"No time for talking," said Declan. "Do it."

Julian's shoulders hunched. His hand tightened around the trigger. Time froze in the shed. Lambert was staring at him. Julian stared back through his mask, their gazes locked, father and son.

Declan was leaning forward, tense and ready. But his own rifle was pointed at Horatio. It seemed that despite what he'd said, he had heeded Princess Seitan's warning.

Then Julian lowered the gun.

"What are you doing?" said Declan.

"I can't do it," said Julian.

"What?"

"I just can't do it." Julian sounded like a little boy who had run away from home and now wanted to go back.

"Oh, fuck this," said Declan.

"Come on, let's go," said Julian. His shoulders were sagging and his gun was pointing at the floor.

"You fucking pussy," said Declan. "If you won't do it, I will."

"No," said Julian, and started to raise his gun. But Declan hit him in the head with the butt of his rifle and he went down.

That was when Nevada kicked the weak table leg and sent crates of vinyl spilling and tumbling towards Declan and Julian.

"*Run*," she said.

We were out the back door, running, the five of us. Nevada and I, followed by Lambert and Horatio and Agatha.

Agatha's car was parked on the far side of the circular village green. But, instead of going around the circle towards it, Nevada ran straight across the centre, through the duck pond, splashing through water up to her knees, and we all followed, scandalised birds squawking and scattering from our path.

Behind us I heard gunfire.

"Get in the car," said Agatha. She flung the door open for us then ran around the other side and got into the driver's seat. Nevada and I scrambled into the back seat. Horatio ran around to the driver's side.

"I'll drive," said Horatio.

"No," said Agatha.

"Let me drive."

"*Get in*." Agatha said this with such force and finality that Horatio got in, sitting in the front seat beside her and slamming the door as she blasted away.

Behind us there was gunfire.

Nevada looked back. "They're getting in a car," she said.

"They've blocked the road with all sorts of shit," said Horatio to Agatha.

"Yes."

"Including a lorry."

"Yes," said Agatha.

"The car's moving," said Nevada. "They're following us."

"You can't jump the lorry," said Horatio.

"I'm not going to jump the lorry," said Agatha.

We were speeding along the arrow-straight road that led out of the village, heading towards the church and the stables. I looked at Agatha's wing mirror and saw the other car speeding after us. Shops and pubs were whipping by. Agatha had floored the accelerator and we were now moving at a very high speed indeed.

There was gunfire from the car pursuing us. I looked into the wing mirror and then it magically vanished. It took me an instant to realise it had been blasted into fragments by a bullet.

"You can't do it," said Horatio.

Agatha said nothing.

"The gradient is all wrong, the power ratio is all wrong and, above all, the lorry is too long," said Horatio. "You can't jump it."

"I am not going to jump the lorry," said Agatha.

We were approaching the outskirts of town now, tearing along, the landscape to either side a blur. More gunfire behind us. Ahead of us was the roadblock consisting of the tilted gate from the stables and, behind it, the length of a huge lorry.

Agatha aimed us straight towards it and floored the accelerator.

"You can't—" said Horatio.

"Silence, Horatio," said Agatha.

We hit the slanting stable gate like a ramp and Agatha wrenched the steering wheel to the right. We shot up the gate and sheared off, not towards the lorry, but over the church wall.

We were airborne for an instant.

Then we were on the church roof.

We were driving along the church roof.

Driving along it, our tyres sizzling on the concrete.

And behind us came the satisfying sound of our pursuers, quite unable to stop at that speed, futilely trying to brake and then crashing into the barrier they themselves had assembled.

We sped along the church roof, along the wing of the bird, along the neck of the bird.

And then off it again.

Launching into space.

Standing by the lorry was a figure in black wearing a Chinese opera mask and holding an assault rifle. Darra or Dermot. Staring up at us in wonder. His weapon quite forgotten.

We were floating over the churchyard, gravestones, flower beds, the church wall, descending swiftly.

And back onto the road with tooth-jarring impact.

We shot along the road.

Past a sign reading *You Are Now Leaving Nutalich*.

28: NEWS REPORT

Famous Broadcaster Held Hostage in Gun Siege

Kent Chronicle's crime reporter Jasper McClew reports on dramatic events that unfolded this weekend.

A village fete on a beautiful summer Saturday was cut brutally short by the shock arrival of a gang of armed robbers. The tranquil hamlet of Nutalich was host this weekend to the Village of Vinyl festival, an exciting new innovation for the sleepy settlement created and crafted for them by the renowned DJ and media personality Stuart "Stinky" Stanmer.

Things began to go terribly wrong, though, when a team of armed raiders cut off access roads, blockading the village and trapping its helpless inhabitants. The masked gang then proceeded to terrorise and rob all the merchants and festival attendees at gunpoint, netting what is reported to be possibly a six-figure sum in cash. Their nefarious activity was immediately reported to the authorities, although the ruthless gun-wielding gang seemed to have taken this into account. "They were clearly working to a tight and disciplined timetable," said one witness, the Reverend Gerald Blanchflower. "But then that discipline began to fall apart."

Apparently the gang began to fight among themselves, possibly in a premature dispute over the division of the spoils. By the time they attempted to make good their escape, they discovered that the very blockade they'd created impeded their own getaway. Before they could reach the vehicles earmarked for their flight, the police had already seized these. Now ensnared in a trap of their own making, the gang seized a hostage and embarked on a tense armed standoff with the police.

The unfortunate victim chosen as their hostage was none other Stuart Stanmer, ironically the mastermind behind the weekend's festival. Expert police negotiators were summoned to the scene but, by the time they arrived, three of the gang had already been identified as the Bolsin brothers, Declan, Darra and Dermot (all 21), who were well known locally.

Their mother and father arrived and pleaded with the boys to surrender, which they proceeded to do shortly afterwards, being immediately taken into police custody. "They're all good boys, really," said their mother Sandra Bolsin (38). A fourth member of the gang was also arrested, Julian Herald (23). Herald had been acting as the manager and Svengali for the Bolsin brothers' boy band, The Trippy-Lits. Before being taken into custody, he was treated for injuries believed to have been received at the hands of the gang during their internal dispute.

A fifth member of the daring daylight robbery team, an unidentified young woman, has so far eluded capture. Stuart Stanmer was interviewed by the police and was thereafter released to return home where he reportedly spent the rest of the weekend under sedation.

29: SPELLING OPTIONAL

Poppy was sitting on the sofa in our living room. I'd considered buying a copy of the *Financial Times* for her to sit on, so she'd feel at home. But she wasn't in her gardening clothes today. Indeed, she was very smartly dressed.

Poppy had driven up from Kent especially to return my records.

These were the records that Nevada had dumped on Declan and Julian to distract them while we made good our dash for the car. Along with all the others we'd abandoned when we'd fled.

The Reverend Gerald Blanchflower had made a point of rescuing this vinyl from the duck shed and carefully repacking it in my crates, and Poppy had volunteered to bring these to us in person, because she wanted to pay us a visit.

I had explained that the records weren't really that important, but Gerry had been insistent or returning them because he felt so bad about what had happened—not only had we almost lost our lives, we'd also lost all of the takings from the sales we'd made that day.

"It's only money," I'd told him, quoting my philosophical darling.

I could afford to take this attitude, not least because Lambert had volunteered to compensate us for our losses that day. Once we realised he genuinely wanted to do this, we'd taken him up on his generous offer. As it happened, Nevada had been keeping track of what I'd earned on the vinyl sales and we were able to give him a very accurate accounting. Not that he cared about scrupulous accuracy. We did, though.

"Lambert's sorry he can't be here today," said Poppy. "But he's busy sorting out Julian's defence."

Julian's defence was going to take some sorting because, on top of everything else, he'd confessed to the police that he'd killed Timothy Purshouse.

What he hadn't confessed was that he'd then planted the corpse on us.

In fact, the official line was that Julian was responsible for dumping the body in the woods.

This was great from our point of view, because it kept us entirely out of things. But Julian hadn't spared us out of the goodness of his heart. And that was what Poppy had come to talk to us about. It was the sort of conversation she didn't want to have on a phone, online or via email. Not via any format which might leave a trace.

"You see," said Poppy, "it's going to be argued that Julian didn't intend to kill Timothy. It was a sudden eruption of rage. He went to visit him to see if Timothy could help us find his father—now that is utter nonsense, of course, because Julian had no desire to find Lambert or bring him home. Quite the opposite. But no one outside the family would know that. To any outsider, it will sound like an entirely plausible idea."

"Well, it is," said Nevada. "Because Tim genuinely was helpful in trying to find Lambert. He was helping us."

"Yes," said Poppy. "So the idea is that Julian went to see him and Timothy said something deeply offensive and infuriating…"

"Again, entirely plausible," said Nevada.

"Yes, and possibly even true," said Poppy. "And then… Julian…" She shrugged.

If she couldn't say it, I could. "He killed him."

Poppy nodded. "Yes. And then what actually happened— not the official version but what actually happened—was that he hid him in the boot of your car, in an attempt to implicate you. But Julian didn't anticipate that you'd find him almost immediately, and then very sensibly and wisely dispose of the evidence elsewhere." She looked at us. "Did you happen to know that the stretch of woodland where you put Timothy was where the triplets did their training?"

"No," said Nevada. "We had no idea. I swear."

"Oh, I believe you," said Poppy. "Not least because there was no set pattern to exactly where they went for their runs. Therefore you couldn't really have known with any precision. But that was not the way Julian saw it. He was convinced it was deliberate. Indeed, a piece of fiendish mockery."

"Fiendish mockery?" said Nevada.

"Yes, well," said Poppy, "Julian is very volatile, has poor judgement and virtually no impulse control. As I'm sure will be argued in court. Anyway, he began to believe you knew all about him and were playing a cat-and-mouse game with him."

"Holy shit," I said.

"Quite," said Poppy. "And it was at this point that he started to get foolishly, murderously reckless. He had spent a great deal of money on all that ecstasy."

Nevada and I exchanged a glance. "You knew about the pills?" I said.

Poppy nodded. "We needed to know what happened, everything that really happened, so we could work out what story Julian is going to use for his defence."

"And he told you about planting the drugs on us," said Nevada.

"Yes, the idea had originally been to buy a large quantity of drugs, resell them and make a great deal of money. Which Julian would then invest in the boy band he was creating. But, instead of that, he impulsively used those drugs in an attempt to frame you."

"He certainly did," said Nevada.

"Yes, Julian conceived a strong dislike for the two of you quite early on, when we hired you to find his father. That was the last thing he wanted. So, he tried to scare you off."

"Which is why he drugged me at the Brixton gig," I said.

"With the help of his green-eyed friend, yes. But you weren't scared off. And then you began to make progress in the search for Lambert, with the help of Timothy."

"So Tim had to go," said Nevada.

"Yes. And I suppose once Julian had committed to the notion of killing someone, sacrificing all that ecstasy seemed like a minor thing. But Declan didn't think so."

"Declan was in on the drug deal, then," I said.

"Yes, he didn't know about Timothy's murder, but Declan was deeply involved in their little entrepreneurial project with ecstasy. He was the only one of the triplets who was."

I remembered the argument Declan and Julian had been having the night we'd arrived for the grand homecoming party. Declan had said something about Julian throwing money away.

I told Poppy this and she nodded. "Declan was very unhappy about their big investment being discarded, although at that point he didn't know exactly what Julian had done with it. He just knew it was gone."

"And Julian was desperate to make good that loss," said Nevada. "He wanted to get the money to invest in the band."

"And to shut Declan up," I said.

"And to shut Declan up and show him he could do it," said Nevada. "Do you remember at the dinner party, me telling Lambert how last year's event in Nutalich had brought in a hundred grand?"

"In cash," I said.

"That's right, in cash," said Nevada. "And at that point Julian suddenly seemed to take a very uncharacteristic interest in the conversation."

"I remember," said Poppy. "It would seem that was when he started to get the idea of robbing the village festival…"

"To make good his losses," said Nevada.

"And, egged on by Declan, he thought he would combine robbery with patricide." Poppy shook her head. "In fact, Julian began to think it would be the perfect cover for murder."

"People would think his father had been killed by unknown armed robbers," I said.

"Yes," said Poppy. "I don't know how Julian ever thought he could get away with it. Or live with himself if he did. But, as I say, when the triplets found Timothy's body in the woods, Julian thought you had put it there deliberately. That you were playing diabolical games with him. And he began to behave very recklessly indeed. His behaviour deteriorated seriously."

I thought this was an understatement. But Nevada brought the conversation back to practical matters. Practical matters of some concern to us.

"So the official version will definitely be that it was Julian who dumped the body?" she said.

"Yes," said Poppy, "because that way—"

"That way the lawyers can argue he was behaving impulsively, in the heat of the moment," said Nevada. "Just as he did when he killed Tim."

"Yes," said Poppy. "And the fact that he deposited the body so close to home suggests irrational behaviour rather than…"

"Being all cold-blooded and carefully thought-out," I said.

"Like cunningly planting the body on us," said Nevada. "So that we'd take the blame."

"Yes," said Poppy. "And also planting those pills on you and on Timothy. If that came out, it would begin to make the entire thing look highly organised and premeditated. As well as implicating Julian in drug dealing on an industrial scale."

"So the drugs have been written out of the official version?" said Nevada

"Yes," said Poppy. "By the way, what happened to the pills he put in your house?"

By an odd coincidence, as she said this, she was sitting on the sofa exactly above the spot where the bag of pills had been planted.

"We gave them to a friend to dispose of," said Nevada.

"Very sensible."

"What happened to the pills in Tim's house?" I said.

Poppy shrugged. "The police found them and assumed they belonged to Timothy. They may even be useful, in that they serve to blacken his reputation and thereby help Julian in his defence."

"Because killing a drug dealer isn't such a terrible crime?" I said.

Poppy gave me a helpless look. "The lawyers are going to use every means at their disposal to reduce Julian's culpability. That's their job."

"Of course it is," said Nevada, ever the pragmatist.

"If possible, they would also be attempting to implicate the triplets in Timothy's murder," said Poppy. "To dilute the responsibility. Or at least implicate Declan in it."

Nobody liked Declan, it seemed.

"But that doesn't seem possible, because—"

"Because the triplets found the body and reported it," I said.

"Yes," said Poppy. "If they'd been involved in Timothy's murder, they wouldn't have innocently and instantly called the police on finding his body. So they can't be complicit in that. But we're going to push hard on Declan's attempt to kill Lambert at the Village of Vinyl."

"Which is absolutely true," I said.

"And on Julian's attempt to stop him."

"Which is true as far as it goes," I said.

Poppy sighed. "Declan's lawyers no doubt will claim the opposite, that Julian planned to kill Lambert."

"And he did," said Nevada.

"Yes, he did," said Poppy. "He actually thought he could kill his father. But, of course, when it came to it, he found he couldn't. And our position will be to deny that he ever had any such intention, and that it was Declan all along and that Julian heroically intervened to stop him. Julian's injuries will certainly support this."

Nevada was watching her closely. "Are you going to ask us to swear to this version in court?"

"No, our intention is that it never gets to court. Julian will plead guilty."

"To killing Tim?" I said. Just because none of us liked Tim didn't mean that he could be murdered with impunity and that his killer should walk free.

"Yes, with extenuating circumstances. Of course, our unconventional lifestyle is about to come under the media spotlight again, and we are all dreading that and bracing ourselves. But the one good thing about it is that it will be a very real and immediate object lesson in the sort of pressure Julian has had to live under, the tabloid circus he has had to endure all his life."

"And the kind of thing Tim was responsible for," said Nevada. "Rave Star Orgy Cult."

"Exactly. We believe this will help create sympathy for Julian and enable him to plead guilty to lesser charges and receive a lesser sentence. No doubt it will still mean years in prison, but as few years as possible."

The strangest thing about this whole situation, for Nevada and I, was the kind of double image we had of Julian. On the one hand, he was the murderous little shit who had tried so hard to harm us, not to mention kill his father. Not to mention actually killing Tim.

On the other hand, he was the beloved child of this family, who were now coming together to protect him. Selena had been particularly impressive in this regard. Watching her work the media was an education. She had cleaned up her act—no trace of sulking or sullenness. Instead, she was the very picture of a plucky mother courageously defending her difficult, damaged, but adored child.

And Lambert was pretty impressive as the concerned and committed father.

"One upside of all this horror," said Poppy, "is that Lambert's records are selling, and in huge quantities. And he's going back into the studio to record a new one."

"At least Julian cleared it out for him," I said.

"Yes, ironic, I know. But Lambert hasn't recorded in years. And if this gets him making music again, at least some good will have come of it. And he's booked a tour. Dozens and dozens of gigs. I've never seen him so busy. All the proceeds will be going to Julian's defence." She looked at us. "We'll send you some tickets to a gig if you like." She smiled. "But no coupons for a food van."

Then she stood up.

"Now, if you don't mind, I've been looking through the window at your lovely garden, and perhaps you'd show me around?"

Speaking of food van coupons, it was worth noting that Princess Seitan—spelling optional— had done a remarkably good job of vanishing.

"Apparently not even Julian knows her real name," said Nevada.

"Was he sleeping with her?" said Tinkler.

"Trust you to ask that," said Nevada.

"Well, it would be pretty cool if he was sleeping with her and even he didn't know her secret identity."

"She's not a superhero, Tinkler," said Nevada.

"You never met her. And Princess Satan is a really cool name. Spelled with an A. Spelled EI, not so much."

"Of course I met her," said Nevada. "At gunpoint."

"Oh yeah, I forgot that," said Tinkler. He held out his glass for more wine and Nevada poured him a refill. We were sitting around our dining table having recently finished a meal, just the three of us. Unless you counted the cats. "What did you think of her?" he said.

"I thought she was the only one of that sorry crew who had her act together," said Nevada. "She was organised and ferociously efficient. Had her eye on the clock and her eyes on the prize."

"Sounds like you admire her," said Tinkler. "Maybe a bit of a sapphic crush?"

"I might not go quite that far," said Nevada, inhaling the bouquet of her wine.

"Darn it," said Tinkler.

"But admire her?" said Nevada. "Yes. She knew what she was doing. She bailed out as soon as it looked like things were going to get messy…"

"When my true love says things were going to get messy," I said, "she means that we were all about to be murdered by Declan and Julian."

"Bummer," said Tinkler.

"But look at it from her point of view," said Nevada. "She was just there for the robbery. For the cash. And when things start to get sticky, she simply cuts her losses and leaves. It turns out she had brought along an electric scooter—she was the only one in the gang smart enough to realise the roadblocks they'd created were likely to impede their own escape. And as soon as the shit started to hit the fan, she got on her scooter and left town via the blocked bridge. There was still enough space to get her scooter through. And as soon as she was past the bridge and out of sight, she ditched her mask and her gun and took a girly frock out of her rucksack…"

"The rucksack with *all* the money in it," I said.

"That's right," said Nevada. "The rucksack with all the money in it. She had the proceeds of the entire robbery. Plus, apparently, a rather nice flowery frock. Which she donned, instantly transforming herself from a black-clad armed robber to a charming young woman breezing along on an electric scooter on a summer day. And she got clean away."

"On an e-scooter?" said Tinkler.

"She only rode that as far as the car she'd left, ready and waiting."

"And they haven't been able to find her?" said Tinkler.

"I'm kind of hoping they never will," said Nevada. She sipped her wine.

"Like I said, sapphic crush," said Tinkler.

We were all silent for a while and then Tinkler said, "I'm sorry."

"For what?" said Nevada.

Tinkler shrugged. "I should have been with you guys when the shit hit the fan. We're a team."

"Don't beat yourself up," said Nevada. "We're glad you weren't there."

"If you had been with us, we couldn't have all fitted in our getaway car," I said. "We would have had to leave somebody behind."

"My vote would have been for Horatio," said Tinkler.

"He certainly proved to be a bit of a back-seat driver," said Nevada. "Even though he was in the front seat."

As ever, when the talk turned to Horatio, even when he'd turned it there, Tinkler changed the subject. "So how much money did Princess Satan—I insist on spelling it with two As—get away with?"

"We think north of a hundred grand."

"Nice work. Now *I've* got a crush on her."

Speaking of large sums of money, we had received an email earlier in the day from Hughie, turntable mechanic, weed farmer and wholesale reseller of ecstasy tablets. There was no message, just an attached image.

A screenshot of a receipt from a charity. It was for payment of a five-figure sum.

And to our favourite charity.

For cats.

ACKNOWLEDGEMENTS AND NOTES

Credit is due to James Swallow for sharing his expertise on firearms. Thank you, Jim.

Although I reopened the Fridge in Brixton for the purposes of this story, that legendary venue unfortunately remains closed. And I've never met the Hartnoll brothers, aka Orbital, but I hope they won't mind their cameo appearance here. I do know Dominic Glynn and his presence in this book is a small thank you for all his help in providing information and reminiscences that evoke the heyday of electronic dance music; Dom was there and generously shared his experiences with me.

And my gratitude to the usual suspects…

Martin Stiff for his consistently beautiful cover art (particularly outstanding this time, I think). George Sandison, Nick Landau and Vivian Cheung at Titan, with special mention for Rufus Purdy who had to put up with me on this book. My indomitable agents, Stevie Finegan and John Berlyne. Ben Aaronovitch for his continuing support.

And Miranda Jewess and Guy Adams, without whom there wouldn't be a Vinyl Detective.

For those who are interested, Hughie Mackinaw and his turntable factory and market garden, scene of an earlier traumatic winter episode for our narrator, appeared in *Written in Dead Wax*. Dr Gerald Blanchflower, the cinephile vicar, was introduced in *The Run-Out Groove*. Tinkler's natural immunity to psychedelic drugs (based on someone I actually know) was also established in that novel. Jasper McClew, the soi-disant journalist whose articles bookend this story, first featured in *Victory Disc*. And the episode of Agatha saving Stinky's sister from drowning takes place in the Paperback Sleuth novel *Ashram Assassin*.

Special thanks to Hannah at CEX in Richmond for letting me use her sawn-off red denim jacket in this tale.

ABOUT THE AUTHOR

Andrew Cartmel is a novelist and playwright. He is the author of the Vinyl Detective series, which was hailed as "marvellously inventive and endlessly fascinating" by *Publishers Weekly*, as well as the Paperback Sleuth series, which features many of the same characters. His work for television includes a legendary stint as script editor on *Doctor Who*. He has also written plays for the London Fringe and toured as a stand-up comedian. He lives in London with too much vinyl and just enough cats. You can find Andrew on Twitter/X at @andrewcartmel and listen to his weekly radio show, Vinyl Detective Radio, via Medway Pride or Reclaimed Radio.

THE PAPERBACK SLEUTH: ASHRAM ASSASSIN

Andrew Cartmel

"An intriguing mystery with an amoral protagonist. Who knew the world of paperback books could be so deadly?"

Ben Aaronovitch, author of the Rivers of London series

"Andrew Cartmel introduces a new kind of heroine, entirely immoral, somewhat venal and slightly foxed."

David Quantick, Emmy award-winning producer of *VEEP*

When a set of rare, impossible-to-find yoga books are stolen from a West London ashram, its leaders turn to Cordelia Stanmer, the Paperback Sleuth, to recover them—a set-up that's a little awkward as they've previously barred her from yoga classes for selling marijuana to their students. But what begins as a hunt for missing paperbacks soon becomes a murder investigation as those involved with the ashram can't seem to stop dropping down dead—murdered with a whisky bottle to the head or a poisoned curry. Can Cordelia work out who the killer is and bring them to justice before they bring an end to her sleuthing for good?

THE VINYL DETECTIVE: ATTACK AND DECAY

Andrew Cartmel

"The Vinyl Detective goes Scandi Noir? Yes please!"

Ben Aaronovitch, author of the Rivers of London series

It starts with a perfectly normal evening in, except for the corpse-faced gentleman dressed all in black, with a crow on his shoulder, staring into the house, of course. And the visit from Owyn Wynter, head of Whyte Ravyn Records, who needs the Vinyl Detective's unique skills.

So begins an all-expenses-paid trip to Trollesko, Sweden, for the Vinyl Detective, Nevada, Tinkler and Agatha to track down a copy of the debut album from demonic metal legends, Storm Dream Troopers. Condemned by the church and banned on release, *Attack and Decay* is a legendary record.

But their trip to the homelands of Nordic noir is quickly thrust into a world of intrigue as the Vinyl Detective closes in on the deal, the band unexpectedly converge on the peaceful town. And, worse, their trip somehow coincides with a visit from Stinky Stanmer... Soon the bodies start to pile up, and the Vinyl Detective is the only one who can solve the case.

For more fantastic fiction, author events,
exclusive excerpts, competitions, limited editions and more

VISIT OUR WEBSITE
titanbooks.com

LIKE US ON FACEBOOK
facebook.com/titanbooks

FOLLOW US ON TWITTER AND INSTAGRAM
@TitanBooks

EMAIL US
readerfeedback@titanemail.com